VICTORIA'S DINER

MA CARTER

Cover Designer: Disturbed Valkyrie Designs
Formatting and Inside Artwork: Designs by Charlyy

For the people who understand that your heart and brain and
feelings get messy dude

PLAYLIST

Criminal by Fiona Apple
Santeria by Sublime
Pain and Misery by The Teskey Brothers
Sugar by Sleep Token
FMLYHM by Seether
Rain by The Teskey Brothers
Lose Control by Teddy Swims
I'm Yours by Isabel LaRosa
Pretend by Bad Omens
Dark Matter by Rivals
Beetlejuice Chill by Life After Youth
Worship by Ari Abdul
Middle of the Night by Elley Duhe
Supermassive Black Hole by Muse
Closer by NIN
Look What You Made Me Do by Taylor Swift
The Love You Want by Sleep Token

AUTHOR'S NOTE

Dear Reader,
Thank you so much for giving my debut novel a chance. I hope
you enjoy it and look forward to my other releases.

A further note: this book contains cheating, aspects of revenge
and betrayal, and BDSM. While this book is ultimately not a
HEA, Millicent's story is far from over.
That being said, suit up and enjoy the ride.

Chapter
One

Relentless thoughts bounce around my overly cluttered mind far too often, giving him ownership of my brain, instead of a rental space. Squatter's rights. That's what he's gained at this point at chateau Millicent with the mind-blowing sex he grants me. His smell is permanently in my olfactory system, subtle hints of leather and musk mixed with something I can't quite put my finger on, exuding an all-out manliness. I suck in a trembling breath as I try and hold onto the smell lingering in my nose as if it'll drift away any moment.

'Mil.'

I shake loose from my daydream and allow myself to bask in his scent a moment longer, a wave of satisfaction washing over me as I realize I'll be up close and personal with him in a matter of seconds. After all, there is only a door standing between us. He's on the other side of this piece of wood, waiting to unleash a fury of pleasure on me - his Millicent.

My mom wanted a strong name for her daughter, a name that would let people know ahead of time that I would command a room. A name associated with the strongest females, who would dominate every aspect of their lives. Millicent, quite literally meaning *strong*, is what she landed on. And I was going to be expected to uphold that name. Today is not that type of day, though. Because while in this room, I am his submissive and he is my dominant.

'Millicent.' I hear the growing agitation in his voice. Best not to keep him waiting.

Grabbing hold of the doorknob, the chill of the cold metal runs up my arm as I open the door. With the light in the room low (as usual), the dark wood walls, sconces placed perfectly throughout, black silken sheets, and the heady smell of his body all add to the sensuality of the space. My breath hitches as I scan the room and see him sitting casually on the leather sofa, one of a few pieces of furniture in the room. The matching ottoman is positioned in front of the sofa, on top of a plush, white rug. A rug so bright compared to everything else in the room, it almost seems as if it shouldn't be there, yet fits somehow. A long, mahogany dresser for the implements, adorns the back wall behind the sofa. Candles sparsely placed on top of the dresser emit a flickering glow. Oh, and let's not forget the bed. A sex room would not be complete without a four-poster bed.

His dark eyes, barely visible due to low lighting and shaggy brown locks, follow me as I slowly approach him. His 10-day shadow makes him look even more primal than normal. Ink in all the right places, down both arms, with just the left side of his chest covered; the right side of his upper back is covered in contradiction with the front. An owl's face adorns his neck, and I see his throat move beneath the tattoo as he studies me intently. He has the physique of someone who doesn't need a regular fitness routine because he does plenty of manual labor. His arm muscles flinch a little as he fists and releases his hands. He's not happy, and the fact he's already positioning himself on the sofa tells me I'm no doubt in for a spanking today.

Cade sits up straight from his far too-relaxed position and runs his hands up and down his jean-clad thighs, never taking his eyes off me. I stop in case I miss a cue from him and notice the top edge of his underwear peeking above the waistband. My nipples are getting harder and harder from the cool air and the anticipation of this afternoon's activities. I'm wearing only his long-sleeved button-up shirt, unbuttoned of course, and nothing else. Just how he likes it.

'What took you so long?' He asks, voice gruff.

'I'm sorry, Sir. I'm a little more in my head than usual.' I squeak, trying to gain control of my breathing.

'You know what happens when I'm made to wait.' His green eyes pierce through my soul and suddenly, there's a heated wetness between my legs. How someone can just look at you and instantly make you soaked is beyond me, but Cade has that effect on me every time.

'Yes, Sir.'

'And what's that?' He huffs, knowing damn well. I just don't want to say what he's going to do.

I let silent tension fill the air, knowing how turned on it makes him when I say he's going to spank me. His frustration grows as his jaw muscles react to the clenching and unclenching of his teeth. His head shakes ever so slightly, no doubt in awe of my noncompliance, as he rubs a palm down the length of his face.

'Millicent?' He's steadily growing more pissed with me, but I can't help feeling even more aroused. The more I annoy him, the hotter the session.

'You'll spank me, Sir.' I can't keep this charade on for much longer unless I want a caning. I love spanking, but a caning is not something I wish to endure again.

A smirk forms on his lips as my words land on his ears. Cade rubs his hands up and down his thighs again, warming my seat for me. He reaches a hand out for me to take, and I do as I know I'm supposed to. Guiding me to lay across his lap, his hand glides up and down the backs of each thigh. Heat from his legs and stomach instantly warms my body. He pulls the shirt up my back exposing my ass, his hand continuously moving gently over my curves.

His fingers slip between my thighs, testing to see how horny I am already. His growl of appreciation vibrates through my body as he rubs and grips my ass harder, preparing me for the initial smack. The anticipation of his hand stinging across my skin has my heart beating up into my throat. His fingers trail along my spine as he brings his left hand to settle between my shoulder blades making it easier to control my inevitable bucking. His right hand lifts, and before I can mentally prepare myself, my scream rattles through the room as it comes down hard on my ass.

He smacks me again and then rubs the spot he just hit. Another smack, this time on the opposite cheek. Smack, rub, smack, rub. I try bringing my arm around my back to block his hand, but he grabs my wrist, holding it in place.

'Oh, Mil. You know I love it when you struggle,' he groans before delivering another blow. 'It means I can go harder on you.'

The spanking continues uninterrupted, increasing in intensity with every swing of his arm. Each time his hand lands on my skin, a squeal escapes my mouth. This is my favorite part of our sessions though. The spanking hurts in the best way possible, and Cade knows exactly how I want to feel.

The longer the spanking continues, the more my legs kick around in a feeble attempt to avoid his hand. He adjusts himself under me, bringing his leg up and over to hold down my lower half. Leaning over my back, effectively blocking my arms from attempting to stop his hands, he has me, and my ass, right where he wants me. I'm completely incapacitated as his hand lifts and slams back down on the sore spots he's creating, over and over again. I have no idea what number he's on but the longer he goes, the louder my whines and cries become.

'Do you think you'll keep me waiting again?' He asks between smacks.

'No, Sir!' I cry out.

'No Sir what?' Smack. Smack.

'I won't keep you waiting again, Sir!'

Smack. Rub. Smack.

'That's my good girl.'

My breath calms to a slower pace as the spanking is replaced with a gentle caressing. My legs now free, Cade traces the details of his handiwork left behind on my porcelain skin. Once holding me prisoner, rough fingers meander softly through my disheveled hair as he tenderly massages my scalp; a release from our moment induced high of one another's energy.

'Stand up,' Cade demands, his voice low and gravelly.

Compliantly, I stand in front of him.

'Turn around,' he says, swirling his pointer finger, indicating for me to face away from him. I hold my shirt up as I do, displaying his handiwork for him to admire.

'Bend over, hands on the ottoman.'

Again, I obey. I'm not usually up for more than one spanking in a day.

Placing my hands down and bending over the ottoman, his palms come to grip my ass while his thumbs rub circles on the memories of his handprints. I suck in a sharp breath as the pinch of canines on my sensitive skin surprises me. The bite turns into kissing as his lips trail all around his five-fingered tattooed welts. His knees come between my legs, and press outward, spreading me open for him. A pleased hum caresses my ear, and peeking back through my legs, his cock threatens to bust through the fabric of his jeans. I love how turned on I make him.

The kisses venture closer, teasing my pussy, and I moan out as his tongue finally finds its target. His licking successfully taking me even further out of my head. My orgasm builds all too quickly with every flick and swirl of his tongue. Gripping the front of my thighs, he pulls me further into his mouth so I can't get away. As the pleasure rips through my body, my arms shake as they attempt to keep me from face planting the ottoman. Thankfully the room is soundproof because I'm sure my moans could be heard for blocks. I reach back and grab his arm to try and release his grip, but his mouth suctioned to my pussy. Another orgasm rapidly builds, ravaging me to my core. He starts to pull away, leaving little licks and kisses in his wake, as my legs quiver and I finally give in to my arms needing relief and drop to my elbows.

His fingers glide down my thighs before his nails rake across my skin as they come back up. I'm still trying to catch my breath when he tells me to stand and turns me around to face him. My sensitive nipples send tingles throughout my breasts as the fabric rubs against them. Trailing up from between my legs, to my abdomen, pausing on my breasts, his eyes finally land on mine. I watch his teeth sink into his bottom lip as he reaches up to push the shirt off my shoulders. Sitting back, he takes in my naked body once more.

The spankings used to be solitary. I wanted them. Needed them even. The submission of it all took me to a place far away. They helped me escape all the bullshit occurring in my daily life. Cade realized just how much I was enjoying them when his thumb grazed my wet center after a hard spanking on a particularly rough day.

'Is this for me Millicent?' He breathed as he bruised my ass under his grip.

'Yes, Sir. I love the spankings.'

'You love the spankings?'

'I love when you spank me, Sir.' With a rumble of approval, he plunged two fingers into my pussy, thrusting them in and out until I was bursting all over his hand with the first of many orgasms.

Now, the sex is assumed to follow a spanking. And I'm completely on board with that. I'm putty in Cade's hands, and the way he works my body is something I've never experienced with another man. Ever.

I watch as Cade's eyes move from my body to his straining cock. Recognizing the sign, I drop to my knees, and keeping my eyes on his as I start to unbutton his pants. He adjusts himself so I can pull his pants and underwear down around his ass, freeing his cock. I don't take his pants all the way off but leave them bunched around his ankles. My own little form of domination. He doesn't seem to mind my small gestures of control.

Salivating over what's to come, I lick my lips and take his cock in my hand, my middle finger and thumb barely able to touch around his girth. Bringing my mouth to hover just above the tip, I linger for a moment, taking in this picture-perfect dick, veins throbbing with want, a glint of cum forming on the tip. His breath hitches as he waits for the warmth and wetness of my mouth. I won't make him wait too long since we both want his cock in my mouth. I tease the head, circling with my tongue before wrapping my mouth around the tip. I look up as he exhales a sigh of relief, letting his head fall back against the sofa. Gripping his cock, I move my hand up and down with my mouth, as I continue my torturous sucking, swirling my tongue each time I come back up to the tip. Fingers find their way into the back of my hair, making my scalp scream as his grip tightens, and I continue to torment him. Cupping his balls with my other hand, I release him and run my tongue up and down the length of him, circling the tip to tease him a little more.

'Get up here.' His words are almost imperceptible.

I don't wait. I stand and straddle my knees around him on the sofa and lower myself down on his waiting cock. The fit perfect as it continues to fill me up until my ass sits flush with his thighs. I start to work my hips up and down his shaft as his hands come to grip my ass tightly. I grab the back of the sofa and my head falls backward as our breathing starts to sync and he starts to fuck me from underneath. His thumb finds my chin, pulling my face down so my gaze is on him. His eyes hold more than just lust for me but neither of us dares to address it. His hand moves behind my neck to keep me from looking away as he wets his other thumb in his mouth before he finds my clit, making me arch forward into him. He forces my face down to his, our moans colliding with each other's as our tongues taste one another.

My orgasm thunders through my body and my eyelids fall heavy with lust. Resting my hand on the front of his neck, I start to squeeze as he finally tumbles over the edge with me. Leaning forward to rest my face in the crook of his neck, I try and regain my breath. Cade twitches under me as he rides out the tremors of his orgasm, one hand fisting the back of my head, while the other squeezes the life out of my thigh. We sit like this until we've both caught our breath and the bumps start to rise on my skin as our bodies cool down. Neither of us wanting to move. Neither of us wanting the moment to end. Both of us wanting to extend whatever this is past the end of the appointment but neither of us willing to admit it out loud. You might think the worst part about my session ending with

Cade would be leaving him, but you'd be wrong. The worst part is that now, I have to go home to my husband.

Chapter Two

The rain beats on my car so loudly the sound seems to penetrate my brain. Loosening my white-knuckle fingers from the steering wheel, I will myself to let go of the wheel completely, grab the door handle, and get out of the car. I open and close my fists a couple times to bring the blood flow back to them. Looking into the rearview mirror, I see my eyes are finally starting to regain their normal color. Inevitable tears shed after a session with Cade make it impossible to drive home or go into the house as soon as I pull into the driveway.

I know Jeremy sees me sitting in the car, and that I have been for a while. The first few times I have come home late, I see our bedroom curtain fall close as soon as I look up. Lately, he doesn't get up to look out the window. I can tell he's awake by his breathing when I walk into the room to grab a change of clothes or use the shower before escaping to the spare bedroom. He's no doubt lying in our bed staring at the ceiling, waiting for me to come inside, contemplating how he can ever fix the situation he's landed us in.

Finally, I muster the strength to get out of the car. Reaching into the backseat, I grab my briefcase before getting soaked by the monsoon that shows no signs of stopping. As I open the door, rain immediately starts pelting my head. I kick the door shut behind me, then walk towards the porch. Before the incident, I would've parked as close to the house as possible to avoid a torrential downpour like this one. Tonight, I invite the rain to soak me to my bones and wash away my sins.

Usually, I can barely see the woods bordering our property, separating us from our neighbors, but tonight the rain makes it so I can barely see beyond the house. My footsteps echo off the gravel, each step screaming out to Jeremy his beloved is home. As if my accidental horn honk when I first pull up didn't do the job.

Stepping onto the porch is louder yet. We live in a home built in the late 1800s and every part of this house aches in pain as you move through it. I would instantly fall in love with the old Victorian home, its perfect mix of gothic and farmhouse vibes, gabled roof, and wrap-around porch. The original house they would keep during the development of the neighboring houses, nestles perfectly into a small opening of trees, and provides the best setting for us to start our journey as a newly married couple. I can picture our future kids playing in the yard. I could hear their footsteps pound on the wooden porch as they run inside after the bus drops them off from school; bursting through the door and announcing they are home. I could hear the creak of the porch swing, and the crickets melodious song to us, as we enjoy a glass of wine once the kids have gone to bed. I could feel all the love that would flow inside and outside of the house.

I find my keys in my pocket and fumble to get the right one into the lock. The sound of the door unlatching is loud enough to shatter the door's glass panes. I step inside as the door creaks open and am hit with a deathly silence. Silence is the only sound heard from this house anymore; that, and the groans from the old wood keeping this house standing.

Since the fighting is few and far between anymore, there's even less talking. Other than the small attempts Jeremy makes to try and smooth things over, of course. I know he's in our bed right now waiting to hear the door shut, my briefcase scraping slightly as it's being set down on the entryway sideboard, and my keys hitting the dish so he can finally breathe. I drop the keys from an obnoxious height, hitting the glass with such force, I'm not sure the dish is even whole anymore. I slam the briefcase down on the table, then turn and kick off my heels into the coat closet. They clatter against the back wall before landing in a pile on top of the other shoes on the floor. I'm not sure why I'm taking my anger out on this poor house. It didn't cheat on me, and it certainly didn't live a double life on top of it. This always seems to be the point in my day where the anger starts to boil over again. After the pleasure of being with Cade subsides, and the anxiety of being with him dissipates, the utter rage drips back in.

I let my sopping wet coat hit the floor, not caring that it'll be wrinkled beyond recognition. I'll take it to the cleaners before my open house Sunday. Dragging myself toward the kitchen without the least bit of consideration for my husband, waiting wide awake in our bed upstairs, I don't bother trying to lighten my steps or avoid the places where I know creaks will sound. Another wife might, but not this wife. Not anymore.

Crossing through the kitchen doorway, I see Jeremy has left a plate of something on the island. I walk over to see if it's anything worth reheating. Noodles and red sauce fall back to the plate as they dislodge themselves from the paper towel I lift up gingerly. Spaghetti. Fucking spaghetti. His idea of a *let's start over* dinner. The dinner I was supposed to be home for about four hours ago.

Sorry, Jeremy. I got tied up. Not literally. Not this time anyway.

Thankfully, my job provides me the perfect excuse for late nights and being seen in different parts of town. I'm lucky enough to be one of the top realtors in the greater Chicago area, which means I'm busier than most. I shouldn't say "lucky", I've worked my ass off to get to where I'm at.

While in college, suffering through my bachelor's degree in business administration, I decided to work on getting my realtors license to supplement my income. Waitressing and working at the local bookstore wouldn't be enough to cut it. I certainly wouldn't get any help financially from my folks, and once Jeremy and I would get together, he could barely support himself. Through the bookstore, I would meet a guy who owns his own realty firm, willing to give me a chance. Now, I'm the star of my own show.

Since my job keeps me busy most days and my husband has unconventional work hours, our choice in careers also provides him the time to run around with his little whore. The girl who *"didn't mean anything"*. The girl he swears to *"never see again"*. The girl who we never should have been having a conversation about because my husband is fucking married.

My face flushes as tears prick my eyes again. I clear my throat, struggling to quell the onslaught of emotions, and grab a glass from the bar cart. I'm so tired of crying all the time. I thought maybe by now the emotions wouldn't be so high, but they only seem to be getting worse. I thought I would be able to come to terms with what Jeremy has done and be well into the rebuilding process with him by now. But here we are, six months later, and my anger only seems to build day after day.

I reach for Jeremy's prized liquor, Johnny Walker Blue Label, and stare at the bottle in my hand. A gift for him on our third wedding anniversary seven months ago. The anniversary of officially becoming Millicent Montgomery. I unscrew the cap slightly and flick it the rest of the way off, watching the cap zing across the kitchen and hit the windows surrounding our breakfast nook. Scent of rich scotch burns into my nose as I pour a heavy glass. I walk, with both the glass and bottle, over to the breakfast nook table and slump down without trying to be quiet. My drinks are no quieter than me as I let them land heavily on top of the wooden table.

I love this table; a gift to us for our wedding, by my grandmother. Her grandmother has gifted it to her at her wedding also, a family heirloom. Usually, items would pass down generationally, mothers to daughters, or what have you. Not this table though, it passes to every other generation. I'm thankful for this strange tradition since she would pass shortly after our wedding and if my mother would have been in possession of the table, I wouldn't be sitting at it right now.

My fingers pass over the deep gashes in the wood where chickens' heads have been hacked off by the women before me. They'd be unimpressed by my lack of motivation to kill, skin, cook, and eat a single chicken. And at this point, I'm not sure it'll pass to anyone beyond me. I'm not sure where my relationship with Jeremy will be within the next year so that puts a wrench in the whole starting a family bit.

Moving past the gashes, I swirl my finger around the large knots covering the table. My wedding ring *tinks* against the glass as my hand runs into my drink. My ring only serves as a reminder of the cheating bastard laying upstairs, instead of a symbol of his undying love for me. I lift the glass to my lips letting the scotch flow into my mouth. I close my eyes as the liquid sits on my tongue for a moment. The burning liquor enhances the torture I bring on myself almost daily now. Finally, I swallow and make myself feel the burn all the way down my throat before landing in the pit of my stomach. The rain has subsided a little bit but the sounds on the windows surrounding me, tell me it's picking back up once again.

These windows have been placed perfectly to overlook the backyard where remnants of a long forgotten garden continues to deteriorate. We've both been so busy with our careers, and now, cleaning up my husband's mess, we haven't had the chance to do anything with the garden. It would be such an experience to plant it together, and eventually, with our kids. We could sit here together, watching our kids run through the yard, eating fresh fruits and veggies right out of the garden, making memories to last a lifetime. My heart stutters from the pain of what may not ever come to be.

I take another drink and lean back until I'm against the windowsill. Only then do I let my eyes flutter open to see who's in the window. I don't know the woman staring back at me anymore. Mascara streaking down her face, showing the world tears have been shed today. Her cheeks still stained red, no doubt a combination of tears and the torturous pleasure being inflicted by some dude at a sex shop. Emerald irises shine brighter than usual thanks to the red background of her sclera. Her skin is as white as the moonlight shining through the windows. She needs some sun. Badly. Her hair once so beautiful - long, brown locks down the middle of her back with an effortless beach curl - now the locks are always wrapping around a pencil in an effort to simply look alive in the least amount of time in the mornings.

I brush back little hairs still plastering to my face from the rain, and watch as the woman looking back mimics me. I test her and take another drink of scotch, never taking my eyes off hers. She does as I do, drinking from her glass. She's good. I grab the bottle of scotch now and hesitate, resting it on my lips, her bottle pausing in the same place. I can't pin the emotion on her face any better than I can explain the emotions ravaging my body day in and day out. A tear glides down from our right eyes at the same moment, before we both take several chugs from our bottles.

As I pull the bottle away, she smiles at me above hers. With a wink, she sets the bottle down and watches as tears pour from my eyes, further adding to the black streaks of mascara on my face. Dropping the bottle to the table, I rip my wedding ring from my finger and fling the ring at her face and as soon as it makes contact with the glass, Samantha's face disappears, the reflection becoming mine again. My heart starts to calm down, and I realize the bottle is on its side leaving very expensive scotch to run across the table. The stream of liquor hits the floor splashing loudly in the stark quiet, sending a shiver down the length of my spine. Pushing up from the table, I grab the glass, toss back the rest of the remaining scotch, then slam the glass back down. Jeremy can clean up this mess too.

Chapter
Three

Why is it so cold in here? I always turn the heat on in the houses before my clients show up. It feels like someone has turned on the air conditioner and now it's a meat freezer.

Mil.

Shit, they're here. My clients are going to be on the fast track out of Chicago if I can't warm this house up.

Mil!

I'm trying to get the AC under control! Stop yelling at me.

Mil!

I can't take it anymore. Give me that blanket! Blanket?

Millicent!

My eyes fly open as I grab for the blanket Jeremy rips off me. It's no wonder I am so cold, with my idiot husband having pulled the blanket off me.

'What the hell are you doing?' I snap.

'It's 9:30 in the morning, Mil! We have a therapy session at 11.'

'Ugh.' I groan, wrenching the blanket from him and flipping over onto my stomach. I must have fallen asleep here last night instead of making it to the spare bedroom. I've been sleeping mostly in the spare over these past few months because Jeremy refuses to leave *our* room. He keeps telling me if we don't continue to live like a married couple, we'll never move past this. And I keep reminding him there wouldn't be anything to move past if not for his sex-capades with the Chi-town harlot.

'Are you going?' I guess that means he's still here.

'Yes, Jeremy. I just need a minute to… to collect myself.' I speak directly into the pillow, my breath reminding me of all the scotch last night.

'Well, you've got about 40 minutes to collect yourself,' he says turning and heading out of the living room. 'Oh, and I cleaned up your mess in the kitchen. What the hell, Mil? That was our anniversary bottle.'

I roll over, flinging the blanket down as I sit up halfway, pinning him with a rageful stare. How dare he remind me what that bottle represents. I'm the one that bought the damn thing. I'm the one who couldn't have been more excited to celebrate my third wedding anniversary with the love of my life - who, unbeknownst to me - was banging the very bartender serving our dinner party drinks that night! I should've fucking known. Every time I would look at him, he would be somewhere else. Not necessarily staring at her; although now, it makes sense. Sometimes I would catch him looking in her direction, but mentally he just would never be with me. It is almost as if he could have cared less about being with me or celebrating our wedding anniversary with our friends. Nonetheless, I know now, he does break things off with her but was terrified she'd blurt something out that night.

Jeremy holds his hands up in surrender.

'I'm sorry. I didn't mean… fuck. I'm sorry, Mil.' Backing into the entryway, he rakes his hands through his brown hair and lets out a long breath.

The same hair Samantha would have been pulling several times a week, no doubt.

'I'm... I'll just wait in the kitchen. Let me know when you're ready.' And, with that, he disappears down the hallway.

I can't stand being in the same home as this man anymore; let alone the same car, where I'm within inches of his body - the body he used to pleasure another woman. The woman he would choose to pleasure in his new car we went together to pick out. Who knows where else he fucked Samantha. He probably fucked her on the bar top at some point, or in our bed. They would have been banging behind my back for almost a year before Jeremy would let the cat out of the bag, so there certainly would have been time for them to experiment.

I look over at him as he drives us to our counseling session. He has been aging over the past few months. The wrinkles around his eyes are deeper, accented by a slight purple tint underneath. He doesn't usually let his facial hair grow out past a five o'clock shadow but from the looks of it, he's way past five. His beard grows so fast he typically has to shave daily. I don't know why he always has done that; I prefer the end-of-the-day Jeremy anyway. He hasn't had a haircut in weeks either, which is also out of the ordinary. Jeremy is always cut and quaffed with his usual brown hair, short on the sides and styled a little longer on top. I have loved how his whole look complements his light brown, almost hazel, eyes. Now, his hair dangles dangerously past his ears, almost covering his eyes. He looks... a mess. But so do I.

I jerk my head to look out the window when he turns and catches me staring at him. His eyes burn into the side of my head as I concentrate on the passing buildings. The air in the car is heavy and suffocating. I hate going to these counseling sessions, because

I'm positive they're not working but I also can't wait to get out of this car.

Jeremy's hand scorches as he settles his hand on top of my thigh. He must have thought I have been reminiscing about the good ole days or craving his touch or some shit. I adjust myself in the seat and turn more towards my door, ensuring sure he knows the last thing I want right now, is for him to touch me. He sighs and puts his hand back on the gear shift. I lay my forehead against the window and close my eyes, the cold sending a shockwave to my brain. Maybe we'll be lucky enough to get hit by a car, putting us both out of our misery, before making it to counseling.

The ticking clock is deafening. My coat off and the top two buttons of my blouse undone, I still can't get comfortable. The underwire of my bra digs into my sides so thoroughly, I feel I'll have indentations for the rest of my life. My pants have randomly started to itch my legs and the waistband seems like it's been slowly constricting around my middle since sitting on this couch. And I'm ready to take my shoes off due to the strangling feeling my toes are experiencing right now. Counseling should be for healing not inducing undue panic. I'm starting to feel laying naked in a bathtub full of fire ants would be more relaxing.

'Millicent?' Dr. Johnson asks.

'Hmm?'

'I asked if you or Jeremy have tried anything this week to make the other smile?'

That's laughable at best. Jeremy has done squat. He's done so little I'm still confused on why he wants to try to work this out. At this point, I might as well just give this woman my money and stay home. Or go see Cade.

'Uh, well, if you call leaving a cold plate of spaghetti on the counter something to make someone smile, then we're headed in the right direction.'

'That's not fair, Mil,' Jeremy huffs slamming his hand down on his thigh.

'Not fair? Don't sit here and tell me what's not fair, Jeremy! I'm not the one who went and fucked the local bartender while my wife was working and is now complaining about her not being fair!'

'Let's take a breath for a moment,' Dr. Johnson redirects, flipping to a new sheet of paper in her notebook. 'Jeremy, do you think you're doing what you can to try and reignite the flame you and Millicent once had? To try and start rebuilding what's been broken down between the two of you?'

Jeremy lets out a forceful sigh that can be heard from Ohio.

'I'm not going to say I've tried everything. I could probably try harder. I made dinner for us last night. I had wine poured and yes, I made spaghetti. All to get a text saying *I'll be late. Don't wait up.* This isn't the first time she's had to miss something because of work but I thought she might also put in a little more effort so we can at least progress a little farther than we have over the past few months. It feels like I just confessed yesterday.'

'What's keeping you from trying harder then?'

'I'm trying to give her space. The space she's asked for from the beginning. It seems like the more space I give, the farther she slips away.'

I see him wiping tears from his face out of the corner of my eye, just as a tear threatens to sail down my own cheek. He's not wrong. I have asked for space. And since he's giving me the space I want, I've had room to explore between another man's legs. I know finding a dominant isn't what the doctor had meant when recommending I find an avenue to release stress. Dr. Johnson was probably assuming I'd join a gym or take a yoga class, maybe even ask Jeremy to go for a hike or something. Instead, I found myself down a Reddit rabbit hole and came across the ultimate stress reliever. Cade.

Need someone to take your mind off things?! -r/596668567

I have never felt so good as I have with my Master... -r/ MasterLover3423423

VictoriasDiner=BestSubmissionOfMyLife -r/subbrat23492735874

Cade is a Master at Victoria's Diner. A great cover when you think about it. The club is almost like a speakeasy of sorts. A sex speakeasy. Your everyday person can come in for a burger, toss back a beer, and not have an inkling of what's happening in the basement. The outside of Victoria's is painted black with a low, warm light emitting through the frosted glass windows. Wooden flower boxes under each window always have fresh greenery hanging down toward the sidewalk. Gold lettering hangs over the double door entrance brandishing the establishment's name. As you walk in, you're met with a seeming "everyday bar" that serves breakfast, lunch, and dinner. There is a beautiful mahogany bar top lined with leather cushion stools. The bar wall is covered with mirrors showcasing the many choices in liquor. Several high-top tables are scattered throughout the main floor, ready to seat you and three of your friends. Around the outside border, plush couches line the walls with coffee tables and candles adorn the tops. Rich, bronze sconces hang around the black walls, in between beautiful, moody, art pieces and mirrors. This is a place for relaxing, enjoying yourself, and staying as long as you want. A very mafia bar-esque vibe overall.

After perusing the online profiles of the Masters listed and making a selection through the website, you're directed to then make an appointment. Once you're all paid up, you receive specific instructions for entrance into the club hidden below the diner:

Thank you for booking your appointment at Victoria's Diner! In order to preserve the privacy of the club, we request the following instructions be adhered to:

1. Please plan on arriving at least 30 minutes prior to your appointment time. Have a seat at the bar in the diner, grab a drink, and take a minute to relax.

2. Once you've are ready, wave the bartender over and ask him this specific question: 'Did this used to be Dom's diner?' This notifies our bartender you have an appointment at the club. Failure to adhere to accurate wording is an automatic forfeit of your appointment, no refunds or exceptions.

3.   *The bartender will ask if you'd like to close out or keep your tab open (you may also want to stop for a drink after your appointment). Please drinks in the club. **There is a small bar inside the club where drinks may be ordered to take into the room with you. Again, this keeps questions at bay.*

4.   *After you've closed out or kept your tab open, the bartender will hand you a key card and direct you to the restrooms.*

5.   *In the hallway of the restrooms, is a sign for "EMPLOYEE BATHROOM". Use your keycard to.*

6.   *Once in the 'bathroom', go to the last stall, continue through the doorway, and down the steps. Please do NOT try and use this bathroom as it is strictly for show purposes.*

7.   *Upon entering the underground club, check-in with the bartender. He'll let you know which private waiting room to proceed to.*

8.   *In your private waiting room, use this time to prepare for your appointment. Note: It is not advised to enter the Master's Quarters before he has called upon you. Please remain in the private waiting room.*

a.   *First-time appointments: Your Master will greet you in the private waiting room so sit tight. He'll let you know what he'd like for you to do during this time should you continue to book appointments. He'll also go over ground rules, safe words, what you're wanting to experience, and any other information he might deem important, or paperwork to sign.*

b.   *Regular visitors: Your Master should have let you know what he expects, and all rules you should follow.*

9.   *Lastly, enjoy!*

Jeremy clearing his throat brings me back to reality. All eyes are on me as I try to figure out if I can answer whatever question Dr. Johnson laid out.

'I'm sorry. Can you repeat the question?'

'Jesus,' Jeremy mutters and turns his head toward the window.

'I'm sorry, Jeremy!'

'Millicent, it seems you are elsewhere today. Why is that?'

I'm thinking about my Dom, and how he has me laid across his lap last night spanking the shit out of me. Then licks my pussy as if his life depends on it. All of that ending with me straddling his lap and fucking him until we both end up coming on each other.

'I just have a lot going on with work, that's all. I have a lot of houses I'm trying to close.' This isn't a lie. I have a lot of houses on the market right now. It's just certainly not the only thing consuming the property in my brain.

'That's understandable. Work can be stressful and feel even more so when you add personal life issues on top of it.'

I stare at her. Stressful doesn't come close to defining this situation.

'So, Millicent, as Jeremy was saying, he wants to make progress with you. He understands you need space but he's afraid giving you that space is having the opposite effect.'

I continue to stare at her.

'Are you willing to accept Jeremy trying to close the space between the two of you? Do you think you might be able to start accepting his acts of apology so you two can start to rebuild? Together.'

'Yeah. I... I can try.' The tears that are constantly threatening to flow begin their descent down my face. I try turning my head toward the wall, but as soon as I do, Jeremy's hand rests on my leg for the second time today. I try hiding my flinch, but the way he moves his hand away, I didn't hide it well enough.

The ride home doesn't go any better than the ride to counseling. The raw feeling I'm left with after counseling, crackles over my skin, sending my brain into a tailwind. It takes all the strength in my body not to rip my hair out, as thoughts ping pong around my head; the silence inside the car further fueling the rate at which they come.

Not able to fight the silence anymore, I switch on the radio. Jeremy makes no move to stop me so he must be over the noiselessness as well. My irritation rises as one commercial ends and another starts. I don't know why I bother at this point. Listening to Sam from Auto-something or other is worse than my husband's breathing. Just as I reach out to change the station, Sam stops trying to sell me a car and the drums of Fiona Apple's "Criminal" start beating, filling the cab of the car.

I remember when this song came out. Just shy of becoming a full-on teenager, screaming the lyrics at the top of my lungs into my brush, giving the best concert I could to walls full of posters. The song would provide an outlet for teenage angst before I could know what it was. Oh, to be able to go back and tell my 12-year-old self to just wait and see what life would bring you. Heartbreak.

Listening to the lyrics today, has the opposite effect of what it did have so many years ago. Now, feeling exhausted and miserable riding along in the car with my husband, thinking about what occurred last night with someone not my husband, the guilt of the situation presses in on me from all sides. How can I do something so wrong when Jeremy is wanting to try to make it to the other side of this? But that's the point, right? I never would have looked for Cade if Jeremy would have remained the wholly faithful husband I always thought him to be. We wouldn't be driving home from counseling right now, and I wouldn't be thinking about Cade nonstop. I could be enjoying my husband's company instead of trying to suppress the never-failing-to rise vomit any time I'm in his vicinity.

Groaning, I reach and turn the radio off. Silence has to be better than this.

Chapter Four

I've been in this bathtub for too long. My water is barely lukewarm, and my fingertips are tiny prunes. I need a good soak after our session today; something to get rid of the *"I've been cheating on my husband, because he cheated on me because I couldn't figure out another way to deal with it,"* grime. Technically, I have found a way to deal with it. Just not a healthy way.

A slight knock at the door, and my first instinct is to try covering up with a sponge or washcloth or something. There isn't really any way to hide, unless I get out and grab a towel, since I'm in a clawfoot tub with no curtain around it. I remind myself Jeremy has, in fact, seen me naked.

'Yeah?'

'I thought I'd bring you up a glass of wine,' Jeremy says quietly as he opens the door and steps into the bathroom.

'Oh, thanks,' I say as he starts walking toward me with the wine. The water slips down my breasts as I sit up in the tub, my nipples instantly hardening from the bite of the chill air.

Jeremy stops, his eyes catching on my breasts.

'Uh, here's….,' Jeremy says, voice raspy. He clears his throat, '…your wine.'

I realize too late what he is staring at, and I sink quickly back into the water.

'Shit! Sorry.'

'No. No, it's fine. I… I should've waited until you were done.'

I reach for the glass while trying to stay submerged. I hate this is so awkward now. Seven months ago, he would've taken off his clothes and slipped into the tub behind me. Water would've been thrown all over the floor from him having his way with me.

Jeremy turns towards the door, stopping short of leaving the bathroom. I hold my mouthful of wine, waiting for his next move. He shakes his head as if dismissing a thought.

'I made dinner. It's just about ready,' he says without looking at me and then disappears from the doorway.

I finally swallow the wine before plucking the drain plug out with my toe.

I towel off, comb out my hair, and throw on a tank top and leggings. Walking to the staircase, I pause at the top. I smell something delicious before hearing Jeremy plate up whatever has been whipped up for our *"let's try harder date"* tonight. I feel miserable standing here, willing myself to go down the steps; but I can't help what this has done to me.

My entire life I have prided myself on being loyal. Not just because I thought that's what I should do but because it also has made me feel good. It's who I am, or have been; people know they can trust me. It's also become a fault of sorts. In my romantic relationships - all of which I have been cheated on in some way or another - my boyfriends would take advantage of my faithful nature. If they would cheat, I would stay devoted to the relationship until *they* would call it quits. I thought Jeremy would be different, but he would prove otherwise.

Prying myself from the top step, I head downstairs and into the kitchen. I stop short in the doorway when I see Jeremy has gone all out. Tonight is already very different from the cold spaghetti on the counter the night before. A huge salad sits in the middle of the table, along with salmon and what looks like Jeremys famous mushroom risotto, and some sort of cake looking dessert. My mouth waters as I take in the well thought out dinner in front of me.

He has another bottle of wine uncorked, and two full glasses sit on the table. Candles flicker around the food and on windowsills, their flames reflecting off the glass. If someone watches from the outside, they would think tonight must be a pretty special night to call for all of this. I can't deny Jeremy's effort makes me feel a little warm inside; I'm also starting to think I might be underdressed. Even though we're in the comfort of our kitchen.

'It smells amazing,' I say as I head toward the table.

'Thank you. I know you love salmon so I thought it might be a good choice,' he says as we both sit down across from each other. He stares at me a moment, a nervous swallow follows.

'I almost feel underdressed.' I look down at my tank top and leggings as a wave of nervousness surges through me.

'You look great, Mil.'

'I look like I'm ready for a Netflix and chill kind of night.' I half laugh grabbing my glass of wine to take a much-needed drink.

'Would you rather do that? We can take everything into the living room and...'

'No, no,' I cut him off before he can finish, 'that's not what I meant. I just didn't expect such a fancy dinner.... date.'

'I wanted to make tonight special, Mil. I'm trying to show you I want to work on things and... I'm sorry,' he lets out a long breath, 'I am so damn sorry.' Jeremy looks down at the table, his head shaking from side to side.

I don't know what to say. A part of me wants to reassure him and say *I know* because I still love this man desperately. Another part of me is so broken I feel we shouldn't even be having this conversation to begin with. Couldn't he imagine he would feel like shit after doing something so… shitty? The moment after finding out about his being with another woman, should've been enough for him to walk the other way immediately. But it wasn't.

Lifting his head up, Jeremy looks out the window and rubs his hand down his face. He's trying to hide the fact he's crying. He takes a shuddering breath of air then lets it out slowly before facing me, shaking his head side to side again. Tears streak his face, and I can see where they land atop his beard. He *is* sorry. He might even be hurting as much as I am.

'I'm sorry, Mil.' He slowly reaches across the table and squeezes my hands in his. It's a squeeze saying more than "I'm sorry". It's saying *I'm in this, and I would never do anything to make you feel so horrible again.*

I manage a half smile in return, because no words will come out. I want to tell him I understand he's sorry; but, at the same time, if I say that, it feels like I'm also in this 100% and I don't know that I am yet.

Our conversation moves on to lighter subject material. For that, I'm thankful because I don't think I would've been able to sit with him for over an hour while he sulks.

I'm also thankful for Jeremy's cooking tonight. Perfectly flaky salmon, the creamiest mushroom risotto that's ever blessed my mouth, and a salad rivaling the best. All before dessert, which can only be described as the best chocolate cake I've ever eaten, and, as a self-proclaimed chocolate cake connoisseur, I can say that.

His food should be amazing, though. Especially since we're still paying down his student loans. He has graduated top of his class with a culinary degree, while managing to also get a business degree at the same time. Now, working as a private chef, I expect his cooking to blow me away daily. I am so proud of him when he is finally done and graduates, and I'm still proud of him. Unfortunately, this is how Samantha has hooked her claws into my husband. She serves as a private bartender for the wedding dinner Jeremy has been hired to cook for. In hindsight, maybe I shouldn't have encouraged culinary school after all.

Finishing my first glass from our second bottle of wine, I stack our plates to start cleaning up. Heading to the sink, I can feel the effects of the wine even more. With the alcohol in our systems, conversation starts flowing a little better and Jeremy even manages to make me laugh a couple of times. I'm reminded of the times we have before the big affair bomb was dropped. He isn't cooking dinner to win me back, but just because he loves cooking and seeing my eyes roll in the back of my head when something is especially tasty.

Standing at the sink rinsing our plates, Jeremy slides between me and the open dishwasher to look for the cover to the cake stand. The second his body glides against mine, I'm met with that familiar electricity shooting through my body. I know he notices it too when he pauses just before the cupboard next to me. I shake it off and go back to my sink full of dishes.

Jeremy packs up what's left of dinner then places the dishes in the sink. His arm grazes mine as he moves away and the electric shock hits me again. Goosebumps pepper my arms and I wonder if a white tank top with no bra is the best choice for tonight. Clearing my throat and rolling my shoulders back, I try to gain some of my composure back. I'm trying my hardest not to reminisce how good Jeremy can make me feel.

He brings over the salad bowl and this time, instead of moving away after placing it in the sink, he lingers behind me a bit. His hands find their way around my waist, pulling me tighter against him, his beard grazes my neck. His lips press ever so lightly onto my neck and my nipples instantly struggle against my tank top.

He waits a moment, as if to gauge my reaction. But then, his lips kiss my neck again and this time, the warmth of his tongue glides along my skin. My eyes close, my head lulls back against his shoulder; his left hand pulls my chin farther to the side, exposing my neck even more to his seductive mouth. My body deceives me when an mmm sound escapes my throat.

'I've missed you, Mil,' Jeremy whispers into my neck.

I feel him lean forward to turn off the water. And when his other hand returns, it finds itself under my tank top, trailing over my stomach up toward my chest. The fabric shifts as his hand moves across my skin inching higher and higher. The tank top scratches across my sensitive nipples as his touch grazes the underside of my tits.

I lose almost all control when his fingers start swirling my nipple, and the wetness pools between my legs as he continues kissing and nibbling my neck. My brain tries pulling me out of the reverie, screaming *you aren't supposed to be enjoying this,* but I can't seem to move away from him. It would be a horrible lie if I say this didn't feel amazing, or that I want him to stop. Maybe we both need this. Maybe this will set us on the track to working things out.

My breath hitches when his right hand slides along my waistband. The other hand holding my jaw now trails up the front of my shirt for its turn with my nipples. His fingers slip inside my leggings, searching out my hot center. Finding his target, he sinks two fingers into me, gathering some wetness before inching back up a little higher. The second his fingers find my clit; I drop the plate I have been holding and grip the sink with both hands. I moan out as he starts circling my clit. My hips instinctively start moving with his hand, and I feel how hard he is as my ass grinds against him. All I can think about is how badly I want him; how much I need him to fuck me right here in this kitchen.

His lips find mine as his fingers continue decimating my clit. His wine-soaked tongue surrounds mine and I can't keep the sounds coming out of my mouth at bay. Fingers plunge into my slit, as I almost instantly cum all over his hand. The burn of the orgasm builds, stronger by the second.

'Is this for me, Mil?' Jeremy groans in my ear, my eyes instantly flying open.

'What?'

'You're so wet baby… are you going to cum for me?'

I grab Jeremy's arms pulling his hands from under my shirt and out of my leggings as I spin around and push him back.

'What's wrong?' Jeremy asks reaching out in an attempt to pull me back into him.

'Why would you say that?' A million questions roll through my mind as my arms cross my chest attempting to guard myself. Does he know about Cade? Or have suspicions?

'Say what? I thought you were feeling good. I thought we were enjoying ourselves?'

'You asked if this was for you! Why did you ask that?' My breathing gets faster, and my cheeks flush, wondering if he somehow knows about Cade. My Cade. Shit.

'I was just trying to be like old times, Mil. You liked dirty talk. I'm sorry. I won't do it if you don't want me to.' Jeremy reaches for my hand again but I pull back, blocking him with my other hand.

'Mil? What is wrong?' He pleads, a look of pure devastation blanketing his face.

'I…I don't think we should…I can't do this!' I turn and run from the kitchen. Grabbing my keys as I pass the sideboard in the hall, and a pair of shoes before I fumble out the front door.

'Mil?! Where are you going?' I hear him yell behind me.

Inside my car, I crank the keys in the ignition, and whip around before heading out of the driveway. Peeking into the rearview mirror, I see Jeremy running onto the front porch.

'Mil!'

He stops there, runs his hand through his hair, then turns, and disappears back through the front door. I don't know where I'm going but I know I can't be here right now.

Chapter Five

I drive for what seems like forever before I find myself in front of Cade's house after fleeing Jeremy last night. I want so badly to go up and knock on the door but can't pull myself from my car. We've had a couple sessions at his house now, but they have always been scheduled ahead of time. So, it would've been the first time showing up unannounced. And for what? For sex? For comfort? Our sessions are already crossing an imaginary line, veering toward a relationship, and if I show up on his doorstep in the middle of the night, that direction might be solidified.

By the time I get back home, Jeremy has been in bed, and the house is dark and quiet. I find a note waiting for me in the dish where I put my keys. As I pick it up, I notice my wedding ring sitting underneath. He must have found it when cleaning up my liquor mess the other night. I hold the ring between my fingers - the metal burning into my skin, before sliding it back on, and heading into the living room to throw myself on the couch.

I didn't even manage to fully open the note, before the paper starts blurring as tears gather in my eyes. *Fuck. Get it together, Mil. It's just a note.* Wiping my eyes, I finish unfolding the paper.

I AM SO SORRY.

LOVE,

JEREMY

I crumple the note in my fist and roll over, planting my face in the pillow. Acting as a sound barrier for my screams, the fabric of the pillow quickly sops up the salty drips from my eyes. I couldn't even pinpoint why I'm crying exactly. Because my husband has cheated? Because he has tried to have sex with me? Because I'm a cheater now and have disappointed myself? Or maybe because I'm feeling stuck now that my husband is actually trying. Perhaps I'm feeling something toward Cade and my husband is getting in the way of that? I do love Jeremy, but the affair coming to light has completely crushed me. Still does every day.

Pulling up to the open house I have scheduled for this morning, I try keeping my wracked nerves in check, still reeling from last night. If a paper bag would have been within reach, I'd shove my entire head into it. I double-check my eyes in the mirror before getting out of the car. I have had to use eyedrops before leaving the house, to combat the redness from my lack of sleep last night.

'Well, hello there! You look like shit.' A voice rings out as I walk through the door and turn the corner into the living room.

'Thanks, Cel. You look amazing as usual.' Rolling my eyes at her, I place my briefcase on the coffee table and take a seat on the couch.

Rummaging through papers, I grab a stack of business cards for potential clients. I'll be lucky if anyone even takes one if I look anything like Celeste says I do. The couch compresses next to me, and I'm suddenly being enveloped in Celeste's arms. I've got to hand it to her, she does give amazing hugs.

Letting myself mold against Celeste's body, a sigh as old as last night, releases into the air.

'What's wrong Mil? Tell Cel all about it?' Ever since Celeste and I met, she refers to herself as Cel. Not because she has always had that nickname, but because she says it makes us more like sisters. I have stopped reminding her long ago, we would be close even if she didn't have a nickname like mine.

'Uuuuuuugggggh,' I grumble.

I pull reluctantly from Celeste's warm embrace and position myself facing her, forcing my gaze upwards. Celeste mimics my actions and scoops my hands in own. Instantly I remember how easy it has been getting close to Celeste. Big, brown, doe eyes gaze into my own, oozing *"trust me, I'm here for you"*. Honestly, we might pass for sisters. Except for our height, and well hair and eye color, we could totally pass. Just kidding, we don't look alike even a little bit. At 5'10" she towers over me and her blonde, neat, shoulder-length bob with no bangs, is clearly shorter than my own, less expensive, home-salon styled hair.

Celeste and I would meet during our first year in college. Both of us shuffle uneasily through the enormous halls housing classrooms, until we reach for the door handle at the same time, our hands knocking into each other. Lost in our own minds of navigating this new world, we look at each other as if not believing there might be another human in our vicinity, before we break into an almost crazed laughter.

'I'm Celeste,' she laughs.

'I'm Millicent.' Explaining, as I take her extended hand in mine.

'And my first friend here.'

'In that case, you can call me Mil.'

Best friend status at 'first-reach-for-the-same-door'.

'Well,' she says, glancing furtively at her watch, 'people will start showing up in 15 minutes or so. Spill.'

'We had a counseling session yesterday. Jeremy promised to try harder, and I promised to stop needing space and start accepting when he's trying. He made a beautiful dinner, we had wine, he touched me, it felt good, we started kissing, his hands ended up down my pants and in my shirt, but then he said something weird, and I pulled away from him, ran out of the house, got in my car, and drove around for several hours.'

Celeste stares back at me, eyes blinking, seemingly just as surprised as I, that all of this comes out without taking a single breath.

'I have so many questions.'

'I figured,' I huff, spinning my body forward, slumping my head against the back of the couch.

'So, he made you a dinner?'

'Yeah. It was delicious too.'

'Did you guys talk about anything? The... you know... affair?' Celeste hates saying the word as much as I do. In fact, when the whole affair did come out, Celeste goes and decks Jeremy square in the nose next time she sees him at an event; while I remain still tucked away at her house.

'No. He did start with an apology. I do believe he's sorry. I just... I just don't know if I can ever get past this.'

'I get it. What he did is unforgivable. And I don't want you to feel bad for a second if you come to find you can't forgive him.'

'I'm trying. I'm just living one day at a time. Maybe it is me? Maybe me wanting space isn't the right thing for this situation.'

'Maybe. I think it's healthy to want and need space. But I guess there might come a time when the space needs to close a little.'

'Yeah, maybe.'

'Now, the elephant in the room. You guys *did* stuff? And it felt good! That's a good sign, right? What did he say that freaked you out?'

'It *was* feeling good. *Really* good. He's always made me putty in his hands when it comes to sex. But he said something weird, and I don't know, I just freaked out.'

'What did he say?' Relentless little thing.

'I can't even totally remember. Something about me being wet.'

'So dirty talk isn't your thing?'

'It is, usually. I don't know. He just said...' The doorbell sounds, cutting me off. Thank God! I never thought I'd ever be in a situation warranting a *Saved By The Bell* quote.

Getting up to let our potential clients in, Celeste's eyes roll revealing her irritation at not having the full story, before reaching the door. And she never will. Celeste doesn't know about Cade. She would disown me. She hates Jeremy for what he has put me through. I know if she finds out I have been doing the same thing while Jeremy and I are supposed to try and work things out, she will think me worse than him.

Shortly after 6:00 p.m., I pull into my driveway. Overall, the open house has gone well, and I have at least seven promising couples expressing interest in the property. In today's market, they will fight tooth and nail up until the paperwork is signed. It's not uncommon to receive constant phone calls and emails on properties that haven't officially closed yet. I have a feeling this will be no different.

As soon as the front door swings open, I hear music coming from the kitchen. Jeremy must be in a good mood. Highly surprising after last night's fiasco. I gingerly set my keys and briefcase down, noticing a very fresh margarita sitting next to my key dish. I hang my coat in the closet, kick my heels off, and drift toward the kitchen. Jeremy appears in the doorway before I can make it all the way down the hall.

'Stop right there!' His playful demeanor bears the half-grin that would always bring me to my knees… before.

'What's going on?'

'Just grab your margarita, head upstairs, shower, if you need to…,' there's that smile again, 'and put your comfiest clothes on.'

I stare at Jeremy, waiting for more of an explanation.

'Go! Seriously. Get moving. And then hurry back downstairs,' he says, shooing me away with his hands.

Eyebrows still knit together, I do as he says and slowly turn to head upstairs, snatching my margarita on the way. I stop after crossing our bedroom's threshold and taking a second to try my margarita; it does not disappoint. The perfect mix of salty and sour. The tequila warms my tongue and throat as soon as it hits, melting the day away, and instantly relaxing me. I take another drink, licking the salt off my lips, before aiming for the bathroom.

I do need a shower. Badly. I have reapplied my dry shampoo three times today, and my deodorant more times than I care to remember. With the shower steaming, I get in, letting the hot water pierce my skin. As the water washes away my sins, I wonder what Jeremy's end game is for this evening. I haven't seen him since frenzy last night, after leaving in a frenzy last night. Not that I have bothered to reach out either, but it catches me off guard to see him in a good mood; let alone ready to party.

Before going back downstairs, I throw on a sweatshirt and some leggings. Realizing it's one of Jeremy's sweatshirts, I pull it off to change it, reconsider, and finally decide to let it fall back down. We're trying to move on, right? Downing the last of my margarita - an extra dose of liquid courage - I go see what Jeremy has in store for us. And also want another one of these amazing margaritas.

'Welcome to Mil Beach!' Jeremy says excitedly, taking my empty glass and shoving a full one in my hand.

'Jeremy, I…,' I am speechless. He's turned our kitchen into a full-on beach party. Little tiki torches flicker all around, light dancing on the walls, beach balls roll lackadaisically across the floor, and island music plays. On top of the table, pushed up against the far wall of the kitchen, to make room for a beach umbrella and towels, sits a taco and margarita bar set up. I'm taking everything in, when a strong arm wraps around my chest, another around my stomach, pulling me into a warm body.

'I thought we needed a getaway,' Jeremy says into my hair with a kiss.

'I'm impressed. Jeremy, really, it's… awesome!' It really is. Before I can talk myself out of it, I reach up and grab onto his arm across my chest, his muscles contracting excitedly as I squeeze.

'Well, then,' his voice gravelly, 'let's check out the taco bar, shall we?' Letting loose his grip, he takes my hand and leads me to the food.

After our bellies are full of margaritas and tacos, we lounge under the beach umbrella singing dreamily to "Santeria" by Sublime, like we have written the song ourselves. This night has gone very well, with neither of us having any weird, sad moments. The conversation hasn't lacked in the slightest and the laughs have come naturally. Maybe this *is* what we needed. Some drinks and a little Jeremy and Mil party to knock the dust off things.

As the song comes to a close, so do our voices. We both look down to realize our glasses are almost empty.

'These are delicious,' I say as I knock back the last of my margarita.

'Want another?'

'If you want to make me one, I'll drink it,' I laugh as my eyes meet his.

He smiles that crooked smile as his eyes fall to my mouth. My heart rate ticks up as I feel the start of a small smile forming on my lips.

Leaning in, Jeremy's hand grazes the side of my cheek as he tucks a piece of hair behind my ear. He brings his hand back to rest on my cheek and instinctively, I lean into his hand, letting my eyes close. The palm of his hand heats my skin and let myself remember how good this used to feel. How good it does feel.

My eyes flutter open to see Jeremy still staring with his smile and finally, let myself return the gesture without all the second-guessing.

'Can I kiss you, Millicent?' His words are so sweet and light, they remind me of the first time we ever kissed. It feels like lifetimes ago. Young and in college, sitting on his dorm room floor playing Mario Kart. Blowing off finals steam, I had just beaten him for what seemed like the 100th time. He tossed his controller down before taking mine from my hands, looked straight into my eyes, and asked 'Can I kiss you, Millicent?' After months of flirting, I thought he'd never ask.

'Yes,' I breath, closing my eyes once more as Jeremy moves closer.

The most subtle kiss at first, like a butterfly trying to decide if it's safe to land, as if he were trying to remember how. His lips are like butter against mine as they brush across the surface, savoring the moment. Parting ever so slightly, they land softly against mine once again, only lingering a little longer. I taste the salt from his margarita as I wait for him to quit teasing and give his all.

His forehead against mine, we're suspended in time. We aren't kissing but neither of us are pulling away either. We're just existing together in this moment. Sitting in the energy around us feels like the ice might be starting to melt.

'Kiss me again, Jeremy,' I whisper. I want him to. His lips just resting on mine are feeling like a taunt. I want his tongue entangled with mine. I want his hand in my hair, pulling me closer to him. I want to feel his other hand gliding down my back, only stopping once he's made it to my ass.

Jeremy lets out a groan as he keeps his forehead glued to mine. His hand moves from my cheek to the back of my neck so slowly it becomes painful to wait for his next move.

'I want to kiss you again. So bad,' he finally manages through gritted teeth.

I start to pull away, his comment throwing me off.

'It's just, after last night, I don't want to rush this. I moved too fast, and I hate that I upset you.' He's staring intently into my eyes now and I can tell, without a doubt, he means to fix this.

'I overreacted. I'm sorry...'

'Don't! Do not be sorry,' he interrupts, 'that was all me. We're going to take things slow. I want to fix this.'

Jeremy takes my hand in his before bringing it to his lips, holding it there. I sit with him as the moment sweeps me up. In front of me is this man that hurt me in the most horrific way and yet, I trust he wants to get back to us. The *us* that existed before Samantha. My mind shoots back to the day I found out about the affair. The day that led to us sitting here, in our kitchen, not tearing each other's clothes off, and holding back kisses to try and take things slow.

'I'm going to fix this, Mil. I promise. I can't lose you,' he says, keeping me from reliving that day in hell. He's giving me everything he's got as I watch the tears slowly start to trickle down his cheeks. My own hot tears pricking at my eyes.

Jeremy jumps to his feet as drumsticks click together, the sound breaking through the air. I take his outstretched hand and he pulls me to my feet. Leading us to the center of the room as "Pain and Misery" by The Teskey Brothers begins its torturous melody, he turns, pulling me in close, one hand settling gently across the low of my back, the other still holding my hand tight in his. I let my head rest against his chest, and I listen as his heart thunders inside his ribcage. We sway around the kitchen in time with the music, and I bring my arm up around Jeremy's neck, his ten o'clock shadow scratching against my forearm. Our bodies fall into a rhythm we haven't had in months, maybe even longer. A rhythm we certainly haven't known since his confession. Our movements are effortless once again, and my body relaxes even further into his embrace, the comfort consuming me.

We continue our dance even after the song has come to a close. Our hearts continuing the tune for us, neither of us wanting to ruin the significance.

Reluctantly pulling away slightly, I look up as Jeremy is wiping away wetness from his face, and I feel my heartstrings tug for another time tonight.

'How about that drink?' he asks as he clears his throat.

'Yeah… yeah, I'll take another.' I manage a meek smile.

Jeremy grabs the back of my neck, pulling my forehead to his lips. The kiss ignites something inside me as he lingers again, relishing the moment and imprinting himself on me.

'We're gonna get through this, Mil,' he whispers before going to refill our margaritas.

'Yeah, we'll get through this,' I mutter to myself as tears fall unbidden down my cheeks.

Chapter Six

A fog is pressing in on me from all sides, even as I sit here in my office. The office, or house rather, Celeste and I bought together for our realty ventures. We went with this old Victorian style home for office space so we could use the downstairs space as a cozy hosting environment for clients when they were closing on their own dream homes. The upstairs bedrooms provided Celeste and I with our own personal spaces for business. We loved it as soon as we stepped foot through the door and both of us saw our future here. We spent a ton of time decorating down to the smallest details to ensure our customers would feel comfortable here and that they would spread the word of how great it was to work with Montgomery Realty, Inc.

The fog further clouds my brain. Not just one cloud either, but several vicious storm clouds ready to drop hail and snow any minute. After Jeremy's surprise Sunday, his promise to move slow, his promise to fix this, and even his cute texts from yesterday while I was working, I'm overwhelmed by the fact that I'm realizing I have no idea what the hell I'm doing. I'm still in a place where I don't know if we can ever come back from this, but I also don't feel like I can leave him hanging. Which is almost absurd considering he's the *why* we aren't in a good place to begin with. I hate that I know his effort is genuine.

Then, there's the Cade situation. Can I continue to see him while my husband is pulling out all the stops? The answer is definitely no. But I also don't think I can quit him. Cade has become a part of my life in a way I wasn't prepared for when I first started going to Victoria's Diner. I'm not even sure whose fault it is that this business relationship has moved into the realm of an actual relationship. A situation-ship if you will. Of course, neither of us has broached the subject but anyone in the room could probably call us out within seconds of seeing us together. Not to mention the fact that I hired this man to punish me and nothing else. I haven't had one of those appointments for a couple of months.

The first time we had sex at an appointment was situation changing enough but our interactions escalated even further during a particularly steamy session. Cade had me standing at the end of the bed, arms high above my head with my wrists tied to the top railing. There was nothing left to the imagination as the only thing I was wearing was a blindfold. He had requested earlier in the day that I bring my headphones with me, which as he placed them in my ears, I figured out why. Silent at first, they slowly sprang to life as Vessel's dark and sultry lyrics snaked their way into my head. I couldn't see anything and could only here the music thanks to my noise cancelling earbuds. With most of my senses drown out, my body reacted wildly as Cade left no part of my skin untouched. His lips seared onto my chin, his beard grazing across my nipples, the sting of his palm on my ass, the bite of his teeth on my stomach, his legs between mine as they spread me further apart, the sweet heat of his tongue as he stroked my clit, igniting crazy waves of pleasure as "Sugar" by Sleep Token blasted in my ears.

I can only imagine the look of pure lust on his face as he stood in front of me while I strained against the wrist cuffs trying to keep myself upright. My head sagging backward as my chest heaved from the exhilaration. He took me by surprise when his lips settled on mine. His tongue immediately opening my lips and coaxing my tongue out to play, claiming me wholly. Leaving me breathless, he reached up and unhooked the wrist cuffs and my arms fell over his shoulders from the shear relief of being released. He pulled out the headphones and slipped the blindfold from my eyes, letting in the view of the near feral man that couldn't wait to be buried inside me. Gripping the backs of my thighs, he pulled my legs up and around his waist. Our mouths collided again as he walked us around to the side of the bed, sitting down and dragging us both to the center of the bed.

Reaching between us and grabbing his heavy cock, he circled my entrance teasingly before sliding easily into my soaked pussy. The fullness immediately making me scream out as I started to move my hips with his. Our bodies slid against each other as we fucked on the bed for the first time. Our voices rising louder and louder the closer we came to shattering each other.

'God damn, Millicent. This pussy....'

'Oh, fuck... fuck... you can... call me Mil.'

'Mil,' he tested the new name out as he seemed to plunge even deeper into me, 'I like that... and this pussy.'

I was so close to coming I could barely stand it. I felt like I was going to burst out of my skin if I didn't find some sort of release but, at the same time, couldn't bear the thought of him pulling out of me once we were finished.

'Phillip... fuck... Phil, I....'

'Call me Cade, Mil... now, cum all over this dick,' he demanded as my pussy clenched around his cock and we both plummeted into a sweaty abyss of pleasure.

That had been our hottest session yet. By far. Even thinking about it now heats my core. I had asked where Cade came from since I knew him as Phillip. Mil is just short for Millicent so it's easy to figure that one out. He told me it's his middle name and typically only business associates know him as Phillip. Only business associates? So, people more than business associates call him Cade? Oh... shit.

Speaking of the devil, I think as I grab my phone when it starts vibrating on my desk.

Client – P. Alderidge: My place tonight. 6:00 p.m.

My heart rate starts to increase as the excitement for tonight spreads throughout my body. I already feel the wetness start to pool between my legs thinking about being back in Cade's house. Our sessions are already intimate, but this adds a whole other level to it.

'Hey!'

'Hey!' My eyes fly up as I slam my phone down on the desk. The typical reaction of someone caught doing something they shouldn't.

'Why so flushed there, Mil?' Celeste asks as she drops into the seat across from my desk.

'Me? I'm not flushed.'

'Right... you look like you're ready to rip someone's clothes off. Jeremy send ya a little somethin' somethin'?'

'Uh... yeah, yeah he did.' I'm fumbling so badly, and Celeste is making it even worse with the stare she's giving me. The *I know something is up here* stare.

'Sorry... it caught me off guard and then you came in and...yeah. Anyway, what's up?'

Not totally believing my story, she adds her quintessential eyebrow raise to the mix. I'm completely unwilling to let her in on any of this, so I return her stare and hope she moves on.

'I have some good news!' Celeste finally relieves me of the most penetrating stare I have ever endured.

'Oh, ok.'

Celeste continues to stare at me instead of giving me the tea.

'Well, what is it?' I add, hopefully to get her to start talking and stop staring. I'm starting to think she was in the room with Cade and me for our last session and she's just waiting on me to confirm.

'We're getting a potentially huge client.'

'Who?'

'So, you know the old apartment building over by Washington Park?'

'Yeah. That's been vacant forever. The owner never wanted to sell.'

'Well, they're selling. And we already have a lead on a buyer!'

'Really? I didn't even know it was for sale.'

'It's coming out of nowhere! I didn't even know until a buyer reached out wanting us to represent them.'

'So, who is the potential buyer? Is it a client we've worked with before?'

'Nope. But it's one we've wanted for a long time.'

'Stop it!'

'What?!' Celeste can hardly contain her excitement.

'Dominus, LLC?!'

Celeste's only answer is her head shaking furiously *yes* with an obnoxious smile smeared across her face.

'Oh my God! This could be so huge, Cel!'

Bolting from our chairs in excitement, we both start jumping up and down, squealing like teenage girls that just determined the guys they have crushes on, like them back. If we can sell this apartment building, if we can build a relationship with Dominus, LLC, we would be set for life. I could sell two houses a year after receiving the commission from this kind of sale. Not to mention, it's the *in* we need to start on the commercial real estate front. And it would be a guarantee that Dominus, LLC would want to work with us for future investments as well.

I grab a bottle of champagne from my office mini fridge to celebrate. Pouring two glasses, I walk over to the seat next to Celeste and hand her a glass.

'A little early to celebrate, don't ya think?'

'No way! We've got this in the bag girl. I just know it. Cheers!'

With a wink, I bring my glass to hers, and then let the sweet champagne slide down my throat.

'You didn't respond to my text today,' Cade says sternly when he finally comes to the door. No doubt making me wait to further solidify his irritation with me for not returning his text promptly.

'I know. I'm sorry.' I can hardly contain my smile as his left eyebrow starts to rise.

'Sir... I'm sorry, sir.' With that, Cade stands to the side and waves me inside. His house is a modest craftsman-style home with dark grey siding and white shudders. There isn't much of a front yard since most of the houses are planted right up by the street, with stairs and little concrete walkways, but the porch is wooden and spacious. The backyard makes up for the lack of space in front, with an attached deck and huge yard. It's the sort of home anyone could think about settling down in and having a family.

Knowing my way around already, I walk straight into the kitchen, taking my jacket off and hanging it on the back of the stool before having a seat at the island. He stalks behind me to his bar cart.

'Drink?'

'Please!' I blurt out. 'Sir!' Why am I acting like it's my first time here?

Cade looks over his shoulder and I see a smirk forming on his lips. He's enjoying this. Probably too much. Filling two glasses with Makers, he comes back to stand across from me, sliding my drink over the granite surface. The only thing between us being is this monstrous counter and I already want to close the gap sooner than later.

'So,' Cade says after he torturously licks the bourbon from his lips.

'So,' I barely get out.

'You didn't respond to my message today.'

'I can explain.'

Cade's response is a slight head shake with the hint of a laugh as he brings his glass back up to those beautifully full lips.

'Sir!' I blurt out again. What the hell is my problem today? I start to fidget with my glass as I wait for him to respond.

'Well?' Cade's eyes are on me when I bring my gaze back to his. They're hooded and dark in that *you are so in for it tonight* kind of way.

'I was reading your text and thinking about you when my partner walked in with some great news. Really great news, sir.' Finally, I remember the sir part. Maybe he'll grant me a little redemption.

'And what kind of news might that be, Mil?'

'We're potentially on the cusp of a huge business deal. There's an old apartment building that's been sitting empty forever. The owner hasn't wanted to sell until now.'

'And the owner wants you to put it on the market?'

'Actually no. Dominus, LLC, this investment company, wants to buy the property.' I'm hardly holding this in, just thinking about it again makes me beyond excited. 'And they want us to represent them!'

The smile that blooms across my face feels dangerously close to touching my ears. Taking another drink, my eyes close to let the moment, and the bourbon, sink in once again.

'That's great news, Mil. Dominus is a prestigious company. I'm assuming that could mean really big things for you.'

'You've heard of them?'

'I have. I do more than just work in the basement of Victoria's Diner, Mil.'

'Well, yeah. Of course, you do. I didn't mean you wouldn't have heard of them, I just....'

'Mil,' Cade interrupts my stammering.

'Yeah?'

'Relax.'

Yeah, yeah. Relax, Mil. Seriously. It must be the combination of the news and being here with Cade, in his house no less, that's making me so crazy. I feel like some sort of violent energy is going to explode from my chest at any moment. The thought of such a huge business deal falling into our laps combined with the pure sexual tension between Cade and me has my brain completely pretzeled.

My phone dings from inside my bag, breaking me from my twisted mess of thoughts. Grabbing it, I sneak a peek at Cade who continues to undress me with his eyes from across the island.

Jeremy: Haven't heard from you. Late night tonight?

Shit. I never told Jeremy I'd be late. Also, why do I care?

Me: Yeah. Sorry. Had some things come up today.

Shoving my phone back in my bag before I can receive a reply, I tuck Jeremy into the closet at the back of my mind and give Cade my full attention once again.

'I fully intended on a punishment for today but since you have a fairly good excuse, I think I've changed my mind.'

'And what do you have in mind now?' My panties instantaneously wet from the thought of Cade doing anything to me. By the look on his face, he knows it as well.

'Stand up.'

I follow his first command without question.

'Back up a few steps.'

I step back slowly, my eyes never leaving his.

'Strip.'

I hastily start to unbutton my blouse and am already on the third button when he interrupts me.

'Slowly, Mil,' he says, his voice gruff.

My breath hitches as I slow my desperate fingers. Once I finish with the last button and shrug the shirt off my shoulders, Cade finally lets his eyes wander down to my chest. I unclip my bra unmercifully slow as I watch him take his bottom lip between his teeth in anticipation. Once my bra hits the floor, I bring my hands up to my breasts and start circling my nipples with my fingers pulling slightly here and there.

'I didn't say you could touch yourself,' Cade murmurs.

'Are you going to stop me?' I'm playing with fire here, but I'd be lying to myself if I didn't also want whatever punishment Cade had planned for tonight.

'No.'

Surprised, I continue playing with a nipple and trail my other hand down to the waistline of my pants. Cade straightens, rolling his shoulders back and cracking his neck as he tries to reign in his impatience. He takes another drink to no doubt steady himself. Bringing my other hand down, I unbutton my slacks and let them puddle on the floor. Stepping out of my shoes and slacks, I'm left in nothing but my panties.

When Cade lets his eyes do the talking, I finally slip my panties down my thighs. His stare darkens even more as he sweeps his eyes over my naked body. Being in a situation like this used to make me cringe but the only thing happening to me now is an increased heart rate, nipples that could cut through steel, and a pussy ready to take on the world, starting with Cade's cock.

He takes another drink from his glass and slams it down with such force I wonder if it was the best decision to make him mad. Before I have time to reconsider, he's rounded the counter and is grabbing me by the back of my head with his hand, lacing fingers through my hair, and gripping my ass like a vice with his other. Lifting me up, I swing my legs around his waist just as his lips claim me. His tongue wastes no time finding mine, his kiss turning murderous, as I float to cloud nine from being on the receiving end of Cade's savage love.

We're all tongues, teeth, and heavy breathing as he moves us from the kitchen. Stopping in the hallway, he slams me against the wall, air escaping my lungs with a moan. His cock, harder than ever before, pins me to the wall. I reach down to undo his pants, but my wrists are almost immediately secured to the wall above me, his one hand, strong enough to envelope my wrists together. Being pinned here under his strength is so hot I'm worried I'll come before he even has a chance to fuck me.

'I still make the rules here, Mil.'

'Yes, sir.'

Wetting his thumb in his mouth before finding my clit, my head lulls and eyes fall shut. His sharp bite on my jaw followed by my neck, I can barely catch my breath as he brings me as close to orgasm as possible before his thumb stops abruptly.

'Fuck!'

'What's wrong, Mil?' he asks as a crooked smile caresses his lips.

'You're punishing me?' My clit continues to throb, begging to be touched.

'Not at all, Mil.'

'Ugh! Then what are you doing?!' I pant as I try, and don't succeed, to thrust my hips and have literally anything rub against my clit.

'I want you to beg for it, baby.'

His thumb rubs my clit again and it takes almost no time for me to start cresting the horizon of an orgasm once again.

'Damn you!' I yelp as he pulls his thumb away a second time.

I start to realize he isn't going to let me come unless I really do beg him for it. Which, I don't know why I didn't believe him a few seconds ago when he flat-out told me that's what he wanted. I guess I just didn't expect this form of punishment.

'Fine! Let me come already!'

'Tsk, tsk, tsk. You know that's no way to ask for something, Mil.'

'Please let me come!'

'Almost baby. Almost.' A jolt of pain shoots across my chest as he pinches my nipple.

'Please let me come, sir!' I scream out ready to do anything for him to ravage my body with orgasm.

'Mmmmm that's more like it, baby.'

With that, he unpins me from the wall and sidesteps through the doorway to his bedroom. Sitting back on his bed, his cock strains against his jeans beneath me. I let him kiss and lick his way down my neck to my nipples. Taking each of my nipples in his mouth, he torments me with piercing nibbles, the resulting tremors threatening to send me over the edge.

'Take my pants off.'

I couldn't have jumped off his lap faster if I tried. I drop to my knees and fumble with his button as if it's my first time. Once his cock is free, I let my eyes linger for just a moment, taking in all its glory. I swear he is the mold sex toy companies use for dildos.

'Quit studying at my cock and put it in your mouth already,' he grits.

Happy to oblige, I wrap my lips around the tip and start circling my tongue. The sounds emanating from his throat are the only clues to my performance. He drops his hand on the back of my head and grips my hair as I start sucking up and down his shaft.

'Fuck Mil. You suck my cock so well.' Cade's words are barely audible. Looking up through my eyelashes, his gaze locks onto mine. He sucks in a breath and sinks his teeth into his bottom lip almost as if to keep from saying something.

'I want that pussy of yours in my mouth,' he breathes, 'get up here and sit on my face.' His eyes are closed so I continue sucking up and down his shaft, making sure to take his full length in. I blink back tears with each punch to the back of my throat.

'Now,' he commands. I pull my mouth from his throbbing cock as slow as possible before climbing up his body. His arms are under my legs lifting me up and to his mouth so fast I barely have time to steady myself. I straddle my legs on either side of his face just in time for him to force my hips down so my pussy sinks perfectly into his mouth. The second his tongue slides across my clit, I know this won't be a long ride.

My hips start to buck against his mouth as he flicks his tongue on my clit and glides down to my opening. I reach down, pulling his hair as he licks and sucks my pussy until I'm shaking. I fall forward onto my hands, unable to hold myself up anymore as a volcanic heat builds low in my stomach. The orgasm that hits, sends shock wave after shock wave, disintegrating me from the inside. Cade's death grip is unyielding on my thighs, making sure I'm drowning him in my cum as the orgasmic tremors continue.

Finally, he wriggles out from beneath me as I try and compose myself. I'm absolutely wrecked, and my clit feels like an electric shock has been delivered to it. Cade's cock presses up behind me as he brings my hips back to meet him. In one fell swoop, he sinks deep into my pussy inducing mumbled moans in response.

'Tell me how good I feel in that pussy, Mil.'

'You... oh, Cade... you feel...' I can't even form words at this point, nor do I care to. His cock moving in and out of me is the sweetest bliss I have ever felt.

'You like my cock in your pussy, don't you, Mil?'

A garbled yes emanates from my throat as he grabs my hair, pulling my head back and causing my scalp to tingle all over. He slams in, takes his sweet time pulling out to the tip of his cock, only to slam back in again.

'Is this my pussy, Mil?' he asks, slamming in again.

'Yes.'

'Yes, what?' Another slam followed by a slow, tortuous pull back out.

'This pussy…its yours…'

'Damn right, Mil. And this cock is all yours.'

Cade lands a sharp smack on my ass as he speeds up to send us both plummeting over the edge. The orgasm that follows is debilitating. The only thing keeping me from collapsing onto the bed is Cade holding my hair back. He stiffens as he pulls a little harder on my hair and embeds himself even deeper into my pussy, letting the euphoria sizzle through his body.

Releasing my hair, he moves and pushes my legs and arms out so I'm flat on the bed. With his cock still throbbing inside me, he covers me with his body. We are a pile of hot, heavy breaths as we both come down from whatever ecstasy that was.

'That was…. fuck…'

'Agreed. Maybe I should edge you as punishment more often.' Cade lets out a snicker as he starts to remove himself from me. The instant chill of cold air washes me in an unwelcome emptiness as he stands up from the bed.

'Shower?' He offers his hand and I take it.

I can't very well go home like this anyway. Shit. Home. The realization hits again that I have a home. A home where a husband is waiting on me. A husband that thinks I'm late coming home because I got held up at work.

I have no idea what Cade does to me that makes me forget the reality I live every day. The entire outside world ceases to exist when we're together. Something that used to happen between Jeremy and me. I really need to figure out what I'm doing. I can't keep seeing Cade if Jeremy is committing to fixing things. If I'm agreeing to fix things. The thought of not seeing Cade anymore though is nauseating to say the least. Especially as I stand in his shower while he scrubs me down in the cedar scent of his body wash. We've crossed a line and I'm not sure if it can be uncrossed. I am so fucked.

Chapter Seven

I wake up in a groggy mess since I didn't get home until almost midnight. I'm not sure how much longer I'll be able to keep up all the late nights without Jeremy starting to question my job requirements. A tidal wave of last night's activities rushes through my brain as I watch the ceiling fan go round and round as I try and will myself out of bed and into the shower.

Thinking about Cade's mouth on my pussy and his cock filling me up has me clenching my legs together. He seems to know my body better than I do. His hands gliding over my skin, the things he says, the way he punishes me, all leaves me feeling so alive. Like he's exactly what I need. The cure I've been seeking. With a sigh, I roll over and grab my vibrator from the nightstand.

Double checking the spare bedroom door is shut and locked before closing my eyes, I let my hands roam down between my legs. The noise from the vibrator seems to echo through the room and I start to reconsider in case Jeremy is within earshot. Deciding masturbation isn't a sin, I place the vibrator directly on top of my throbbing clit, not wanting to waste any time. Just wanting that sweet release from Cade being on my mind.

I skim the vibrator over my clit a few times, sending jolts of electricity to my core, before plunging it into my now-soaked pussy. Teasing myself, I glide it back up to my clit, switching between that and my slickening center. My teeth bite into my bottom lip as slight moans start to fall from my mouth. Feeling my orgasm about to crest, I grab a pillow and pull it over my face so I can't be heard. Bringing the vibrator to rest directly on my clit, I'm falling off the cliff in a matter of seconds as I whimper into the pillow. My body convulses under the covers as the orgasm starts to subside and visions of Cade with his tongue in my pussy start to fade.

The buzzing of my phone from the nightstand replaces the sound of my vibrator as it sweeps me away from my post orgasm bliss. Ripping the pillow from my face, I roll over, and toss the vibrator back into the drawer before reaching for my phone. I have an open house later today so it might be Celeste needing something or hopefully adding more great news on the apartment building.

Jeremy: Get your beautiful ass out of bed and get down here. Breakfast is almost ready.

Impeccable timing. I hope this text wasn't prompted by him hearing me in here. Knowing Jeremy, he probably would have said something to allude to me playing with myself or even knocked on the door in the middle of it.

Me: I'll be down in 15.

Jeremy: Ok ;)

Tossing the covers off, I trudge from the spare bedroom to the master bathroom to jump in the shower. Waiting for the water to heat up, I stare into the mirror at the naked woman looking back at me. Anxiety instantly riddling my body. My husband sent me a message about making me breakfast right after I finished making myself come to visions of another man. The man I was with last night while I told my husband I was stuck at work.

Cade is on my mind more and more with every passing day. Jeremy also seems to be slowly starting to creep back in. What is happening to me? I haven't ever cheated in my life. I don't consider what I started doing with Cade to be cheating since it was strictly business... at first. But now? We've already ventured into new territory that feels strangely similar to a relationship. Throw in Jeremy putting in all this new effort and me saying I'm also willing to try. Am I becoming the villain in my own story?

I pull up behind Celeste's car outside of our open house. I'm not ready to be here for hours after the weird morning I've had. The shower didn't absolve me of my wrongdoings as I had hoped, and the ante was upped once I came down to breakfast. Jeremy had eggs benedict waiting on the kitchen island for me along with a steaming cup of coffee. He noticed I seemed distracted, but I was able to play it off by being stressed about work and thankfully he didn't push. My briefcase ready to go for me and as I headed out the door, he handed me a fresh to-go cup of coffee coupled with a tender kiss on my cheek.

After several deep breathes, I grab my briefcase from the passenger seat and get out of my car. I don't have time to sit and think about my morals right now. We've got houses to sell.

'Good morning!' A familiar sing-song voice floats from the kitchen as I stop by the entryway table to put some cards out for the potential buyers.

'Hello, Cel,' I chime back. Walking toward the kitchen, I

notice she's already turned all the lights on. I love her. She's the best partner I could ever ask for. The most incredible best friend I could ever ask for. She's my person through and through. I knew immediately that I could drop my mask with her, and she would accept me unequivocally. If she told me she didn't want to work with me anymore, I don't have the slightest idea of what I would do but it would leave me devastated, in a catastrophic ruin.

'How are you, my darling?' she asks as I pass through the kitchen doorway and sidle up to the island.

'I'm fine… I guess.'

'You guess? What's up?'

'Nothing. It's fine. I'm fine. Just tired.'

'Long night with Jeremy?' she asks with a wink. As much as she hates Jeremy for what he's put me through, she's ultimately in our corner for working through this. She'd support me whether I worked it out or not, which is one of her attributes I love. But I think she'd really like to see us happy again. Like we were before.

'No. I was finishing some stuff up for work and barely saw him last night actually.'

'Boo,' she says tossing her pen at me playfully, 'what were you working on? Did I miss something for today?'

Shit.

'No! No, not at all. I was just researching some stuff on that apartment building and just… s-some other stuff,' I stutter trying to regain my composure after the slip-up. She knows I wouldn't have been working late because there isn't anything to work late on!

'Oh, ok. Well, you can tell me if I miss something. I'm not one to let you do all the work.'

'You didn't miss anything, promise.'

'Good! Do you want to grab a drink after we're done here? Or does Jeremy have some elaborate dinner planned for you?'

'No, that works. Drinks sound great. Jeremy is attending some cooking seminar in Milwaukee. He's probably getting ready to leave now and won't be back until Friday morning.'

'How are you feeling about that?' she asks, concern etched on her face.

'I'm fine. Really. I can't tell him no anyway. It's for his career. I've got to start giving him some rope if I'm going to work on this, right?'

'Yeah. I suppose you're right.'

'I have to trust that he's not going to make the same mistake again.' And strangely, I do. It's me I'm worried about now.

'That's very big of you, girl. Better than I would be doing. I'm not sure I could even work on my marriage after my spouse cheated.'

'Yeah,' I sigh pinching the bridge of my nose.

'I'm sorry. I don't mean to judge you for working on this with him. I'm only trying to commend what you're doing,' she says as she comes around to give me a hug. I sink into her arms, absorbing her warmth. I know Celeste didn't mean anything by it. It does make me feel silly sometimes. There are so many people that would've walked away immediately. I chose to stay and wallow in the pain. I agreed to counseling and am now agreeing to putting in real effort with my husband. I still don't know if I'm stupid or strong for it, nor do I know if I could classify it as commendable.

Sometimes I wonder what Celeste would say if I told her about Cade. She is against cheating regardless the circumstances. It wouldn't matter to her that Jeremy cheated first. I know she would be irate with me. I wouldn't be surprised if she walked away from me completely. I just wish I had someone to talk to about this whole thing. Celeste is the best for the job. She'd be able to tell me if I'm being stupid and should stop seeing Cade immediately or if I should ultimately leave Jeremy and explore things with Cade. Or, worse yet, stay single and work on myself. That sounds like the worst option possible.

'It was great meeting the both of you! Have a great night!' I say closing the door behind the last couple leaving the open house. I switch the lock before turning around and letting myself slide down to the floor. That was the longest open house ever, I'm exhausted, and it's already 7:00 p.m. The open house was supposed to end at 5:30 p.m. but the people just kept coming. And who am I to turn away potential money?

'I feel it, girl, I feel it.' I open my eyes to see Celeste headed down the hallway with a bouquet of flowers in her hand.

'What's that?'

'These are flowers and they're for you.' Standing up, I take the vase from her.

'They're beautiful.' I sit the vase on the entryway table and take the card from the envelope that was stuck in the bouquet.

'Who are they from? Who are they from?' Celeste squeals as she claps her hands together. She gets so giddy with stuff like this. A true romantic.

'Relax woman!' I give her a playful side eye before reading the card.

Mil,

I wanted to send beautiful flowers to my beautiful wife to let her know I will miss her while I'm in Milwaukee and that she will be on my mind the entire time.

I'll be home Friday morning sometime. I know you've been crazy busy with work so would you be my partner in crime and play hooky with me Friday afternoon? I promise it'll be worth it. I'll be ready and waiting in the car at 2:00 p.m. Wear something comfortable ;)

- Jeremy

'Well??' Celeste is so impatient.

'Jeremy wants me to play hooky Friday.'

'Oh! You're doing it, girl! I've got you covered.'

'I don't know...'

'Stop! There isn't anything going on that I can't handle myself.'

'Ok, ok. Fine.'

'Thata girl. Let's go get those drinks.'

Chapter Eight

Friday afternoon came faster than it ever has before. Honestly, I thought I would get to relax with Jeremy being gone. I was also hoping to swing by Cade's house for an impromptu visit, but I was left to service myself again after having to cover an open house for Celeste since she woke up Thursday morning with a migraine. I think the migraine started coming on Wednesday night. The drinks hit her way faster than normal and she was spent after only three.

I tried calling Cade this morning to let him know I wouldn't be able to meet him for our appointment tonight. I'm more bummed than I probably should be, but he's become a staple in my life. The only good thing that will come from missing my time with him is that he's a huge fan of punishments for missed appointments. I suppose they don't want their time wasted in the Dom world.

I've been sitting on the couch since 1:30 p.m. just waiting on my 2:00 p.m. surprise. It's five till two and I haven't seen or heard from Jeremy. I figured he would've been here getting ready for whatever he's got planned but I guess not. I reach for my phone to send Cade a text since he never called me back when a text from Jeremy comes through.

Jeremy: Let's go pretty lady!

I didn't even hear him pull up. I really need to get my head out of the clouds, or off Cade rather, and pay attention to what's right in front of me. I jump up from the couch strangely excited to see what Jeremy has planned. Grabbing my purse, I tuck my phone inside, and out the door I go.

When I open the passenger door, I'm met with a huge smile on Jeremy's face. I hate that my body threatens to crumble at the sight that smile still. It's always made me feel some type of way, and even more so once we got together. Maybe because I knew it was for me and for me only. I feel like it is still for me in a way, but I also have to tell myself it's for me nowadays. An affair will have that effect on you.

'Where have you been?' I ask sliding into the seat.

'I had a few errands to run. You ready?'

'Yeah. As ready as I'll ever be.'

'Don't sound so excited.' Jeremy senses my apprehension and his face falls a little.

'Sorry! I'm excited. I'm just worn out from the past couple days.'

'If you're too tired we can stay in…'

'No, it's ok. Let's go. I'm ready.'

'Atta girl!' He shifts the car in drive and lets his hand fall to my thigh. My eyes immediately go to his hand, but I manage to keep the flinch at bay. I hope I'm not starting to get myself in a situation where I need alcohol around him. Those are the only times I've been relaxed enough to let him touch me lately. I didn't recoil this time so maybe we are making progress.

'This ok?' he asks, noticing I'm still staring at his hand.

'Yeah, it's fine.' I give him a small smile he returns with a squeeze of my leg. We both give our attention to the road ahead and my curiosity takes over as I start thinking about what he's got up his sleeve.

No wonder he wanted me in comfy clothes! We've been to the arcade, played laser tag, went go-carting, stopped for a picnic he set up ahead of time, and went for ice cream. We finally end up at one of the bars we used to frequent in college. I don't realize until we're in the bar, beers in hand, how much I needed today. It was the perfect stress reliever and it let me enjoy my time with Jeremy without having to talk about anything too serious and question what I'm doing with my life.

We haven't been to this bar in a while and sitting here is starting to bring back so many memories. Thankfully they're happy ones. The night he proposed being one of them.

We were sitting in these exact seats and joking about how we would propose to each other.

'I'm going to propose to you before you get a chance to propose to me.'

'Like hell you are!' he laughs, and I almost spit my beer out.

'What's wrong with that?'

'I mean, nothing, but I want to be the one to propose to you.'

'Well, better hurry.' I joke since we had only been together for 8 months.

'I hear ya. I'm curious now. How would you do it?' I hadn't really thought about it honestly. I was just trying to give him shit. I knew we'd get engaged and married eventually. He was my best friend, and I just knew he was it for me.

'Uh, well... I'd probably do a big surprise party with all our friends. And I would do some over the top karaoke and dance. The finale would be me down on one knee with a ring. And you would no doubt say yes!' I snort and laugh before taking another swig of my beer.

'Wow. You've really thought this through haven't you.'

'Not at all,' I say as we both start laughing.

'Ok, ok. How would you propose to me? That is, if you get to it first.'

Jeremy takes a sip of his beer and starts thinking of the perfect proposal.

'Well,' he starts as I spin my bar chair to face him. I want to hear all of this. A crazy sort of excitement rolls over me thinking about how he might eventually propose.

'It would probably just be an ordinary day… like today.'

I nod my head letting him know I'm all ears.

'And I would probably do it somewhere that's special to us… like here.'

Oh! Ok. I like where this is going. I haven't thought a lot about the whole proposal process, but I do think I'd appreciate a more intimate approach.

'I would probably just pull a box out of my pocket randomly. Ya know, when you were least expecting it,' he says this as his hand goes to his pocket mimicking the move. Except, a small box starts to appear.

'Then I would just get down on one knee and open the ring box to show you the ring.' He slowly lowers to one knee in front of my bar stool, opening the ring box. My beer is stalled right at my lips as I try like crazy to catch my brain up to the hypothetical situation turning reality. This cannot be happening.

'And then, I'd ask you if you'd marry me,' he says with tear-filled eyes. 'Will you marry me, Millicent?' he finally chokes out.

I can't believe this is happening. This situation could not have played out more perfectly if it had been planned out for a movie. The first tears hit my cheeks as I jump down from my stool joining Jeremy on the floor, throwing my arms around his neck. I bury my face in his neck and inhale all of him, his bergamot and citrus scent, inhale the moment, so I can make sure I keep it forever.

'Are you serious?' I ask as I pull my face from his neck.

'Of course, I'm serious Mil! I love you with everything. I can't imagine spending the rest of my days with anyone else.'

'I love you,' I breathe out bringing my lips to his. The kiss we share is unlike any other we've shared before. The intensity of it burns and melds our lips together. This must be it. This must be what they always talk about in the movies.

'So, is that a yes?' he asks pulling away from our kiss.

'Yes! Absolutely yes!' And with that, he takes the ring out of the box and slides it onto my ring finger. A sob escapes my throat as I take in its beauty. A massive, solitaire diamond with a diamond-encrusted band. I had never felt like my finger was naked until now. A feeling of completeness washes over me as I stare down at my hand. This simple piece of metal with the most exquisite diamond I've ever had the pleasure of gazing upon, means so much more than I thought it would. A symbol of Jeremy's love and adoration for me. A symbol I can carry around everywhere, showing the world that I'm his. I'll have to shield it in the sun, so it doesn't blind anyone. It's breathtakingly beautiful.

'Watcha thinking about?' Jeremy asks pulling me back to the present.

I stare down at the ring on my hand resting on the bar. It's still just as beautiful as the day Jeremy pulled it out of the box and put it on my finger. Only now it's tainted. Tainted by my husband's infidelity. This ring is supposed to represent our love, our till death do us part, our commitment to each other. What does it represent if someone cheated? What does it represent if I'm the one that's cheating now? A lie.

We head home shortly after we finish our one and only beer. My good mood was completely dismantled by my amazing memory turned nightmare. I hate that we could have such a good day for it to all be burnt to the ground in an instant. I shouldn't feel bad about it, but I do for some reason. I know I wouldn't have any bad memories if it weren't for Jeremy's actions but if I could just get over it, maybe we could fully move on. But moving on with Jeremy would also mean not moving on with Cade. The fact that I'm even considering Cade to be an option is ridiculous. For one, I have no idea if he even has feelings for me. For two, I am married. Supposed to be working on my marriage with my cheating bastard of a husband and here I am doing the same goddamn thing to him.

Pulling into the driveway, we're both completely silent and have been for the entire ride. I know Jeremy sensed my shift in demeanor, but he hasn't said anything. He's switched from a sky-high level of confidence to walking on eggshells as he holds the door to the house open for me. Dropping my stuff on the sideboard, I walk into the living room and fall onto the couch. Today exhausted me mentally and physically.

'Tea?' I look up to see Jeremy leaning in the doorway wringing his hands. His classic sign of anxiety showing through.

'Yeah, tea sounds good.' I smile weakly.

My phone vibrating on the side of my leg makes me jump. Pulling it from my legging pocket, I see it's Cade. Fuck! I was going to send him a text about tonight after he didn't answer when I called him this morning. I completely forgot and it's almost 7:30 p.m. already. He is going to be beyond pissed.

Client – P. Alderidge: You know what happens to no-call, no-shows

Fuck. Fuck. Fuck!

Me: In my defense, I did call you this morning.

Me: Sir.

I keep my eye on the screen as the three dots take turns changing colors.

Client – P. Alderidge: No voicemail?

*Me: No, I didn't leave a voicemail. I was going to
send you a text and then something came up.*

Me: I'm so sorry!

Me: Sir!

Sweat starts to bead on my forehead as I wait suspensefully for his response. Cade's punishments seem worse now that I'm no longer paying him to hurt me. Sometimes I wonder what I was paying him for in the first place. I can only imagine the gratifying torture I'm in for after this stunt is going to far exceed the intensity of my usual spankings. The thought of it has me adjusting my thighs as I try and quell my pulsing pussy. I shouldn't be having this reaction knowing Cade is going to hurt me. Of course, to me, the pain is worth it.

*Client – P. Alderidge: No worries.
I'll see you Sunday.*

His change in mood has the hairs on my arms raising. No worries? I don't think I've ever heard him use that term. This can't be good. In fact, this will be very, very bad. Reading the message again, I realize he threw seeing me Sunday in there. I open my Google calendar and scroll to Sunday. There definitely isn't an appointment with him. The only thing scheduled is my open house. My anxiety starts to skyrocket as I respond to him hoping I didn't double book appointments. There's no way I can miss this open house since it's the first one for the apartment complex.

*Me: Sunday? I don't have anything
on my calendar for Sunday, sir.*

I gawk at the screen waiting for the three dots to appear, but they never come. I hear Jeremy coming down the hall so I shove my phone back in my pocket before he can round the doorway.

Chapter Nine

If I'm being honest, I'm beginning to doubt how much Dr. Johnson is even helping. We've been in counseling for a little over six months now and I feel like we lead the conversation. She just sits in her chair with her notebook saying, 'and how does that make you feel?' or 'is that working for the both of you?' and, my personal favorite, 'I see.'

I've heard of people having fantastic luck with marriage counseling and love the therapist on top of that. This one seems disconnected. Maybe that's not even it. It's hard to nail down. Again, it feels like she doesn't provide us with much direction, and we have to get to the point ourselves. Maybe that's how therapy is supposed to go. I'm new to this so I could be judging this when I should be sitting back, listening, and taking the lessons home we've taught ourselves and applying them.

'So, tell me more about the date day you all had yesterday,' she says as she relaxes back in her chair waiting for one of us to speak up.

Jeremy and I share a look before he finally starts. If I didn't know any better, he shares the same sentiment as I do about this therapist.

'I planned a day for us to just have fun,' he breaks off glancing at me, 'we did a bunch of stuff and then ended up at a bar we used to frequent when we were in college.'

'Mmhmm,' Dr. Johnson scribbles something in her notebook, 'and how was that for you, Millicent?'

What is she even writing in there anyway? Is she really noting that we hung out and went to a bar.

'It was fine… we had fun, actually.' Clearing my throat, I let my gaze go back to the notebook.

'But how was it for you? How did you feel?' Here we go again. Feelings. Maybe I am the problem. I try my best not to roll my eyes while my 14-year-old self screams *let 'em roll!*

'We had a great time. Honestly. It was good to just be around each other and not think about anything that's happened.'

'Do you think it's helpful to not think about what's happened? Or do you think it's a beat around the bush situation?'

'Uh, I don't know. I thought the point was to get back to normal.'

'Yeah, do we have to constantly rehash what's happened when we're trying to reconnect?' Jeremy swoops in for the save and I couldn't be more relieved. Dr. Johnson burrows further into my skin the longer we sit in this room.

'I don't think you need to constantly rehash things but to talk about what's happened as it comes up naturally, would be beneficial.'

Jeremy and I stare at her, waiting for her to continue.

'For example,' she clears her throat after realizing we aren't doing her job anymore, 'was there ever a moment yesterday where one of you thought about what had happened? If it comes up, I think it's beneficial to talk about it instead of skirting around it.

'So, was there anything that triggered memories, happy or sad?

Or something maybe reminding you of the affair?'

Jeremy lets out a sigh as he runs his hand down his face and looks out the window. I see where she's going with this.

'I guess I had a moment yesterday. But should we really be bringing down a good mood between us to talk about something so terrible? I don't know how much sense that makes.'

'Well, let's talk about the moment first, shall we?'

Fuck.

'Uh, yeah... I guess. I, uh, was just thinking about the day we got engaged since the bar we were at is where he proposed. His proposal was amazing.'

'You didn't tell me that,' Jeremy starts, full of worry, 'I asked what was on your mind because I felt your mood shift... you got sad all of a sudden.'

'What turned the good memory sour?' Dr. Johnson asks. Her eyes drill into my soul, already knowing what turned it sour, but she wants me to say it out loud.

'Well, I started thinking about what my ring represents and then it turned into what it represents once a person has cheated.' I trail off as I try and quell the tears that are threatening to fall.

The couch sinks down as Jeremy scoots next to me, enveloping me in a hug. My body shutters with grief as I let myself lean into his hug. Damn it. When will this stop? I'm so tired of crying and thinking about what happened. I thought these counseling sessions would help keep the tears at bay, but it seems they just bring them on even stronger.

'How did that make you feel, Millicent?' Dr. Johnson asks over my sobs.

'Please, just... stop.' I hear Jeremy say. I already know he's talking to Dr. Johnson. Without a doubt, Jeremy wouldn't try and stop me from feeling something.

'Let's go ahead and wrap up for today. I'll give you two a moment alone. I'll see you next week.' Dr. Johnson stands and steps out of the room without either of us acknowledging her leaving.

It seems like forever, but it's only been a couple of minutes before I start to pull myself together. Jeremy holds me as patiently as ever just waiting for the flood gates to slowly close. I do appreciate that about him. He's never been one to rush anyone. Especially in a moment like this.

'Look at me,' Jeremy finally says as he lifts my chin with his hand, 'let's go home.'

I don't say anything. I simply nod my head *yes* and let him lead me out of the room, out of the building, and to the car.

When I finally come downstairs from my skin-melting bath, Jeremy is waiting on the couch with wine and a movie queued up. After the emotional roller coaster that is counseling, I need a night to just chill on the couch in some pjs with some wine.

Jeremy was wonderful today. The way he took control in counseling and how he's been so comforting all afternoon. Sometimes I think it hurts him more to see me in pain from all of this than it does me to endure the agony. If I could get through conversations without breaking down, I think I would be in a better place. I know it's only been six months but at the same time, it's been six months. This didn't happen yesterday or even last month. When will I be able to talk about things, the affair, I mean, without my mind taking me back to ground zero. Why does every day continue to feel just as bad as the day he revealed what he'd been hiding?

'You know, I don't want you to hold anything in, Mil. I really don't.'

'I just feel bad ruining a good time.' Damn it! Why am I being so empathetic?

'Stop!' he looks exasperated, 'I don't want that. Not at all. I think Dr. Johnson was right today when she said we shouldn't skirt around the affair.'

'I loathe talking about it.' Tears are already springing up in my eyes, so quick to come back.

'I do too. But if we don't talk through these things, the moments when you're feeling sad, or even when I'm feeling sad, are we really helping each other? Is it really best to keep a good mood going when one of us is hurting?'

'I guess not.'

'I knew something was wrong yesterday. You went from being happy and carefree to completely bummed out. I'm trying not to push you but I'm also thinking that we owe it to each other to just let it out. I mean, I had an affair for christs sake. You can tell me anything at this point and I will not be upset in the slightest.'

Jeremy pulls me into his chest and wraps me in another all-consuming hug. The tears fall unbridled as he holds me and finally, I start to soften and be in this moment with him. Maybe he's right. What good does it do to keep my feelings bottled up simply because we're having a good time? He can't help me through it if I'm silent.

'I love you, Mil. More than anything. And I know I screwed up, so badly. But I wouldn't be here trying with my all if I didn't want to show you how fucking sorry I am. How much I regret everything that happened. So, please, if you start feeling any kind of way, no matter what we're doing, let me have it. Let it out! Scream at me. Beat on my damn chest if you have to. Not only do I deserve it, but I want to help you. I want to help us get through this and come out on the other side stronger than ever.'

Each of Jeremy's words force the sobs out harder, and I'm transported back to the counselor's office where I couldn't control my blubbering this morning. The worst part is, I believe him. I believe with everything that his words are true and he will do anything in his power to make sure we overcome this massive hurdle.

Gathering what's left of my broken soul, I readjust myself to watch whatever movie Jeremy has ready to play. He keeps his arm around my shoulders, reassuring me he's here. His fingers brush across my cheeks as he reaches over to dry up any remaining tears. Pulling me closer to his side, his soft lips connect with my temple creating a sense of comfort I haven't felt with him in a long time, six months at least, that settles into my bones. He hands me my wine glass that I don't remember him taking, and guzzle back an overdue drink.

'So, what do you want to do tomorrow?'

'Oh, actually, I have something going on tomorrow.'

'Oh, ok. I don't remember you saying you had plans. I'm sorry.'

'Don't be sorry. I forgot to mention it. It's kind of a big deal actually...'

'Yeah? Let's hear it,' Jeremy says as his lips tick up on the ends.

'Well, I have an open house tomorrow for an apartment complex. There are some big investors interested in it too. This could be huge for Cel and I if we can land this sale!'

'That's awesome, Mil!' Jeremy squeezes my shoulder and leans in for a kiss.

I give his kiss the permission to sweep me away. His playful lips and warm, wine-soaked tongue carry me back to a happier, simpler time. I shouldn't be enjoying this, but I am. And if we're going be in the present, I should appreciate the good just as much as the bad, right?

Chapter Ten

This is a bigger deal than I could have ever imagined. I've been rubbing elbows with investors, exchanging information, answering questions, all with a smile plastered on my face since 10:00 a.m. The sheer volume of people that have walked through this building today is unfathomable. It will be an investor blood bath when they all start submitting their offers. I know this part of Chicago is really starting to pop but I figured it would be a few years before people were looking to buy in this area.

I'm relieved I was able to get some good rest last night. It was by far one of the best sleeps I've had in months. Jeremy and I finished our movie after sharing a bottle of wine and were in bed before 9:00 p.m. We're still in separate beds but it didn't seem so depressing last night like it has. It was more akin to a date ending. He stood at my door, kissed me goodnight, and then headed off to our master bedroom. It was cute, really. The guilt didn't start to rot me from the inside again until after I put my vibrator back in my drawer. Masturbating to your Dom/boyfriend/situation-ship after spending a couple of good days with your husband will do that to you.

I spot Celeste across the main hallway and mouth that I'll be in the bathroom. It's slowing down a bit so I think she can manage while I slip away for a second. Before I can head up the stairwell, someone approaches her to ask what is most likely the same questions we've answered all day. We've been on auto repeat for the past several hours.

Celeste and I set up a bathroom in one of the apartments on the third floor ahead of time so we would have somewhere to escape to. A rush of relief guides me through the door of the empty apartment, and I shut the door behind me. My brain has been dying for respite, even if it's only 10 minutes. After my much-needed bathroom break, I walk over to the window in the living room area. The third floor is going to be prime space for these apartments, or condos, or whatever the buyer plans to do with them. The view is amazing. Not only can you see all the high rises of the city, but you can see the Chicago River and Lake Michigan. They'll be able to rent these or lease them for thousands a month.

I reach for my phone in my jacket pocket as it buzzes.

Celly-girl: OMG! The woman that walked up to me when you were going to the bathroom....

Me: Yeah?

Celly-girl: She was with Dominus, LLC!!!!! Girl, I'm dying!

Me: Oh shit! Really?! I'll be down.

Celly-girl: Take your time. She's left. Said she already walked around and will be in touch!

Me: Holy shit!

Me: This. Is. Real.

Celly-girl: This is our time girl!

This is real. It's happening. The chances of working with the buyers of this property in the future are high. If we can pull this off, we'll be working with other big investors and working on the commercial front rather than the residential housing front. And that means much bigger gains.

Celly-girl: Seriously though, take your time. It's more of a happy hour now. Everyone is mingling and drinking. The champagne was a brilliant idea. I wouldn't be surprised if we have offers tonight.

Me: You're welcome HA

I press send just as a hand shoots out from behind me, grabbing my phone and yanking it away from me. As I start to twist around, ready to slug whoever is waiting there, a strong hand seizes my right arm, forcing it to bend across my back. With my arm pinned, I'm pressed against the glass of the living room window before I can even think. My breathe accelerates as my left arm is bent backward to meet my right, my hands pinned together, and I find myself smashed between glass and a huge body. Unease races through my veins as I try and shake the massive person off me and fail.

'I don't know why you followed me up here, but I can assure

you the other realtor will realize how long I've been gone and will come to find me.'

I try to keep my voice as steady as possible while my heart starts beating hard enough to crack the glass. My attempts to catch a glimpse of who has me restrained are futile, even with my head to the side. They're keeping their face perfectly out of my field of vision.

'Oh baby,' a gruff voice caresses me ear, 'I can assure you; you'll be dying for someone to come to your rescue in a few minutes.'

My heart slows as realization hits of just who exactly has me highjacked.

'Cade!' I gasp, 'You scared the shit out of me.'

'Good. That was the point.'

'How did you know where I was?'

'Now, now. I can't very well give away all my secrets now, can I?'

'Uh, I guess not. Can you let me go? I'm kind of uncomfortable.' His grip tightens around my wrists as I try and jerk free once more.

'Are you?' he asks as his muscular body presses me harder into the window. My nipples harden as he runs his tongue up the side of my neck, finishing with a sharp bite. I cry out from the pain, instantly ready for him to take me any way he sees fit.

'You didn't think I was going to let you get away with skipping out on our little meeting Friday, did you?'

'I told you; I called you and meant to text you, but something came up.'

'Sounds like an excuse to me.' The sound of metal against metal fills the room and before I know it, he's cuffed my hands behind my back. The cold metal against my skin chills me to the bone.

'I... I... I'm sorry, sir.'

'What's the matter, Mil. Cat got your tongue?'

I am so utterly fucked. My heartbeat returns to its rapid rate from a few seconds ago when I didn't know who was attempting my kidnapping as I'm pulled from the glass slightly, providing room for Cade's hand to reach up and rip my blouse completely open.

'Fuck, Cade! I have people... I have investors downstairs... I can't.'

'You can and you will. Maybe next time you'll think twice about missing our time together.' I'm given a small reprieve from the glass once more as he reaches up with both hands, pulling my bra down and exposing my tits to the world. Forcing me back against the glass, my nipples are so hard I could etch our names for all to see. Fuck! As much as I'm freaking out right now that Celeste is downstairs by herself or that someone might find us, this whole scenario has my pussy begging. Cade hasn't been this rough with me yet and I don't I hate it. I could come from pure adrenaline.

His cock strains against my ass as he uses his body to keep mine immobile against the window. Biting down at the base of my neck again, he lets out a feral snarl before spinning me around to face him, my back slamming and shaking the window. I chance a glance down. My shirt is completely ripped open, and I already notice a missing button. Thankfully I have my jacket and button it up to cover the destruction. Cade cups my tits callous hands, massaging the supple mounds, before pinching my nipples hard, eliciting a moan from deep within my chest.

'God damn, Mil. Your tits are so fucking perfect.' His mouth joins in the fun, laving my nipples in sweet saliva and grazing his teeth across my overly sensitive buds. There is no controlling the moans that are growing louder and louder. Coming up for air, he smashes his lips into mine, shoving his tongue into my mouth. His kiss is wounding and so full of passion, you would think I had missed months of appointments with him. And I'm loving it. I feel as though a beast has been unleashed within me and I'm not sure there is any returning. His mouth against mine, our tongues twisting together, sends me into a euphoric bliss I haven't known before.

'Here's what's going to happen, Mil,' his words invade mouth between kisses, 'You're getting handcuffed to the closet rod in the next room. These pants are getting ripped off and then I'm going to take my belt across that sweet ass of yours. Once I know you regret skipping out on our appointment and won't miss another, I'm going to fuck you so hard the only thing that'll keep you standing is your hand cuffed above your head.'

'Cade, I... I...' My words are barely coherent, I'm so nervous, anxious, turned on, excited, freaked out, and a million other emotions I can't even name. My breath is coming so fast now, it's becoming erratic and my heart rages inside my chest cavity.

'And you will be quiet. Am I understood?' he asks pressing his finger to my lips.

All I can do is nod my head yes. Besides, the last thing I would want to do right now is say anything to make this punishment even worse than it's going to be.

'Oh, and one more thing,' his voice low and seductive as he pulls away slightly, his eyes meeting mine, 'you will not come. But you will walk out of this room with mine running down your leg.'

With that, a grunt flies out of my mouth as I'm thrown over Cade's shoulder. He hauls me across the living room and into the bedroom, my back hitting the closet wall as he brings me back to the ground. A hot hand grips my throat, gently squeezing, while the other works the buttons on my pants. My chest heaves from pure thrill as my pants fall down my legs, puddling around my feet. He steps back, admiring my pussy, knowing it's already dripping for him.

'Get rid of those pants.'

I try and step out but almost fall over as it's harder than it sounds to be able to kick off pants while wearing heels with your hands cuffed behind your back. Finally, I'm able to kick them off and to the side. My cheeks become rosier by the millisecond as I wait eagerly for my next command, barely able to catch my breath. I haven't been able to get a good look at Cade until now and I realize he's wearing a suit with a tie and all. He's dressed to the nines, looking ready as ever for some very important business. Where did he come from? And why the hell does he look so hot? His brown hair is slightly disheveled with wildly hungry eyes, he has the look of a man ready to eat me alive any second. Untamed energy radiating from him.

He takes off his suit jacket while his crazed eyes stay pinned to mine. Throwing it to the side, he takes a step toward me. Reaching up to his tie, he slowly undoes it while I slowly melt into a heated pool of lust. He wraps the tie around his fist before reaching down for his belt buckle. Shit. Shit. Shit. He wasn't kidding about taking his belt across my ass. This is going to suck. How the hell am I supposed to stay quiet? I want to scream just from smelling the leather. With hooded eyes, his belt is unbuckled and yanked out of the loops in one swift move. I swallow hard.

'Turn around.' His deep voice commands as a smile plays at his lips. Oh fuck.

My body is hot and cold all at once. My hands are starting to clam up and goosebumps are rising all over my body. My mouth has suddenly turned into the Sahara Desert and my eyes are blinking so rapidly they might flutter away. The anticipation is going to kill me before he ever gets to use that belt. The worst part about all of this is that my pussy is so wet that I won't need his cum to have something running down my legs.

'Hands above your head,' he instructs as he uncuffs my right hand. I didn't realize until now how tall these closet rods are. Whoever owned this building before must have had this exact scenario in mind. If I were any shorter, I'd need to stand on my tippy toes to reach. He cuffs my hands in place and I stand completely pants-less in my heels, blazer, and ripped-open blouse. My tits still hanging out over the top of my bra.

'You look so fucking sexy like this, Mil.'

'Ready for your punishment,' he pauses as he runs his hand down my back to my ass, 'remember, you're going to be quiet.' His words sink to my core as he places the tie across my mouth, tying it behind my head, leaving me unable to say much even if I wanted to.

'Now spread those legs and stick that pretty ass out for me,' he commands as he steps back from me. I'm so exposed, and it's by far the sexiest thing I've ever experienced. I don't even care that his belt is about to own my ass. I'd let him do much worse than this.

He stands back and stares at my ass for what seems like an eternity. No doubt building the anticipation for what's to come. It does nothing to stamp out my nerves and I start panting harder than ever while I wait, my saliva starting to soak into his tie already.

The belt cracks as he holds it in half, snapping it tight at either end. I can tell he's soaking in the situation since he's taking his time, dragging the moment out as long as possible. I think he likes to torture himself as much as he loves to torture me. The suspense has my clit pulsating like it'll explode any minute as sweat starts to roll down my spine.

The first hit lands across my ass so hard my eyes instantly well with tears. My head falls back as I try to steady myself. I can barely even moan with this tie in my mouth.

Another crack of the belt lands as I struggle to keep my legs apart and ass out.

Crack! Fuck. The third time feels even more intense than the first two strikes, the sting spreading from my ass and down my legs. Tears are running rampant down my face and my knees start to buckle. I try and stand up a little straighter attempting to change the area he keeps hitting. The pain that radiates through me with each swing does nothing to quell my starving pussy. It's hungrier than ever.

'Eh, eh, eh, Mil. Ass out.' I start to shake my head no, trying to barely pop my heated cheeks toward him, hoping it will appease him.

'Now, Mil. Or you'll get more than I already had planned.' A muffled cry escapes my throat as I force my legs apart and stick my ass out as far as I can. My legs quake beneath the weight of my body as I wait for another blow.

'That's my girl,' he growls before smacking the belt across my ass three more times. The only reprieve between hits being the time it takes his arm to swing back and forth. I'm starting to worry that I'll pull the railing down from the closet, I'm straining against it so fucking hard. My ass has been set ablaze and my pussy gets wetter with every hit. What the fuck is wrong with me?

Cade unleashes three more swats of the belt on my ass before I hear it drop to the floor. My head lulls back as relief sweeps over me. I'm spent already and decided after the first hit that I won't be missing any appointments from here on out.

I hear the zipper of his pants and let out a whimper as he steps up behind me, his hard cock settling against my soaked and swollen pussy. Gripping my throat, he pulls me back against his chest as his free hand reaches down to my clit, his caress is almost my undoing.

'That's my good girl,' he whispers against my ear as he places kisses before moving his lips down my neck. I sink into his touch and start to shake as he brings me to the brink of orgasm.

'Such a good girl.' His tongue glides along the outer shell of my ear. 'But we're not done.' He takes his hand away and I slump forward at the reminder.

'I'm going to fuck you now, Mil. Don't you dare come.' He doesn't even need to threaten me as I'm unwilling to receive the belt anymore after this.

'Now, stick that ass back out here for me,' he commands as he slaps my ass, nearly bringing me to my knees.

Without warning, he shoves his cock all the way into its base, his hips slapping against me. If I didn't have a tie in my mouth, I would've screamed out. Everything is muffled with the tie. He starts to pump in and out hard and fast showing me no mercy. He's definitely not here for my pleasure and I'm fine with it, if I get to feel him inside me.

'Fuck, Mil. This pussy is so tight... and wet,' he grits out as he fucks me harder than ever before, like he's trying to split me in half. He drives into me fervently as my insides slowly rearrange. The heat of an orgasm starts to build deep in my belly, but I lose all hope of sweet release as he slams into me one last time. His fingers bruise my hips as he holds me against him to ride out the waves of orgasm. His cum coats my swollen insides as he twitches against me. Leaning forward and placing a hand against the wall to steady himself, his weight lifts from my back, and face still in my hair, his breathing mellows. This whole show fully drained both of our energy reserves.

He was right. I can barely stand after all that. I'm slumped forward under his weight. The only things keeping me upright now being that I'm cuffed to the railing, and his arm around my waist. He kisses into my hair one last time before he pulls out, releases the tie, and uncuffs one of my hands. I almost fall to the floor when my hands are let loose.

Cade catches me and slowly lowers me down to sit on the floor. My ass is still throbbing from the belt and my pussy is swollen from being used and not being allowed to come. Fuck. I'll have to break out my vibrator tonight. There's no way I'll make it until Tuesday without getting off. Not after this.

While I sit on the floor of the closet still trying to regain my composure, Cade replaces his pants, suit jacket, and puts his tie back on. He looks like he just came from the office. Not like he just beat my ass with a belt, fucked me so hard I could feel his cock in my lungs, and then left me high and dry with no orgasm. Kneeling in front of me, he takes my chin in his hand and brings my eyes to his.

'Don't you dare clean that pussy up. I want my cum streaming down your leg when you walk back downstairs.' He places a kiss on my lips so tender you wouldn't believe he just belted me a few minutes ago.

'I'll see you Tuesday.'

With that, he stands and heads to the bedroom door. Before he crosses through the doorway, he turns, takes me in for a second, and adds, 'Don't be late.' Then, he's gone.

What. The. Fuck. Was. That. Never in my life have I experienced something so intense. I don't know if I'll even be recovered by the time Tuesday rolls around. And why the hell am I still turned on after all that? The urge to have an orgasm is overwhelming. All I want now is for him to come back in here and eat my pussy until I'm dissolving into a puddle of bliss. Then he can rail me again and again until neither of us can dream of walking out of this place. A shiver runs throughout my body as my mind starts to run wild.

Standing up, I scan the room for my pants. I find them in the corner of the bedroom. How they ended up all the way over here I have no idea. As I pull them up, I realize he left the cuffs shackled to my wrist. Son of a bitch! I look around quickly for a key, hoping he left it but there isn't one. I can't go back downstairs with a handcuff on one hand and a button missing from my blouse. One I can hide, the other will be impossible. I shove my tits back in my bra and get my blouse situated, confirming the button right between my tits is completely gone.

Damn it! I fumble in my blazer pocket for my phone and see I have six missed texts from Celeste and two from Jeremy. Shit. How long have I been up here? Looking at the time, I've been missing for 35 minutes and counting.

> *Celly-girl: Are you good up there?*

> *Celly-girl: A couple more investors just left.*

> *Celly-girl: Yo bitch! Did you fall in?*

> *Cel: Uh, for real. Where the hell did you go??*

> *Jeremy: Hey babe. Just wondering when you were going to be home. I was going to make sure dinner was ready when you got here. No rush.*

> *Celly-girl: WTF Mil! Did you leave? I went to our hideout and the door was locked.*

> *Jeremy: Mil! Everything good? Cel text me and asked if I'd heard from you.*

> *Celly-girl: I'm sorry! I messaged Jeremy. I'm starting to freak out.*

Shit. Damn you Cade. Couldn't he be normal and punish me at his house when people wouldn't be worried about my whereabouts?! Ok, ok. Calm down. I can tell Celeste I left sick. I'll tell Jeremy the same thing but that I pulled off the side of the road to throw up or something. I take a few deep breaths to calm myself down. I need a level head if I'm going to keep up this lie.

> *Me: Girl! I am so sorry. I got up here and I started feeling sick. I threw up and I'm headed home.*

> *Me: Hey babe. I got sick and left. I'll be home shortly. Don't worry about dinner.*

I peek out of the apartment, take off down the hall, and hit the back stairway hoping to God I don't run into Celeste. I plow through the exit door and speed walk to my car. I pull my keys from my pocket and unlock the car before I've reached it. Opening the door, I throw myself in and shove the keys in the ignition, put the car in drive, and speed off, trying to put the apartment building, and my lies, as far behind me as possible.

Chapter Eleven

Uneasiness consumes me as I race home, "FMLYHM" by Seether blasting through my speakers to drown out my transgressions. I slow to a death crawl before hitting my driveway, so Jeremy won't be alerted to me being home just yet. I need to get in the door and upstairs without running into him. Great plan, Mil. You're really nailing this. Ok, get in the house. Get upstairs. Figure it out from there. This is my only option.

I shove the open handcuff up my jacket sleeve trying to conceal it as much as possible. My heart quivers inside my chest as I slide the gearshift into park and exit the car, speed walking to the porch. I stick my key in the lock, turn the knob, and dive through the door. I don't even bother pulling my keys from the lock or shutting the door. I hear Jeremy's voice as soon as I hit the steps.

'Mil? Are you ok?'

'I'll be fine. I need the bathroom,' I yell as I sprint up the steps, trying to disappear around the corner before he can see me.

I fly through the spare bedroom and skid into the bathroom, slamming the door behind me. I made it. I fucking made it. I start to catch my breath when the knocking starts.

'What do you need from me, babe?' Jeremys asks through the door.

'Nothing, I'm not feeling well. I just need a minute.' I flush the toilet for added effect. My eyes scan the bathroom quickly as if the key to the handcuffs will miraculously appear.

'Are you sure? I can hold your hair. I'm pretty good at that.'

'No, you don't want to see this,' I lie, 'just give me a minute.'

'Ok, ok. How about some chicken noodle soup? That might settle your stomach. We might have some sprite in the pantry too.'

"Yeah, yeah that's fine.' I make a gagging noise to add some effect and flush the toilet again. Anything to get him from this damn bathroom. I just need to get these fucking handcuffs off. It'll be no problem to fake sick after that.

'You got it babe. Yell if you need me.'

I sit down on the toilet lid once Jeremy walks away. Clearing my head is top priority now if I'm going to get out of this.

I start pulling open drawers, looking for anything I could use to unlatch this fucking lock. Nothing. I'm not sure if anyone has ever been able to use a toothpaste bottle to pick a lock but I doubt it. The cabinet yields the same results. Zilch.

I sit down on the floor and lean against the door. Pulling my knees to my chest, I drop my forehead to my knees. How the hell am I going to get these off? I have no way of hiding them. Jeremy and I aren't exactly touching each other but I'm pretty sure he'd either hear the metal or see them through even my bulkiest sweatshirt sleeve. Besides, I can't take a chance like that. There would be no explaining my way out of that one.

Stretching my legs back out, I look down at my feet and tap the toes of my pumps together. Think, Mil. Think. Using the toe of one heel, I slip a shoe off, then the other, and flex my toes. One of life's greatest pleasures, taking heels off. Its right up there with getting rid of your bra at the end of the day.

I shake myself back to reality. I don't have time to relax right now. I sit up and cross my legs, and rub my face into my hands, the cuffs jangling when I move my arms. I sigh into my palms and wipe my hands down my face. My eyes open as my fingers slide across my eyelids and that's when I see it. A lone bobby pin under the vanity. A fucking bobby pin!

I scramble to my belly, slide my arm under the vanity and grab the bobby pin. I sit back up and stare down at my little lifesaver. Now, to pick this cuff. I pry the bobby pin open and shove the end in the hole and start digging around. They make it look so easy in the movies. Why isn't this just automatically popping open? Why would I be able to handle it quickly and be on my way to my evening? Because I'm an idiot that's why.

Google swoops in for the win. I click the first video that pops up and watch it with the sound off. Trying to decipher what they're telling me to do in silence. Thankfully, someone or something is on my side because it only takes me three rewinds to finally pop them open. The pure relief I feel as soon as they're off is unexplainable. I rub my wrist and think this must be how an actual prisoner feels once they've been released. In reality, this probably doesn't compare in the slightest but for what I've just been through and for what I'm able to avoid, I'll take it.

I open the cabinet of the vanity, unroll a towel, and reroll it back up with the cuffs inside. This'll have to do until I can get them out of the house completely. I stand and flush the toilet again for good measure and start the hot water at the sink so I can rinse my face off. I run my wet hands through my hair to add that sweaty effect and brush my teeth. I give myself a once-over in the mirror. It's the best it's going to get. The biggest issue has been hurdled.

I turn around and open the door of the bathroom.

'Feel any better?' Jeremy asks standing up from the bed to come and comfort me. Great, I should've known he'd be waiting on me.

'Here, let me help you,' he suggests as I start to shrug my jacket off.

'I can get it,' I say as I pull away.

'Mil, it's ok, just let me help you get comfy and into bed.'

'I've got it, Jeremy.' My words come out sterner than I intend, and I see the hurt reflected in Jeremy's eyes.

'Right, sorry,' he starts to back away, 'I'll just run downstairs and grab your soup. I'm sure it's ready by now.'

I take advantage of Jeremy being gone and run into the master bedroom, slip out of my clothes, and toss them in a pile on the closet floor. I grab a pair of sweatpants first so I can make sure my ass is covered. My illness charade would end as fast as it started if he caught a glimpse of the welts. I wouldn't be able to begin to come up with a cover for that.

I must have had a crease in my pants that indented into my ass cheeks when I was driving.

I was sitting on a really weird chair at the showing.

A man showed up, cuffed me to a closet rod, and beat my ass with his belt.

Even the truth would be unbelievable. I pull a sweatshirt over my head and let it fall around my body. Going back to the spare bedroom, I slip under the covers and let my eyes close. Honestly, I'd take this over still standing and forcing small talk with a band of white, male investors. The only woman in attendance today was the one with Dominus, LLC. Having more women around might have made it more enjoyable but here we are. I hate that I left Celeste there by herself. She's going to kill me. Except she thinks I'm sick, so she'll be very concerned. Which I also hate.

Jeremy comes back in the room bearing soup and Sprite on a bed tray. He's even got a small vase with a single rose. Damn him. I sit up in the bed so he can sit it across my lap. The soup smells amazing, and I realize I haven't eaten since this morning. I'll have to pace myself if I'm going to keep up this rouse.

I take a spoonful of the liquid and sip it. As expected, it's delicious. Jeremy lays on top of the covers next to me, propping himself up on his elbow as I shove another spoonful into my mouth.

'Take it easy. You don't want it coming back up,' he says with his most sincere smile.

'You're right.'

I set the spoon down and opt for a couple swigs of the sprite.

Sprite was always the go-to when I was sick as a child. The bubbles instantly made any ailment better. I think they could wipe the pharmacy shelves and replace everything with the magic potion. It never failed me anyway.

'I was worried about you when Cel texted me.'

'Yeah, sorry. I should've told her I wasn't feeling well.' Except I couldn't because I was cuffed and being fucked by my Dom. 'It came out of nowhere.'

'Well, you're home now. I'll take care of you.' He raises up and places a soft kiss on my cheek.

'Thanks. And thanks for the soup. And the sprite. And the flower. It's very sweet.'

'Anything for my favorite girl.' My face flushes and I turn my attention back to the soup.

Jeremy sticks around while I pretend to have a hard time getting food in my stomach. We chat idly about nonsense. Things he saw from our friends while scrolling on social media, the new coffee shop that's going up, the new book he wants to read that just came out. I'm thankful for the easy conversation. The hard, weighted ones are too frequent for me. And I'm entirely too exhausted after today's activities to struggle through a serious conversation.

A yawn takes over and Jeremy takes that as his queue to let me get some rest. Which I need desperately. Who knew a belting as punishment would take that much energy out of you?

Jeremy takes the bed tray and sits it outside the door of the room. He comes back and makes sure I'm tucked in. Leaning down, he presses a kiss in my hair and lingers for a moment. Tucking my hair behind my ear, he whispers that he loves me before leaving me to sleep. I can feel him standing in the doorway, watching me. I wonder what might be going through his mind right now. Is he trying to figure out if I'm actually sick? Was I a good enough actress? Or maybe he's just wishing he could snuggle up with me. Trying to decide if I might welcome him in bed or tell him I need some solo rest. I hear the door shut as he must have decided it's best to leave me be.

Chapter Twelve

My body shakes with nervousness like I've been on a cocaine bender for the past two days. Not that I would really know what that felt like because I haven't ever used cocaine, but if one could guess, this is what it feels like. The adrenaline from my run-in with Cade, lying to Jeremy and Celeste, rushing home to try and get off handcuffs without my husband seeing, and faking an illness the rest of the evening is still fresh in my veins.

I wasn't off the hook the whole time with Jeremy. He was certainly a stellar caregiver, not leaving my side, at my beck and call for anything I needed. His being so far up my ass really put a damper on satisfying myself. My vibrator taunted me from a few inches away for two days. I suppose I could've let him have some fun with me. He's always been a giver in the bedroom and would've been even more so with my sickness and all. But he would've been sweet in bed and my body is craving the opposite. I want to be violently used and put away wet. I want to question my very existence after being fucked into another timeline.

Here I am a couple of days later and the thought of the belt biting across my ass is still making my pussy tingle with anticipation. I'm just now able to shake Jeremy's presence enough to get out of the house. He had canceled a private dinner last night to stay home with me and probably would've canceled another tonight if I hadn't faked a doctor's appointment.

Regardless of how turned on I was, and still am, I don't want the belt again, so I'm at Cade's house a full 20 minutes early. As I hit the top step leading to the porch, I notice a white piece of paper hanging from the door. Grabbing the note, I open it up, hoping this isn't him canceling on me. I haven't been checking my phone too much in case Jeremy was looking over my shoulder but I'm sure I would've caught a message from Cade if there was a change of plans.

Looking down, I read what Cade needs from me in his very neat scroll:

Door is unlocked. There is a white button-up for you. Put it on and nothing else. I'll be waiting in the living room.

Back to the white button-up, I see. I'll do whatever he needs me to as long as he lets me come all over him. My pussy is on the verge of exploding with all this pent-up sexual energy. Death itself couldn't provide me solace right now.

Opening the front door, I slip inside and start taking off my clothes. I feel like I should make some loud noises, but the living room is right off the entryway so I'm sure he knows I'm here. Goosebumps coat my skin as I remove layers. The white button-up hangs on the coat rack and I grab it to try and warm up. The shirt does nothing for my cold skin but I'm sure to be heated up once I step into Cade's living room.

Crossing the hall into the living room, I find it empty. What the hell? Maybe he doesn't know I'm here. I am early. Knowing he was expecting me, you know, with the shirt and all, I decide to venture deeper into the room where it transitions into his office. I might as well take advantage of some snooping while I wait for him. He has a bibliophile's dream bookcase, floor to ceiling on all three sides with a huge mahogany desk in the center. Leather chair and leather couch in front like he conducts some sort of business here. This drives my mind a little crazy as I start to wonder if he does conduct business here. Does he bring his other subs here as well? The thought makes my stomach roll over itself and I want to ask him, but I have no right to.

Sauntering behind the desk, my fingers glide along the edges of the spines. So many of these books are classics. He has several titles from John Steinbeck, Tolstoy, and Tolkien. It registers that I really don't know much about him other than the fact that he doles out one hell of an orgasm and punishment. Venturing a little farther down the shelves, I see he also has some books on business. Maybe he has a degree in business? I wonder if one needs that for the Dom world. Ah, there it is. Dartmouth? He graduated from the Tuck School of Business at Dartmouth. With a Masters! Holy shit! I certainly didn't take him for a stupid man but he's brilliant. Who have I been in bed with?

I lean down a little to give the degree a closer inspection. I'm sure it's real, I'm just surprised. I guess I shouldn't be since, again, I'm realizing I know nothing about him. I'm standing in a badass library office in a very nice home. Who am I to question the Dom business? I know what I was paying for his services and if he only had a few clients at that price, he would be rolling in cash from Victoria's alone.

'It's real.' I jerk upright and spin around, my back slamming against the bookshelf at the sound of his voice. Standing on the other side of the huge desk is the brilliant man himself and he does not look impressed.

'I, uh, I, was just... just thinking that... I'm impressed. And I don't know anything about you, I guess.'

'You've never asked,' he deadpans.

'Right. You're right,' I say and wait for him to say something else. One thing I do know is he's a man of very few words. I start to flounder not knowing what else to say and realize I'm clutching my arms so tight around my chest that my fingers are starting to tingle from loss of blood flow. I loosen my arms and let them hang at my sides. The shirt gapes open from the change in position, effectively giving Cade a front row seat for cleavage and pussy.

Cade's eyes roam up and down my body as I stand backed against his bookshelf. I watch as the hunger builds in his eyes and feel the throb grow between my legs in response to his gaze. After all these months with this man and still, just him looking at me practically brings me to my knees.

'Come here.' His demand is hard and direct. I walk around to stand between him and the desk. He can't still be mad about last Friday, can he? After the punishment he put me through two days ago, I'm still paying for it standing here today since I haven't been able to come. He steps forward abruptly making me step back, my ass hitting the edge of his desk. My breath hitches from the jolt and I instinctively reach back to grip the edge of the desk. He seems bigger. Meaner. There is an air of annoyance about him tonight.

'You still have me some type of way over last Friday and I can't, for the life of me, figure out why.' His voice is gravelly as he reaches up and strokes my cheek with his finger.

'I'm sorry, sir. Really, I am. It won't happen again.'

His deep stare scratches at my soul as I practically hyperventilate under the pressure.

'Sir!' I add in louder than I cared too. This can't be good for my health. Getting my heart rate up like this without even moving my body. It's insane. My chest rises and falls violently with each breath.

'There's also the issue of you leaving the open house after I was done with you. What were your orders?'

'I had to get out of there. You ripped a button off my shirt, *and* you left the handcuffs on!'

'And?'

'What? I couldn't…someone…somebody… how was I supposed to hide those things? The button was one thing, but I couldn't walk back down there with a handcuff hanging off my arm. Cel would've called the cops! There was a room full of investors. Wait... How did you even know...' My breathing becomes sporadic as my mind starts going a million miles in every direction.

Cade takes another step toward me and his lips crash against mine effectively saving me from my impending panic attack. His tongue warm and wet in my mouth sends electrical pulses spurring throughout my body. His left hand grabs my hair as he pulls my head back and starts kissing and nibbling his way across my jaw and down my neck. He grips my right leg and guides it around his waist lifting me up onto the desk. I wrap both legs around his waist as his hand travels up my back pushing me against him. My body melts as the heat from his skin caresses me. His touch so fucking hot, I come apart at the seams as everything else dissolves away. He's going to have one hell of a wet spot to clean off this desk when we're done.

Continuing the attack on my mouth, his hands string heat up my sides as they reach my tits, kneading them in his rugged palms. Rolling my nipples between nimble fingers, I whimper against his mouth as my back arches further into his grasp. His cock, stiff under his jeans, grinds between my legs, and I want nothing more than to strip him down. Deciding I've had enough, I reach down between us and start to unbutton his jeans. My plan is quickly dismantled when he grabs my wrists, pulling my hands away.

'Ah, ah, ah.' He continues to abuse my mouth before biting onto my bottom lip and stretching is out, before releasing me, and taking a step back.

My lungs burn like I've just ran a marathon from how ready I am for him. The outline of his cock in his jeans is begging to be freed so I can slide my mouth up and down his silky skin. My eyes find his and I glimpse something behind those green pools. It's the quickest flash so I can't nail down the emotion, but I know I saw something. What is happening? He almost seems as though he doesn't want to be doing this. Which completely contradicts the fierce makeout session we just had. There's an internal warfare waging inside that beautiful head of his. He rubs a hand down his face as he lets out a long, exhausted breath before giving me his direction.

'Turn around and bend over the desk. Hold onto the other side.'

Swallowing hard, I do as I'm told. My breath hitches as cold shoots through my body sending chills clear to my feet when my skin meets the wood. I reach my hands forward and latch onto the opposite side of the desk.

'Don't move your hands.' My hands are firmly planted, and my mind is a whirl. For some reason, I can't shake the feeling he's upset about something. Is he upset with me? Or did something happen today? My concern piques and I suddenly feel out of place.

His hand smacks down on my tender cheek just as I'm about to ask him if something is wrong. Fuck! The tenderness from Sunday is immediately reignited and my ass is set aflame. Smack! Smack! Smack! My hands tremble and sweat gathers on my palms as I force them to keep holding onto the desk. He's not taking it easy on me today for some reason. Even after Sunday.

Regardless of the pain, here I am again, dying for him to touch me. My pussy is a trembling mess just waiting on his fingers, or cock, or something. Hell! I'd take a wine bottle at this point. I get my wish when a hand slides up my back and stops, holding me in place on the desk. His free hand rubs across my blazing ass cheeks easing some of the pain. As I start to catch my breath, his deft fingers start roaming around, teasing across and around my clit but not entering my wet and waiting opening. I moan into the desk, my hot breath clouding the surface, just from him grazing my pussy. I push my ass out to try to get more from him but his hand on my back is keeping me completely still. I'm a needy little bitch.

Finally, he sinks a finger into my dripping core. I tremble around his one finger, my psyche frazzling further. His weight presses down on me as his mouth trails up my back before a second finger joins the first. Cade's hand between my shoulder blades renders me motionless as his teeth bite along my back. Rigid fingers pump in and out slowly, torturously, as I try as hard as I can to buck against his hand.

'Oh, Cade….' I murmur out, barely able to stand the feeling of his fingers sliding against my walls and stroking against that sweet spot, after two days. I berate myself for being so pathetic as I try and will myself to come from the tease of his fingers alone. Heat builds in my lower belly, and I know with just a couple more strokes, I'll fall into an orgasmic abyss.

He works me closer and closer before stealing his fingers away.

'Cade,' I huff out pissed beyond belief that he didn't take me over the edge.

'Don't talk back to me,' he snarls as his hand slaps my pussy. Not once but twice. I yelp at the bookcase straight ahead. My only audience. 'I'm sorry, sir.' My pussy is so engorged I'm sure I'll die before this night is over and tingles in the most delicious way from his strong swats. Cade stands behind me as he starts to massage my ass cheeks. His hands and fingers burn his memory into my skin as he grips and pulls. He glides his thumbs around my pussy, spreading me open, pulling yet another moan from my feeble body.

Grabbing my hip in one hand, he circles the tip of his cock around my swollen entrance, stimulating fibers in my body I didn't know existed. Barely pressing inside of me and pulling back out to circle the tip around again, I'm firing on all cylinders as my entire body begins to shake. Every nerve inside my pussy is sending vicious pleasure signals to my brain. Finally, even he can't hold out any longer. He buries his cock into me, and I scream out, mostly from the relief of him finally filling me up. He pulls completely out before slamming into me again. Then continues his torture with rough and long strokes. One hand grips my ass while the other stays firmly in place in the middle of my back. I lay my cheek onto the surface of the desk, mouth gaping, eyelids heaving with desire. I let my face slide back and forth with each pounding movement of his cock. I can barely breathe, and my knuckles are white as I barrel over the edge of my orgasm. My face is sticky with sweat against the desk as I ride out the remaining convulsions. Cade isn't far behind me with his own orgasm as he slams into me with finality. His hot cum shoots inside of me with a grunt and his cock twitches with satisfaction, as I come down from my high.

Cade brings his lips to my back again, kissing along my spine as we both savor the moment. Waiting two days for an orgasm made the experience much more intense but I can't say I want to do it again. I still feel pent up and could use a round two if I'm being honest.

Cade's weight lifts from my back with one final kiss. He pulls out, leaving me feeling empty and void of warmth.

'I'll see you Friday.' And with that, he walks out of the room.

Chapter Thirteen

I remain sprawled across the desk for too long after Cade leaves the room. Stunned isn't even close to describing what I'm feeling right now. Bewildered? Dumbfounded? He fucked me on his desk, pulled out, and just walked off. He used me. Did he just use me? We've had our weird goodbyes when I was seeing him at the diner but that's because I was paying him for a service. Aren't we passed that by now? I slowly peel myself up from the desk as the feelings of being compared to an old rag doll that's being thrown out come rushing in.

I stand for a moment trying to collect my thoughts and reign in the tears that are waiting at the edge of my eyelids. I can't seem to move my legs forward. Looking around the room, waiting for Cade to come back and let me know it was just another scene to play out, I realize I'm alone. I have no idea if he's even still in the house. My bottom lip starts to quiver as a sob breaks the silence. I throw my hands up to cover my mouth to stifle my cries as the tears stream down my cheeks and start to soak the cuffs of the button-up. I've got to get out of here.

I walk as fast and light as I can to the front door where my clothes and jacket wait. I peak over my shoulder to check I'm alone in my humiliation before I peel off the button-up and throw it onto the floor. I dress as quickly as I can, continuing to glance behind me every so often. My heart feels like it's breaking and I don't know why. I hope Cade left the house and doesn't know how long I stayed after he left me lying used on his desk. My stomach twists with the thought of him listening and waiting for me to leave. Fuck. Fuck. Fuck!

Throwing on my jacket, I twist the handle and pull the door open. Standing halfway outside, I take a chance and wait for just another moment in case Cade is ready to jump out and keep me here. The button-up is lying on the floor where I threw it, and I can see where the cuffs are soaked through from when I dried my eyes. A lone tear falls to the floor as I finally muster the courage to pull the door shut and leave. My shame trails behind me like smoke from a fire as I speed across the porch, down the sidewalk, and to my car.

Dropping into the driver's seat, I let the floodgates flow. My cries filling the silence of my car. The sounds coming from my body are guttural and I wonder if I even cried this hard when Jeremy confessed about fucking Samantha. I keep thinking I feel used but I'm not sure that's what this is. Listening to Cade say *I'll see you Friday* and realizing he's just leaving me there, to fend for myself, to not even see me out, is worse than if he had kicked me out immediately after our session. Our incredible session. Fuck.

My sobs finally slow, and I let my head fall forward to rest on the steering wheel. I push my key into the ignition and turn the engine over. The car comes to life and the last remnants of a cheesy greeting card commercial reverberates from my speakers. My fingers fumble around for the heat as I keep my eyes pinched closed.

I let what just happened sink in a little further and the realization that I'm hurt sweeps over me. I'm hurt. Cade hurt my feelings. Feelings I shouldn't even have because he's my Dom. My Dom I'm seeing while I'm still married to my husband. The dull ache coming from my chest is screaming what I won't admit out loud.

I lift my head and look into the eyes of the woman staring back at me as the sounds of "Rain" by the Teskey Brothers infiltrates my ear drums. Of all songs, this one. Can't a girl get a reprieve from the heartache for just one damn second? Is that too much to fucking ask? I let out a scream that rings my ears and lay into my steering wheel, pounding my fist into it like it's that bitch Samantha's face. That whore. I wouldn't be having this moment in my damn car if it weren't for that homewrecker.

'Ah, fuck!' I scream after about the sixth hit and grab my hand.

'Shit!' That fucking hurt. I start to rub the pinky side of my hand and hope I didn't break anything as a result of my battle with the steering wheel. That would be embarrassing. If I'm going to break my hand, I'm going to do it after throwing a punch right into Samantha's pretty little mouth. I allow myself a couple more massages around my pinky before taking a few calming breaths. I catch my reflection in the rearview mirror once more before pulling out of my spot. You're a fucking mess, Mil. An absolute mess.

I drop my stuff on the sideboard and bring my fingers to my temples. My head would feel better if I had an ice pick sticking into it. I popped two Excedrin on the drive home and washed them down with an airplane bottle of vodka that's been living in my glove box for who knows how long. In hindsight, that probably isn't helping my headache.

'Mil? Are you ok?' Jeremy asks from the doorway of the kitchen. I drop my hands and look over at the man drying his hands on a towel and watch his face transform from mild concern to completely distressed.

'What is it?' he asks dropping the towel as he strides toward me. My bones liquefy as he wraps his arms around me and lowers us to the floor. The tears I dried earlier start making another grand appearance. Jeremy lets me unleash my waterfall as his hand rubs up and down the length of my back while the other clutches my head to his chest. With his legs spread on either side of me, I snuggle tighter into his chest and sob. I know I shouldn't be letting him console me right now, but I can't help that his arms still have a hint of home in them. I let my body shutter against him as the tears start to subside, and I start to relax. He places the softest kisses into my hair, not once trying to drag my reasons for being upset out of me. Just letting me feel what I'm feeling, and I couldn't appreciate him more than I do in this moment.

'I'm sorry, I just got overwhelmed on the way home and....' I say as I start to pull away, but Jeremy immediately shushes me and pulls me back into his chest. I let him hold me a little while longer before moving to look up at him. His eyes are pools of concern as he examines my whole face. I know he's willing me to open up to him but there's a mammoth of a reason why I can't. The reason finally having nothing to do with the man in front of me and everything to do with the man I just left.

'Why don't you change into some comfy clothes, and I'll meet you on the couch.' He kisses my forehead before releasing me to get changed. As I round the top of the stairs, I spare a look down to see Jeremy still standing there looking torn between following me and keeping his promise of meeting me on the couch.

In just a few minutes, I'm on my way back downstairs and find him waiting in the living room with wine and a blanket. I take up the open spot next to him and take my glass of wine from him as he covers us with the blanket and throws his arm around my shoulders, pulling me closer to him.

'Do you want to talk about it?' he asks after a few minutes of silence.

'Not really.' I stare down into my wine hoping he'll drop it. I'm exhausted and lying right now feels like it'll send me to an early grave.

'Mil… you know we need to start talking to each other about stuff. I'm trying not to push but if you start feeling sad because of us, I want to talk through it with you.'

'I know. It wasn't…' Fuck.

I wasn't upset about us Jeremy. I was upset that my Dom left me feeling empty and alone and I'm struggling hard, real hard, with that.

'What is it then?'

'I… I… ugh…' I try and stall as much as I can, trying to find a legitimate reason for why I was in shambles a little bit ago. My mind is a blank space, so my only option is to use what's in front of me.

'I was driving home from my appointment, and I saw a girl walking and she looked like Samantha. It just… ya know… reminded me…' I fade off on purpose because I'm having trouble finishing up my fabrication. The lies are getting harder and harder to string together the longer this goes on.

'Of my affair?' he finishes the sentence for me.

'Yeah.' I say to my wine glass.

Jeremy adjusts his body slightly away and clears his throat as he prepares to talk through this incredibly uncomfortable subject. Feeling him squirm next to me reminds me of when he admitted to what had been going on for a year.

I had just come home from work and was ready to celebrate the first sale that Celeste and I had landed as a new realty company. I had put my stuff on the sideboard like I would any other day and began yelling for Jeremy as I started down the hall to the kitchen. I looked around the kitchen with no Jeremy in sight and decided to check upstairs. Maybe he didn't hear me come home. As I walked back down the hallway, something caught my attention out of the corner of my eye in the living room.

'There you are!' Finding Jeremy.

'I yelled for you, dork,' I say as I cross over to the couch where he sits staring at the old wooden floor, 'I've got great news!'

Kneeling down in front of him, I see his eyes are so bloodshot it looks as though every capillary has exploded. Even with me right in front of him, I almost start to think he doesn't realize I'm here and he's stuck in some sort of catatonic state.

'Hello, earth to Jeremy. Is everything ok?' I wave my hand in front of his face to try and break him from his trance.

He clears his throat and adjusts himself slightly toward the wall, away from me. I watch him as he brings his hand to his face covering his mouth and blinking away tears.

'Jeremy, you're starting to freak me out.' I sit back onto the ottoman that's directly in front of him and put my hands on top of his thighs. His immediate reaction to move his legs away from my hands startles me and I scoot farther back onto the ottoman, squeezing my hands together in my lap.

'Jeremy, please, what's wrong?'

'I uh… have to tell you something,' he chokes out as another stream of tears falls from his eyes. Oh my God. Someone died. If he's reacting this way, then someone really close to him had to have died or he doesn't want to tell me because its someone close to me. My dad? His brother? Tears prick at my eyes as I start going down the list of people who could've died that would have my husband reacting this way. Jeremy finally moves and sits up on the edge of the couch placing his legs on either side of mine. He reaches up and takes my hands into his shaking ones with a strained breath.

'Jesus Jeremy, just tell me what the hell is going on.' I'm starting to get pissed. Who makes someone wait for news like this? Just get it over with already.

'I've been having an affair.' I stare back at him. I obviously didn't hear him correctly.

'Who's having an affair?'

'I am, Mil.'

I continue staring at him while my mind tries like hell to wrap around the information he's feeding me. My hands start to sweat in his as he massages my hands. I can't tell if it's for my benefit or his.

'You're having an affair.' I repeat, almost breathless, the words stick like glue on my tongue. My chest constricts as my breathing picks up pace as the room starts to spin.

'It's been going on for a while now… with Samantha… that bartender from the Pour House…. I've been wanting to tell you, but I just couldn't… I don't want to lose you, Mil. I fucked up, ok. I fucked up....' Jeremy is talking a million miles a minute as he tries to get out as much as he can. I know he's still talking but a static sound starts in my ears and gets louder and louder, drowning him out and threatening to burst my ear drums.

I don't realize I'm standing until Jeremy stands up in front of me saying something, but the static is making it impossible to hear anything. He continues to plead as the heat in my face rises and sweat droplets fall down my back.

'Mil!' Jeremy yells, shaking my shoulders and breaking through the static. My eyes connect with his as the gravity of what he's just told me bears down on me. He cheated. My husband cheated on me. The person I shared a first kiss with in my dorm room, cheated. The person who got down on one knee and asked me to spend the rest of my life with him, cheated. The person I planned to have kids with, cheated. The person I planned a future with, cheated. The person I was supposed to grow old with, cheated. The last person on earth that was supposed to cheat on me, cheated. My forever person slept with another woman.

'Is that all?'

'What do you mean is that all?' he asks with pinched eyebrows.

'Is that all you had to tell me?' I repeat, suppressing a choking sob.

'Uh, yeah, I guess...' he says, confusion spreading across his face as I square my shoulders and head back toward the front door.

'Mil! Please!' He follows me as I make my way through the front door and onto the porch.

'Mil! Don't leave, please!' I hold up my hand not wanting to hear anything else that's going to come out of his filthy mouth. A mouth he's had on another woman. I get into the car and start the engine as he drops to his knees on the porch, the tears puddling around the neck of his shirt. I wonder if he ever got on his knees for her as I reverse out of the driveway and head in the direction of nowhere.

'Was I not enough for you?' I ask coming back to the moment with Jeremy.

'Oh, Mil,' he pleads as he turns toward me and takes my hands in his, 'you've always been enough. More than enough. I swear to you.

'At the time I was being a selfish bastard. You were so busy with work and getting your realty company off the ground with Celeste and I felt like I barely saw you anymore.

'Things started with Samantha at a time when I was feeling down and neglected. Instead of coming to you, I ran to someone else. And I hate myself for everything that happened with her. Apologizing to you will never be enough to fix what I did, and I understand that, but I'll spend the rest of our days trying to make it up to you.'

Jeremy reaches up and places his hand gently on my cheek. His thumb slides toward my mouth and brushes against my bottom lip. Finally looking up, I find my reflection in eyes, blazing with desire. His eyes fall to my mouth before slowly moving in, taking one last breath before tenderly placing his lips on mine. His tongue teases between my lips and I let them fall open, inviting him in for a taste. His hand moves back, fingers entangling in my hair at the back of my head, pulling me closer into the kiss that's becoming more savage by the second. This time, I let him. I will let him fill in this starving void that started with him and now, seems to be ending with Cade.

I find my arms moving up and hugging around Jeremy's neck. This is the only queue he needs to start pushing me into the couch. Lying back and letting my legs fall to the sides, he settles his weight on me. My scalp tingles as he pulls my hair slightly, forcing my head back farther, opening my neck up to his mouth. His hips start to roll, and my shameless body reacts when his stiffening cock presses against my pussy. A greedy moan emanates from the depths of my chest as his other hand slides up my shirt and caresses my nipple.

My hands move down the sides of his sculpted stomach to grip the bottom of his shirt and I pull it up over his head. His lips are back on mine in seconds before he mirrors my movements and tosses my shirt to the floor with his. Sitting back on his knees between my legs, he stares down at me with lustful eyes. He licks his lips before sinking his teeth into his plump bottom lip, rolling it out slowly.

'Mil,' he breathes before planting his mouth on my nipple, running his tongue in slow, languorous circles. My back arches and

I wish I would feel the heat of his hand move smoothly up my chest to squeeze around my throat. The pressure of his hand on my neck with his tongue on my nipples would have goosebumps rising all over my body and the heat of a sweet release collecting between my legs before our pants were even off. But Jeremy wouldn't do that. He's a sweet lover. Hand necklaces are something I learned to love after being with Cade.

His mouth moves farther south, kissing down my belly. I quake under his touch as he runs his tongue along the waistband of my pants. Looking down, our eyes meet, and I'm reminded again that its Jeremy down there and not Cade. He grins up at me, biting into his bottom lip again, before pulling my legs up straight in front of him. Gripping the waistband under my back, he strips my pants off effortlessly. Pushing my legs apart, his arms reach under my thighs, and gripping my waist, yanks me closer to him. His tongue glides teasingly along the inside of each thigh, letting me feel the hotness of his breath on my bared pussy. Before he devours me wholly, he lightly flicks and grazes my clit, and my hands grip the couch cushions as if I'm preparing to take flight. Finally, seemingly over teasing me, and himself, his whole mouth covers my pussy as he fucks me with his tongue. My fingers prickle with numbness from the grip I have on the cushion as he slides his tongue up and sucks my swollen lips into his mouth.

'Fuck baby, you taste so damn good,' his voice husky, 'I missed this.' His tongue moves knowingly up a little further around my clit, pulling sounds from my body I never thought he'd hear again. I grip his hair as I start rolling my hips, grinding my clit against his mouth. He pushes on, punishing my pussy with his mouth and I don't think it's ever felt this amazing as my cries grow louder.

'Cum for me baby,' he breathes as he two fingers inside me, curling and stroking me into oblivion. My walls contract around his fingers and cum saturates his hand and mouth as the orgasm overtakes me. My forearm flies to my mouth and I bite down to keep from screaming Cade's name. His hungry swipes continue over my pussy, not wanting to leave any arousal behind, draining me of life.

Sitting up, I see my orgasm glisten on his chin before he wipes is forearm across his mouth. With a wild look in his eyes, Jeremy grabs my wrists, pulling me up to sit in front of him. Gripping my thighs, he picks me up as he stands, my legs wrap around his waist. With his back facing the couch, he sits back down so I'm straddling his cock. Grabbing my face, he brings my mouth to his as our tongues wrestle with each other. Remnants of Cades cum from earlier ignites across my tastebuds. I taste even better mixed with him. We're nothing but breathes and moans as his hands find my ass. He twitches against my eager pussy before he lifts me and sits me down on his waiting cock.

'Jesus Christ, Mil. You're so fucking tight,' he grits, 'ride this cock, baby.' And I do. I'd do anything right now to keep my mind off Cade. Except this position is one of Cade's favorites and I can see him underneath me from our last session at Victoria's Diner. The way he spanked my ass. The way he ate my pussy from behind. The taste of his cock on my tongue. The way we both came apart after I fucked him just like this on that leather couch of his.

Jeremy's hands grip my ass tighter, urging my hips to keep moving.

'Does that feel good baby?'

'Yes,' I moan as I buck my hips even faster.

'Yes, baby. Just like that.'

I move faster and faster as visions of Cade flash through my mind. The way he'd pull my hair. They way he'd choke me until my vision would blur, only letting up at the perfect moment. The way he'd force me to look at him while I covered his cock in cum.

'Oh, Ca... keep filling me up.' I catch myself before Jeremy sends me into a fit of pleasure.

'Fuck!' Jeremy grunts as he finds his release right after me. I drop my head to his shoulder and pretend for a moment that its Cade's cock spasming inside of me. We sit like this for a while letting the pleasure fade. Jeremy moves my hair off my face and kisses my cheek gently.

'I love you, Mil,' he whispers into my neck, bringing me back to the reality again, that I'm not back in Victoria's Diner nestled against Cade's neck. I press my lips to his neck, trying to return some of the love he's giving to me.

'Do you still love me?' he asks as he wraps his arms around me, molding me against his body.

'I do.' It's not a lie. I do still love him. He just isn't in first place anymore. I think he hasn't been my number one for a while now. Since the day he came clean about Samantha, his spot as my forever person started moving backward. Now, there is someone else that's taking his place. It's up to me to figure out what to do about it.

Chapter Fourteen

My brain is speeding through the traffic of Cade, Jeremy, and this damn apartment deal. The string that is my sanity is slowly starting to fray and I need to keep it together at least until this sale is closed. Jeremy and I having sex the other night really added an extra layer to the crazy episodes I call my life that I didn't expect. It wasn't my plan to sleep with him but, damn it, if it didn't feel good. Great, really. Jeremy is a conscientious lover and his dirty talk always seemed to have me reaching the big O faster than just his dick. The icing on the Jeremy cake. It was easier for him to break through my cracking walls after my disaster of a night with Cade. Lucky for him, he caught me in a weak moment. Unlucky for me, since our sexual encounter only added fuel to the forest fires blazing within myself.

I haven't heard from Cade since Tuesday when he left me shaking and sobbing on his desk. I called him a few minutes ago, on my way to meet up with Celeste for a late lunch at Kirk's Brunch Bar, but I was met with his voicemail. I followed up with a text, but my phone has failed to alert me of a missed text message over the course of the 20-minute drive. I pull into the parking lot of Kirk's and park next to Celeste's car. She's always annoyingly on time. I was hoping to get a mimosa down before she got here to calm my nerves. My time management skills are subpar considering I'm already 10 minutes late.

Kirk's is a regular haunt of ours. The owner is a cool, older dude that you would definitely want to hang out with. Friendly and full of sarcastic humor, he whips up an all-day brunch full of delectable dishes, ensures a constant flow of mimosas and bloody marys, and keeps the customers coming back for more. I wish we could sit on the patio but with the chill in the air, its inside seating for us. The patio has an outside Italian cafe feel with small tables covered in floral tablecloths and large plants everywhere. Vines cling to the sides of the brick building while cute umbrellas shield you from the blazing sun in the summer. The inside is just as cute, of course. The brick left exposed on the inside with copper lighting and décor consisting of antiques from around the world. Old photos of people before our time are sprawled throughout the restaurant and more plants can be seen hanging from the ceiling, bringing the outside in.

Celly-girl: Are you standing me up?

Celly-girl: or just curled up in Jeremy's arms after a hot sack sesh?

Jesus. I suppose I could've let her know I was running late but she should be used to it by now. Her 'on time' is 15 minutes early and mine is anywhere between 10 to 20 minutes late.

Me: Just pulled in. Order me a drink :)

I back out of Celeste's message and press Cade's thread. *Read.* Are you kidding me? He's leaving me on *read?* Heat rushes to my face as the nausea starts to slosh in my empty stomach. He's just busy, Mil. Like he said the other day, he doesn't only spend his days in the basement of Victoria's Diner. I open messages and forget to respond all the time. Other than to him. I will walk completely out of the room where clients are to answer a call or text from him. Shit. Stop it! Stop it. I close my eyes and count to 10. I'm sure he'll message or call me back by the time I leave here. That's what I'll tell myself anyway.

'Hi,' I sigh, plopping into the seat across from Celeste. Her eyes widen at my appearance as I throw my purse onto the table and start to drag myself out of my coat.

'You good?' she raises an eyebrow at me in that look that's all her own. Half concern, half 'the fuck is wrong with you'.

'Yeah, yeah. Everything is fine. Why?'

'You just came in here at a hundred. Did you run a marathon before you got in here?'

'No,' I chuckle wiping my sweaty palms on my pants, 'this apartment deal is just stressing me out.'

She waits to respond as the waitress bring my drink to the table and I take a second to let the champagne cleanse my soul. The bubbles burn away my shame and nervousness as they roll down my throat. Celeste's eyes drill into mine, startling me as I open my eyes.

'Are you sure everything is good?'

'Yes. Just this...'

'Apartment deal.' She cuts me off before I can finish my sentence. I guess I am being repetitive. What else does she want me to say? *We have this huge deal on the line but on top of that, I'm dealing with my cheating husband whom I fucked two nights ago, and I'm catching feelings for my Dom.*

'I don't think the Jeremy situation is helping either.' I give a half-truth since the full truth would have her throwing her drink in my face and leaving me to drip dry in my own humiliation.

'I don't think this apartment deal is anything we can't handle. I know it's our first of its kind, but we've managed several houses at once with closings and crazy clients. We've got this,' she says, her voice full of concern.

'You're right. You're absolutely right,' I say, nodding my head in agreement. Now I'm really going to have to keep it together.

'What's new on the Jeremy front?' she asks, eyeing me like her pupils are trying to pierce through into my inner workings.

'Fine… It's ok,' I grab for my glass to down another drink, 'good, I guess.'

'Nothing new going on? You guys have been having dinners and other dates. Do you feel like those are going well?'

'Yeah, they are. He's really apologetic and understanding. He's almost better than the pre-affair Jeremy.' Oh God. Why did I say that?

'Well, that's good. Really good,' she implores.

Yeah, I suppose it is. Before Samantha, Jeremy was a great man. He was always attentive making sure I wanted for nothing. Hell, even during the months he was involved with that whore, I still felt like I was his whole world. Aside from his infidelity, that was one of the things that hurt the most. Besides sinking his dick into her whenever he pleased, what else was he doing? Was he also giving her the princess treatment that once was only reserved for me? Was he leaving her little notes in her briefcase before she left for work or sending her thoughtful texts throughout the day? Was he asking her what she wanted for dinner and making sure it was ready before she came in the door after a long day? Was he rubbing her feet while she laid back on the couch, sipping wine, recounting her crazy day, while his hand eventually trailed up her thigh? Did he follow his hand with needy kisses up to her pussy that waited eagerly for his soft lips and tongue on her clit?

Did he hold her as she dropped to the floor as the phone slipped from her hand when she got the call that her mom had died? Did he go above and beyond to help with arrangements, so she had the time to grieve instead of picking out places to hold a celebration of life since her dad was also in shambles? Did he cup her face and wipe away her tears when it all became too much for her to bear on her own? What about when she made the decision to open her own firm with her coworker and best friend? Was he encouraging through it all, making sure she felt supported on her worst days? Was he there by her side for the ribbon-cutting ceremony on the first official day of business?

This is where my mind immediately goes when I think about what he did. The things he did with her, then coming home and doing them with me. The moment he decided to step out of our marriage and into bed with her was the day I stopped being his whole world whether he continued to make me feel that way or not. Regardless of whether she was just a side piece, some skank he banged when he was feeling like I wasn't giving him enough attention, she was something to him I was supposed to be. She was filling a void for him and replacing me when I was supposed to be irreplaceable. These are the thoughts that have plagued my mind for months. These are things that bring on the wildfires of grief even my streams of tears can't extinguish.

Celeste's comforting hand squeezing mine breaks me from my intrusive thoughts. I grab the silverware napkin and blot my wet cheeks. I clear my throat, roll my shoulders back, and adjust in my seat, slipping my hand from Celeste's grasp to down the rest of my champagne. It doesn't feel right to accept Celeste's love and concern anymore. Not since I'm in bed with another man while my husband is going above and beyond to make sure we get over this mountain. A mountain that grows more comparable to Everest with every passing day.

My belly is beyond full after smashing some much-needed eggs benedict and several more mimosas. Neither of us probably needs anymore but who can say no on thirsty Thursday? The waitress brings more drinks, and we continue our discussion about how we're going to celebrate once the apartment deal is closed. I can only think of one way I want to celebrate and that's by being throat deep on Cade's cock in a cabana somewhere in the Caribbean. I check my phone for the 70th time to see if I have any messages from him only to find I'm still on *read*. That's just rude. There is a message from Jeremy though.

> *Jeremy: Would you give me the pleasure of your company for dinner tomorrow night? I'm thinking the Japanese steakhouse and all the Saki we can drink.*

Ugh. Why does he always try to do things with me when I'm supposed to be laying over Cade's lap with fire red ass cheeks. I guess I'm not even sure what Cade is anymore considering he isn't returning my messages. Again, Mil, people get busy.

> *Me: Raincheck? I have an open house.*

> *Jeremy: Bummer. Another day this weekend?*

> *Me: It's a date :)*

'Who are you mad thumbing over there?' Celeste snorts and I look up to see her mimicking my so-called mad thumbing.

'Jeremy,' I smirk and sit my phone down.

'Ooooohhhh, and what does Jeremy want?'

'Just to take me out to dinner this weekend.'

'I'm glad to see you guys moving forward even if it's only a little bit at a time.'

I smile and take another drink of mimosa, so I don't have to agree with her out loud.

'I will say, he seemed pretty concerned Sunday when I couldn't find you,' she adds, and I almost choke on my drink. I wasn't expecting to have to rehash that evening today, or ever.

'Yeah, he had messaged me too. I'm sorry about that. I was a mess,' I fumble as I try and puzzle together the lie I fabricated days ago.

'It's ok. It was getting slow anyway. Obviously, you're feeling better.'

'Yes... much.' I want so badly to change the subject of conversation, but my brain is a barren wasteland.

'You know you can talk to me, right?'

Her question catches me off guard.

'Yeah, of course.'

She stares at me, and I feel my buzz wain a little as a weird reality starts to set in.

'When I read your message, I went upstairs to see if you needed any help. The door was finally unlocked but you weren't up there.'

Fuck. Fuck. Fuck.

'Yeah... I had bolted... I just needed to get home.' Sweat beads on my forehead and the heat that is radiating down my back is threatening to catch the booth on fire.

'Uh huh...' she says unconvinced. I start to fidget with my glass, spinning the stem between my fingers as I wait for the other shoe to drop.

'I saw you running to your car from the window, and you certainly didn't look sick, Mil. Especially with those handcuffs dangling from your wrist.' My jaw drops and my eyes widen at the words that just spewed from her mouth. Although her facial expression doesn't quite match up to what I think she's thinking. She's smirking at me.

'I...'

'You and Jeremy are into some kinky shit, aren't you?' she winks and tosses back the remaining drink of mimosa. I'm stunned into utter silence as her words bounce around in my hollow head.

'Listen, I like to get freaky occasionally, too, girl. You could've just said Jeremy was wanting to role play.' She waves at the waitress and holds up two fingers letting her know we need refills. And boy do I need a refill.

'Yeah, Jeremy, uh... Jeremy wanted to get freaky.' I repeat unable to form my own thoughts, let alone a solid response.

'Here I am asking you about your dates and he's handcuffing you to God knows what at one of our open houses.'

'Yeah.' I blink.

'What did he handcuff you to anyway?'

'The closet rod.' My voice is barely above a whisper.

'I knew it!' she cackles and slaps the table hard enough that it draws the attention of some of the other patrons. I do my best to force a smile. I can feel the color changing in my cheeks as blips from that evening play through my head. The only problem being that it wasn't Jeremy in the apartment with me.

'Well, anyway, next time, just tell me that man of yours is looking to play out some wild sex scene and I'll give you whatever time you need,' she snickers like a schoolgirl, 'I'd rather not be worried about you thinking you're puking your guts out or you're being murdered.'

'Ok,' I clear my throat, 'ok, yeah, for sure.'

We finish our drinks and I tell Celeste I need to get home under the guise I've had way too much to drink even though any alcohol that entered my body quickly evaporated when she let me know she saw me leaving the open house. With handcuffs hanging off me no less. Now she thinks Jeremy and I are in an even better place than I'm putting on. Thankfully she thinks Jeremy was just playing along with her when she called him Sunday, worried I had been kidnapped. Now I have to make sure these two don't get together and start talking about that day like she did with me. I don't see Celeste having this same conversation with Jeremy as she would me, but I wouldn't put it past her to put in little plugs trying to be cheeky. Great. Another thing added to my plate. Close this apartment deal, figure out what I'm doing with my husband, decide if my feelings for Cade are something I should pursue, and make sure Celeste and Jeremy are not alone in any capacity.

Chapter Fifteen

I check my phone again before walking out the door of Kirk's. Nothing. Still on *read*. I break into a frantic sort of sprint/walk toward my car knowing exactly what I'm about to do. The tension sears through my body as I race across town to Cade's house. Even after trying to check if we were still on for our regularly scheduled appointment tomorrow, he still left me on *read* and didn't return my two other phone calls. I could've called more than that. Thankfully, the mimosas succeeded in drowning the urges, if only temporarily. My eagerness is teetering on the line of stage five clinger. The anxiety I've been plagued with over the past few months isn't helping the situation either. I try and tell myself I don't care if he never messages me again, but my brain is right there to remind me that I, in fact, do.

I'm having a hard time seeing anything past these appointments. They are all consuming and it's not even about relinquishing control anymore. Because, if I'm being honest, a lot of the sessions recently, I've grabbed onto the reins. It's the man. It's all about this man who has carved his way into my brain and made a bed there. The only way I'll be able to get rid of him is to find someone to perform a backyard lobotomy.

Turning onto his street, I drive past his house first, like the creep I am, just in case there's something, or someone, else going on. Continuing to the end of the street, I turn and head back around the block. The anticipation mounting the closer I get to parking in front of his house. Fuck it. He brought this on himself. If he had just answered me then I wouldn't be stalking him and showing up completely unannounced on a non-appointment day. Yeah. That's right. All he had to do was respond and I would've been satisfied seeing him tomorrow evening like normal. I think.

That's what I tell myself anyway as the courage seeps into my blood giving me the motivation I need to park and walk up his steps. Before losing my nerve, I knock a little too hard on the door. I hear a muffled voice followed by heavy footfalls coming from somewhere in the house and, when I see his clouded form approaching through the opaque glass, my heart instantly jumps into my throat and the instinct to run the other way nearly takes over.

'Mil?' he questions in surprise as he pulls the door open, running his hand through his shaggy hair. His emerald eyes shine in the last bits of sun that remain above the horizon as they search mine for an explanation for showing up on his doorstep. He's wearing jeans and nothing else. I let my eyes skim down his body, taking in his bearded jawline, muscled chest and abs, and the ink that covers his skin. The way his jeans hang just so, letting that v of muscle peak above his waistband.

'Mil? Is everything ok?' he asks as he nudges my face up with his finger and strokes my chin with his thumb.

'Yeah! Great! I just... you didn't respond to my messages, so I wanted to make sure *you* were ok.'

'I'm fine. Just crazy busy today. My phone hasn't stopped,' he snickers, his hand falls away from my chin. He places his hand high on the door frame, leaning against it. He is absolute perfection. Michelangelo himself would sculpt this man if they were living at the same time.

'Ok, good. That's good. Well, I guess I'll see you later since I know you're fine.' I turn and start for the steps.

'Mil, stop,' Cade says as he grabs me by the arm, spinning me around into his chest, 'would you like to come in?' He tucks a strand of hair behind my ear as he waits patiently for my response.

'Yeah, yeah I'd like that.' Relief spreads over my body as he brings his lips to mine, pressing ever so gently, threatening to make me melt directly into the wood of his front porch. Releasing my lips, he takes my hand to lead me into his house. Closing the door, he turns and takes my jacket to hang on the coat rack.

'Drink?'

'Please.'

'I'll grab us one and meet you in the living room.'

'Ok,' I say as he heads down the hall toward the kitchen and I amble into the living room. I make myself as comfortable as possible as I wait for him to come back which isn't hard because this is by far the most amazing couch I've ever had the pleasure of sitting on. It has just the right amount of structure but still lets you sink in a little, molding your body into it. I pull my legs up to sit crossways but straighten them back out since that might be too casual. *Mil. You have been sleeping with this man for months. Sitting on his couch* is *the most casual thing y'all have done together.* After deciding I'm acting like a teenage girl, I cross my legs again, tucking them under myself. Finally getting settled, I cast my eyes across the room to where his office is. His desk taunts me from 30 feet away and seems to grow larger, reminding me a few short days ago, Cade was buried in my pussy, my body coming apart around him, only to leave me lying there alone and exposed.

The desk immediately shrinks back down to size when my vision refocuses, and I see there are papers and folders spread all across the top. It certainly looks like he's been busy from here so at least he wasn't lying. I need to stop letting my anxiety get the best of me. At least wait a full 24 hours before I really start to panic anyway. My eyes continue around the room and spot a Bluetooth speaker. It's old school style, one of those fancy Marshall speakers. I notice for the first time its emitting a sound. Cade comes back into the room, stopping by the speaker for a moment to adjust the volume. "Lose Control" by Teddy Swims plays, filling the room with sensual vibes.

'Here you go,' he says as he approaches the couch, and I take the glass that's being held out to me.

'Thank you. I needed this.' On top of all the mimosas I had today, I surely needed more booze. I don't think I need to mention that though.

'Sounds like your day has gone about as good as mine,' he says before taking a drink of bourbon. I watch as he pulls the glass away from his mouth. The way his tongue peeks out to clean up any remaining liquor from his lips. His teeth capture his bottom lip and I look up, registering that his focus is on me.

'What are you thinking about?' he asks, eyes smoldering.

'You,' I breathe.

'Well, then, stop thinking and get up here.'

I stand up and send the entire contents of my glass down my throat in one go. I run my forearm across my lips like a true lady and set my glass on the table, my eyes never leaving his. I reach for his drink, and he gives it up willingly so I can get it out of the way.

Before I can make my move, his hands are on me, cradling my face. Towering over me, his eyes burrow into mine so deeply that my body heats from his stare alone before he brings our mouths together in a frenzy. The kisses are maddening, and I can feel how much he wanted me, missed me even, in each sweep of his tongue against mine. Like he can't get enough of me, and never will.

I let him consume me body and soul as his hands wander down my neck to my chest, to my waist. Moving around my hips where he grips my ass, our bodies are forced even closer together. I throw my arms around his neck and revel in his torridness. The heat we're creating together. Grabbing the bottom of my shirt, he pulls it up and over my head, throwing it somewhere behind me. He reaches for the cups of my bra, and I gasp as he rips it apart, my tits bouncing free, leaving it completely useless to me after today. One by one, my nipples pebble in his mouth as his tongue roves over them. I release a moan, reveling in the satisfaction of his hands imprinting themselves on my tits as he massages them in his palms.

Dropping to his knees, he unbuttons my pants and has them around my ankles in seconds. He helps me step out of them and my pussy can hardly stand the anticipation when he looks up at me through thick lashes. My panties are becoming steadily more wet with every touch. He makes me feel like a fucking queen. This man, my Dom, is down on his knees ready to worship me. And to think I showed up here without an appointment. He didn't want to punish me for veering away from the plan, he wants to reward me. His breath hitches and an emotion flickers across his face. I put my fingers into his hair, ready to ask him what's on his mind, when his hand comes up to cover my mouth.

Rendering me speechless, he licks my clit through the fabric separating me from his mouth, and my knees shake from the burst of pleasure spreading from between my legs. He taps my ankle with his free hand, signaling me to spread my legs open further for him. I have never been so glad to follow a command in my life as he reaches up, slides my panties to the side, and begins his assault on my clit. Two fingers are rough against my tongue as he slips them into my mouth, gripping my face with his thumb and other fingers, forcing me to suck. His free hand pushes the skin above my clit, forcing it to stick out, giving him unfettered access. I try and suppress a whimper when his mouth fully covers my clit, but a full-on moan escapes around his fingers as he brings me closer to orgasm.

Everything stops and I huff in exasperation as my eyes spring open. My anxiety spikes as the feeling of being left slams into me like a wrecking ball. My chest rises and falls faster and faster. He's not going to leave me again, is he? Cade stands up in front of me, unbuckling his belt and unbuttoning his jeans, and then pulls them down to meet the floor. He sits back onto the couch and stares up at me, taking in my almost naked body.

'Drop your panties,' he demands seemingly answering my question.

I obey.

'Turn around and sit on my lap.'

Again, I cooperate.

Sitting down, he immediately pulls me back into his chest. Gripping my face, he turns my head toward him until his tongue finds my lips. His other hand moves down my belly and palms my pussy. Fuck. I can barely stand this. My nipples harden further as I soak his hand from him simply sitting it on my pussy. He deepens the kiss and begins to move his fingers in and out of me while his palm applies pressure to my clit. My hips start to rock against him, and his cock fully hardens underneath me, digging into my back.

His hands leave my pussy and my face to lift me up and sit me back down, his cock sliding into my pussy for a perfect fit. I revel in the feeling of fullness, the feeling of pure joy that swallows me whole whenever we're together.

'Damn, this pussy,' he whispers hotly, grabbing my face to kiss me again. His cock fills me up and I'm consumed by pure need. Pure need for him to fuck me today, and every day until we die.

I start grinding my hips, both of us giving each other lifesaving breaths, and losing ourselves in one another. His fingers locate my clit with ease and my insides clench as I feel my orgasm come within reach.

'Whose pussy is this, Mil?' he asks against my mouth.

'Yours.'

'Say it again,' he demands.

'It's yours, Cade.'

'Damn right, it is.'

My brain fogs as he brings me closer and closer to that burst of pleasure he evokes effortlessly. I rock my hips harder as he fucks me from underneath. His cock sends carnal shockwaves through my body with every plunge deeper. His mouth leaves mine when he switches hands and grabs my throat, pinning my head back to his shoulder. He brings his fingers to my mouth, gathering saliva, before moving back to my throbbing clit.

'Mmm, love this pussy, Mil,' he pants into my neck before biting onto my tender flesh.

My eyes roll back in my head from the desire he's eliciting with both his body and his words. I want him to own this pussy. I want him to own my whole body. My life.

'This pussy is mine and this cock is yours, understood,' he grits out through ragged breaths.

'Yes, yes...' I can't get out another yes before I plummet into oblivion.

'That's it... That's my girl... Soak my cock,' he grits, 'I want to feel your cum running down the sides of my dick.'

Shockwaves ravage my body as Cade walks off the same cliff as me. We grind against each other as we regain our composure after what qualifies as the best orgasm I've ever had in my life. We finally settle, neither of us willing to move. Which is fine with me because the last thing I want is for this moment to end.

I'm sorry,' he whispers into my hair.

'Sorry?'

'Last week... leaving you.'

Oh. Ok. What the fuck was that then? I want to ask but at the same time, I'm just glad he recognizes it was fucking weird.

'Ok. I was starting to think it was something I did.'

'No, I just... I've had a lot on my mind lately.'

'Ok.'

He kisses my hair again before "I'm Yours" by Isabel LaRosa fills the silence that stretches between us.

Chapter Sixteen

I swipe the lipstick along my bottom lip one more time and roll my lips against each other. I lean in for a closer look, puckering at the mirror. My eyes look clear today and I feel lighter than I have for a while. After showing up at Cade's last night and the amazing sex we had, coupled with all his claiming words, the weight has shifted some on my shoulders. I slept incredibly well, closed on a house today, Jeremy is at an event, and I'll be heading out the door in the next few minutes to let my sexy ass Dom have his way with me yet again.

A flush colors my cheeks as Cade's figure slips into my mind. I want to be tangled up with him right now. I want to feel his skin sliding against my body, feel his breath on my neck, and listen to my voice fill the room as I scream his name. The only thing I could want more at this point is to be able to stay with him for longer than a couple hours. I'll take what I can get for now but to be able to lay in the same bed, not have a time limit, not needing to constantly be on alert for my phone going off, to wake up in the morning and let him fuck me all over again, sounds divine.

I walk into the bedroom to give myself another once over before I leave. My red pumps paired with black slacks are giving my ass that perfect lift. I decided on a black lace corset underneath my black jacket. The only color on me being red lipstick and the matching pumps. I'm glad I ran home before meeting Cade because I'm feeling like an 11, especially after I refreshed my curls. If this outfit doesn't have him drooling, I don't know what else to do.

I need to get moving if I want to get there a little early. I pause "Pretend" by Bad Omens, put my earbuds in the case, and toss them into my purse. I throw my purse over my shoulder just as I hear a familiar voice echo from downstairs.

'Mil?' Jeremy yells as he opens and shuts the front door.

Fuck. He was supposed to be at some event. Or something. I guess I can't remember what he said now.

'Mil? You home?'

I stand frozen in my room as I listen to his footsteps move toward the kitchen. I listen to him rummage around in what I assume is the fridge and I can only hope he'll faint so I can sneak out the front door undetected. Quickly, I reach down and start to close the buttons on my jacket. It does little to conceal the corset but at least he won't see the lace. Now, for an excuse. Shit. Why couldn't he have just stayed wherever he was?

'Mil?' he calls again.

Here we go.

'Yeah?' I yell as I start into the hallway and down the stairs.

'Hey baby,' he greets me as I round the bottom of the stairs. He heads straight for me, arms wide open, and envelopes me in his signature Jeremy hug. He squeezes his arms around me, and I let it happen so as not to let him know anything is wrong. Nothing is wrong exactly. Aside from the fact I'm dressed a little unusual and am headed to meet my Dom. Oh, and I'm supposed to be at work.

'I thought you had to work late,' he starts to say as he pulls away, his hands moving to my shoulders. He holds me away from him, examining my face and outfit. Damn it. He's going to ask questions. Think. Think.

'Damn babe, you look… you look sexy.'

My answer is a simple smile as I try to slide past him to grab my keys.

'I thought you were going to an event tonight?' I ask attempting to change the subject.

'No, I just went into the restaurant to get some prep done for a wedding Sunday morning. I'm surprised to see you home since you said you were going to be late,' he says as he crosses his arms and leans against the wall eyeing my back, no doubt, as I pretend to be looking for important items in my purse.

'I am going to be late, I just needed to run home to freshen up a bit. We're… meeting clients.'

'Oh. You and Celeste?'

'Yeah, who else?' Shit. I don't usually tie her into my shenanigans, but I wasn't expecting him to show up just before I walked out the door.

'Right, of course. So, when do you think you'll be home? I can have dinner ready.'

'Oh, uh, I'm not sure. It'll probably be late. And, I don't want to have to try and end the night prematurely, ya know.' I put the strap of my purse over my shoulder and finally turn to face Jeremy. When my eyes reach his, the disappointment is clear. I know what he wanted me to say. He wanted me to say I could be home by 8:00 p.m. and we could eat dinner together. We could share some wine and I might let him fuck me on the kitchen table like I used to. And then after he's wined, dined, and given me an orgasm, he might be able to talk me into sleeping in our bed together. But I'm not interested in dinner with Jeremy. Or sex with Jeremy, for that matter. The only dinner and sex I'm interested in right now is waiting for me across town in the form of Cade's cock.

'Ok, well, try not to be too late. Maybe we could open that new bottle of wine,' he says, pushing himself off the wall to stand in front of me. His hands come to grip my arms while his thumbs burning reassuring circles into my biceps.

'Yeah, I'll try. Just… just don't wait up. In case, ya know, it goes really late.' I watch as he deflates a little further.

He leans in and kisses my forehead. He lingers a bit, not wanting to take his lips away from my skin. When he finally pulls away, he stares intently into my eyes, and I think he can see what I'm getting ready to do. He can see me with Cade. All the things we're going to do to each other. My head falling back as his mouth grazes my neck. Cade gripping his cock and teasing my opening before making the plunge into my aching pussy. He can hear us yelling each other's names into the air thick with sexual tension. He can see himself sitting here, alone, waiting on his wife to come home after being with another man.

'I love you, Mil,' he whispers as he grabs my face and sweeps his thumb along my cheek.

'Love you,' I say, barely audible and break from his touch, leaving him standing in our entryway.

I can't get through the door fast enough. Getting into my car and down the driveway feels like fighting my way through syrup. Everything is slow since I'm trying to look like I'm not in a hurry, but my heart is beating a marathon runner's cadence inside my chest cavity. Deep breaths, Mil. Deep breaths. How the hell did he keep this shit going for a year? How did he look at me before and after he was with that girl? The look in his eyes just now was almost enough to bring me to my knees, screaming my confession. Almost. I'm calling it disappointment, but it could've been defeat that shadowed his eyes as he silently willed me to cancel my plans and stay home with him. Stay home with him and let him show me how sorry he is. To show me what I would be missing if I decided to leave him.

My phone sounds from my purse and I hope it's Cade. I can't get to a red light fast enough.

Jeremy: just a friendly reminder that I love you, Mil. so much.

Jesus. I look up before I reply and see the light is getting ready to turn green.

I drive a little farther until I find myself at another red light. I grab my phone so I can appease Jeremy, hoping that'll be the last of his messages tonight.

Me: I know :)

I watch as the three dots light up before setting my phone in the cup holder in anticipation of the next green light.

Ding.

This is NOT a good time, Jeremy. I gun it, trying to get through the next couple of lights without having to stop. Jeremy has taken up enough of my time. I should've been at Cade's already.

'Fuck,' I squawk as I hit the brakes for yet another red light. Damn. I need to chill, or I'll never make it to Cade's in one piece.

I grab my phone to see what kind of whiny message Jeremy has sent. Probably something about me not saying I love him back in some super cute way.

Client – P. Alderidge: Are you on your way?

Oh! It's not from Jeremy. In fact, Jeremy didn't even respond. Probably best. I don't need him in my head while I'm with Cade.

Me: I am :)

He doesn't respond before I speed off again and signal for the exit onto the interstate. Cade lives just far enough away that I don't think anyone would ever see me. And he lives close enough that I can make it to his place in under 30 minutes.

Ding.

I look down, tempted to check the message, but refocus on the road before I rear-end someone. Again.

I pass cars in the slow lane like I'm auditioning for NASCAR while the message waiting for me weighs more and more on my mind. What if he's trying to reschedule? No. He hasn't ever rescheduled. I'm the idiot who's missed appointments. And paid dearly for it. Maybe he's just excited that I'm coming over? That could be it. Yeah, maybe. Or maybe not. I know his words lately have felt like he has some sort of feelings for me, but can Dom's really love anyone? Do they *do* relationships? It dawns on me that I really know very little of what comes along with the Dom life. Surely, they exist outside of it. I mean, even from my little experience, I see how things have shifted with Cade and I. Completely business in the beginning. Very transactional. But after that first time we fucked, our business relationship moved towards something else. I can't name it, but it did. And even more so after the first time I met him at his house.

Regardless, he's still my Dom and I have no idea how many other women he is working with. The thought crushes my heart and I quickly push it from my mind. Fuck it. I reach for my phone and see a message waiting from Cade. There's not a ton of traffic on the interstate right now. It's after the rush of people racing to get home. Why am I thinking so hard about this? I could've already checked the message and responded by now.

> *Client – P. Alderidge: Good :) I'll open a bottle of wine. See you soon. Be careful.*

Oh my God. Oh my God. Oh my God. It's good that I'm on my way. And he put a smiley face in his message. This is a first. And he's going to open a bottle of wine? He'll see me soon? He wants me to be careful! My thoughts bang around my brain and into each other as I replay is text over and over again. Here I am again living through another shift in our situation-ship. A shift I'm actually present for this time. Every other moment that was leading to something more slid past me only for me to realize later something had changed between us. I blame that on the stress of my cheating ass husband. But not today. Today I'm more present than ever for this steppingstone. I'm still not sure what we're stepping toward but I'm present for it, nonetheless.

I glance at my watch. 5:45 p.m. I should be there in 15 minutes or so. A whole hour early. I get to add an hour of sweet bliss to the evening. With that thought, I turn up the radio, sink back into the seat, and let "Dark Matter" by Rivals and the gas pedal take me straight to Cade's.

Chapter Seventeen

I let myself in the door and can hear Cade talking in the other room. I listen for a moment and confirm he must be on the phone. I check my own phone one last time to make sure I don't need to keep Jeremy pacified before hanging my purse on the coat rack by the door. I move toward Cade's voice in the living room and see a glass of wine sitting on the coffee table. Looking over, Cade's back is to me, and a matching glass of wine rests atop his desk making it obvious this one must be for me. I reach down for the glass and smell the wine before bringing it to my lips.

The wine smells delightful. I seal my lips onto the glass and let the cold liquid flow into my mouth. The flavor ignites taste buds on my tongue I didn't know existed. I close my eyes so I can eliminate a sense and rejoice in this wine even further. It's exquisite. I want to brush my teeth with it. I want to get naked and relax in a bathtub full of it. I need to taste this exact taste every day for the rest of my life. This *has* to be insanely expensive because I have never tasted any wine like this. Ever. I need to know its name so I can purchase it in bulk.

I take another drink and it's even better than the first. I run my tongue around my lips making sure I don't miss any drops of this magic elixir. God, I hope he has more than one bottle. I'm about to drink the rest of the glass but decide against it since this is something I want to savor.

My eyes flutter open when I notice I don't hear Cade's voice anymore. I see now he's hung up the phone and is leaning against his desk, legs crossed at the ankle, hands gripping the desk on either side of his lean, sexy body. I watch the veins bulge in his forearms as he flexes his hands, holding the desk tighter then loosening his grip like he's holding himself back. As I start to move my eyes up his body, I notice the black slacks and belt. The sleeves of his shirt that have been rolled up to his elbows showing off his forearms. The few buttons that have been undone at the top, his smattering of chest hair peeking out. I see his 10 o'clock shadow before I notice the flex of his jaw. Then, that bottom lip of his, that always has teeth sinking into it. His appraising eyes overflowing with lust.

'Hi,' I manage as though the word had to travel over mountains and through rivers to make it out of my mouth. I clear my throat as I wait in the silence.

'Hi,' he says in his low, sultry voice that sends instant vibrations to my core, 'you look amazing, Mil.' His words massage my ears, and the flush starts to creep from my cheeks to my chest. The energy crackles between us even from opposite sides of the room.

'Thank you,' I smile and toss the rest of the wine into my mouth, 'this wine is also amazing.'

His mouth ticks up on one side giving me his half-smile. He reaches for his own glass and makes the wine disappear in one go.

'Would you like another glass?'

'I would love one.'

He hesitates, letting his eyes roam over my body once more

before turning to grab the bottle of wine.

My shoulders relax when he walks out of the room. His stare is so intense it feels like it could burn my clothes off in a blink. I should probably get my heart checked also. I'm positive it stopped completely when I realized he was standing there taking me in. Either that, or it was beating so fast, it was one constant thump. My legs move toward his desk without being told to do so. My unconscious brain making me close the gap between him and me.

He strides back into the room, wine in tow, and a look of determination chiseled on his face. My knees wobble from the pure desire he exudes.

'Glass?'

I stare at him blankly. I can't tear my mind away from this God of a man. This God of a man that wants me and isn't afraid of showing it.

'Mil, where's your glass?' he asks as he grips the front of my chin between his thumb and pointer finger.

'On the coffee table.' I realize I must have set it down sometime between downing the wine and my legs carrying me over to his desk.

He releases my chin and walks to the coffee table. He fills the glass as he starts to make the trip back across the room. Pausing halfway, he pulls his phone from his pocket, seeming to select some music, and places the phone on top of the radio. Turning to me once again, he closes the distance and hands me my wine. A spooky sort of sound starts to pour from the speakers as Life After Youth's "Beetlejuice Chill" snakes its way around the room. Cade fills his own glass and sits the bottle down on the desk behind me. His chest barely grazes my shoulder, but I can feel the heat start to rise like lava from my core.

'A toast,' he says raising his glass.

'A toast to what?' I mimic his movement and bring my glass up near his.

'I got some good news today.'

'How very vague of you.'

I'm rewarded with a chuckle and a full smile that lights up his face more than I've seen before. The entire room seems to warm up by degrees from the genuine happiness that spreads across his face. The joy he's feeling seems to flow from him to me and I find myself not wanting this to end. I want to stare at him smiling forever. I want to be around him. Forever. Now, I just need to figure out what he wants exactly. If anything.

'Cheers to good news… and, good company,' he clinks his glass to mine.

'Cheers,' I repeat and we both drink at the same time, our eyes glued to each other's.

'What kind of wine is this by the way? Its…'

'Amazing?' he finishes my sentence, smiling. He reaches for the bottle to show me. Its Argentum Bonum – Elena Walch. The label is simple, adorned with a yellow wax embossment at the bottom. Just looking at it, I know it cost a fortune.

'My brother sent me a case from Italy.' A case? He has a case. Thank God. I want to finish my glass and ask for another just so I can watch him uncork it. And suddenly I have a new kink for someone uncorking a wine bottle. Not just anyone. Cade. Cade uncorking a wine bottle. I can envision his hand flexing around the bottle, the condensation seeping between his fingers, while the other hand grips the wine corker. His forearms flexing as he twisted the cork free with a *pop*. Yup. New kink unlocked.

'I didn't know you had a brother.'

'You never asked,' he chides.

'Fair enough. I suppose you're right. So, this brother, is he as good looking as you?' I try and hide my smirk by taking another drink of wine.

'That's a bold question coming from someone who is subject to punishments,' he states simply as his eyes narrow on mine. Swallowing, I try to think quickly of how I can back pedal out of this situation I got myself into.

'I'm sure he's not… I mean, I didn't mean… I'm sure he's attractive, but… fuck,' I ramble and struggle to take hold of a meaningful sentence.

'Mil,' he laughs and puts his finger on my lips to shut me up, 'stop. Relax.'

And I do. My smile lifts across my face as I realize he's enjoying watching me flounder in my agonizing discomfort.

'You'll be glad to know that I'm the better looking one.'

'Is that so?'

'Yeah. The only thing he has on me is the salt and pepper hair all the women seem to love.' I picture Cade with salt and pepper hair and know his brother is probably gorgeous. And that Cade will only get better with age. Like this wine.

'Well, I hope I'm around long enough to see you with salt and pepper hair.'

'Is that so?' he asks as he sets his glass next to me on the desk, his eyes darkening further as he takes me in. His finger sweeps along the top of my corset, creating goosebumps on my skin and stirring a chemical reaction deep within myself akin to when potassium meets water.

'It is so. You'll be even more irresistible.'

His eyes flick to mine. A hint of concern plays across his face as his brows pinch together ever so slightly before being replaced with hunger. He moves forward and pushes his body against mine, forcing me to lean backward over the desk. He sticks two fingers in between my breasts, grips my corset, and pulls me to him. Staring down at me as I struggle to catch my breath, the tension between us is unmatched.

I watch as his tongue slips out, licking his lips, followed by his teeth grating across his bottom lip and my entire mouth goes dry. A gruff sound emanates from the depths of his chest before he moves his mouth closer to me. I tilt me head back and close my eyes, just waiting to feel his lips on mine.

The second our mouths meet; I'm transported to another galaxy where the only people in existence are Cade and me. And I never want to leave this place. His kiss is seductive, slow, and burning. He takes his time, letting his lips explore mine, committing them to memory. I feel his breath and can smell the sweetness of the wine as he grazes his lips across mine, kissing the sides of my mouth.

He hovers just inches from my lips, seeming to take in the moment like I am. Seemingly wanting to live in this moment forever like I'm wanting to. When his mouth meets mine again, his lips part and his tongue dips out for a taste. My mouth instinctively opens, inviting him in for more. He licks across my lips teasingly before taking my bottom lip between his teeth.

Releasing my bottom lip, our tongues collide. My reaction is visceral, and I groan into his mouth as we massage and play with each other. Neither of us willing to part for a breath of air. His body continues to press into mine and I reach up and grip his shirt. Low and throaty sounds roll up from his chest as he feels me grip his shirt to pull him closer than either of us thought possible.

He breaks the kiss and stands up straight leaving me wanting and panting. Again, my mind goes straight to the last time we fucked on his desk. I hate that him breaking a kiss, or moving away from me is a trigger for me now but damn it, that killed me when he left me standing here. In this exact spot. I keep my hands firmly attached to his shirt in case he decides to run for the hills.

His breathing is labored, and he clearly doesn't intend to leave me high and dry because he reaches up and starts to unbutton my jacket. I look down and watch as his fingers nimbly release each button, and my jacket finally falls open. He pauses before trailing his fingers up the opening and shoving the jacket off my shoulders. I lean forward off the desk to let it slide past my ass and hit the floor.

'This new?' he murmurs as he runs his fingers along the top of my corset again.

'Yes.'

'Perfect,' he says, 'you're perfect.'

My heart skips a beat with his words. I'm perfect? He thinks I'm perfect. My breathe comes faster and reach back to balance myself on the edge of the desk as his hands drag down along my sides. He grips my hips and brings his mouth to meet my exposed skin above the corset. His tongue for the first time across the top of my tits makes me feel like I'll fall into a fit of convulsions any second. The bite that follows threatens to make me spontaneously combust.

He continues kissing and nipping at my skin across my chest before he brings his hands up, grips the inner cups of the corset, and rips it open in one swift motion. He admires his handiwork while I think about needing to replace my wardrobe with items that'll easily tear because watching him rip my clothes to shreds has awoken a lascivious beast. My nipples are already hard from his teasing and ache to be taken into his warm mouth. As if reading my mind, he takes a nipple in his mouth, twirling his tongue round and round while his hands grasp onto palm-fulls of soft tissue. I watch him as he runs his tongue all over my nipples and tits. My head lulls back as he reaches up to grip the front of my neck.

'So,' kiss.

'Fucking,' lick.

'Perfect,' a bite.

He creates a path of kisses down my stomach as he settles on his knees before unbuttoning and unzipping my pants. Sliding the pants down, he picks up each leg to take them off without removing my heels. He reaches up and takes hold of my panties, if you can call them that, and pulls them down my legs. Once I've stepped out of them, he bawls them in his fist before tossing them to the side.

Sitting back on his heels, he silently praises me standing in front of him in nothing more than my red pumps and ripped open corset. He takes his time roaming over my body, stopping here and there to take in the sight. His eyes finally connect with mine and I see the fires burning within. Gazing down at him, I want nothing more than for him and his fire to consume me in the worst way. His hands squeeze my thighs and I feel him leaving an impression on me that'll last forever.

'I want to worship you, Mil,' he says, voice hoarse.

I'm silent as I try and decipher what it is that he means.

'Let me worship you,' he pleads, more of a question than anything. Something breaks in me as I stare down at him. As his eyes pool with wanting, desire, and yearning, what I need to do hits me like a Mac truck. I want this man and everything he is. I just hope he wants me the same way.

'Then worship me,' I finally manage, and with that, his bruising grip pushes my legs apart.

He wastes no time teasing his tongue across my clit. My legs start to quake under my weight as he alternates long strokes with quick flicks. My moans rival the volume of the music as the pressure starts to collect low in my belly when he pushes two fingers inside my swollen pussy. I look down at this man devouring my pussy and I have never witnessed a hotter sight. My hand gets a mind of its own when I reach down and slip my fingers into his hair. I grip onto a section of shaggy locks and tilt his head slightly back, forcing him to look up at me while his tongue is buried inside of me. A gratifying hum skates across my pussy from his mouth as he licks my clit, effectively finishing me off.

I come all over his mouth as Ari Abdul finishes up her song "Worship". His tongue continues to torment me, our eyes never breaking away from each other. I've never watched someone go down on me before and after today, I think I'll look every time Cade has his face buried there. It's the sexiest thing I've ever witnessed, and the orgasm is all the more intense because of it.

Cade finishes with a couple more strokes around my pussy, pulling his fingers out of me. Sitting back on his heels again, he licks me off his fingers as if luxuriating in his last meal as a man on death row. He stands up and takes a couple steps back from me eliciting my fight or flight once again.

'Where are you going?' I pant.

'I'm not going anywhere.' He reassures me as he wipes his arm across his mouth and my panic eases slightly.

He stalks over to me, squats down, and tosses me over his shoulder as he stands back up. I squeal out as I find myself staring down at the ground. He turns and walks from the room, and I grip his jeans for dear life.

'*We're* going to my bedroom,' he says with a slap across my ass drawing out another scream from me. He strides away from the desk as Elley Duhe starts to serenade us with "Middle Of The Night". As we head out of the room, the only thing I want is for Cade to tame me and I crave nothing more than his taste.

We're in his room in no time and before I know what's happening, he's tossing me onto the bed. He rips off his shirt, a button flying across the room. Next, he slides his belt from the loops, throwing it to the side, and loses his pants before climbing onto me. He takes my corset off the rest of the way and flings it to the floor. Our mouths crash together as his hard cock rubs the engorged opening of my pussy. My hips start to roll, seeking him out immediately.

'I want you inside of me... now,' I huff as I try to maneuver my hips so his cock can slide in with ease.

'You got it,' he smiles and plunges straight into me. I'm instantly filled up as the tsunami of electricity blows through my body. He brings his weight down on me and drops his face into my neck. He starts to move languidly, stroking in and out impossibly slow, as he scrapes his teeth along my neck before biting into my shoulder. I inhale a sharp breath through gritted teeth as I'm forced to arch into him.

'So fucking tight, Mil.' He pushes up and sits back on his heels, grabbing my hips and pulling me closer, I'm impaled on his cock. He pushes down on my knees, making my legs spread farther to either side and I hope like hell that I'll be able to stretch that far. Picking up his pace, he pumps in and out of me relentlessly.

'Come for me, Mil?'

'Yes... sir,' I can barely speak as I reach out and grip the sheets, the pleasure starting to erupt in my core. He licks his thumb before bringing it down to my clit to massage the throbbing bud.

'That's my girl,' he gnashes, pounding into my pussy. He reaches up to grip my throat and my eyes flutter shut as he squeezes.

'Look at me, Mil.'

My eyes fly open.

'Eyes on me baby.'

I bring this beautiful man back into view.

'Thata girl... I want to see that pretty face as you come on my dick... just like you watched me when you came in my mouth...'

The orgasm creeps closer as my vision blurs with tears from the pressure on my throat and know that any second I'll be done for.

'Oh Cade...'

'You liked that didn't you Mil? Watching me eat your pussy. Watching me lick up your cum.'

'Yes, Cade... yes, fuck.'

'Come, Mil... that's it baby, come for me.'

And as if pushing a button, I'm completely undone. My whole existence unfurling. My back arches off the bed as he continues to annihilate my body, pumping in and out of me fervently before he's spent as well. He comes with a feral groan and drops down on me, letting his weight sink me into the bed.

We lay there, listening to each other regain our breathes, as the music I can't quite make out tapers off from the other room. The silence slowly overtakes us. Finally, he lifts his head and kisses me tenderly on my lips, then my cheek, then my neck, before getting up and reaching for some sweatpants.

'Should I grab the wine?'

'Absolutely.'

Chapter Eighteen

I roll over, reaching for my phone on the nightstand. My hand slams the top as I continue my search across its surface. I peel my eyes open when a familiar arm wraps around my waist, pulling me closer into an even more familiar chest. Cade. I'm still at Cade's. His face snuggles into the back of my neck, and I start to relax into him before I jolt upright, springing from the bed.

'What's wrong?' Cade asks sleepily as he leans up onto an elbow, his eyes still closed.

'Uh, I can't find my phone and I… have an early appointment in the morning.' I stumble around his room looking for my purse, but I must have left it hanging in the hallway.

'It's probably in your bag, hanging on the coat rack,' he huffs, letting his body slam back onto the bed with exhaustion.

What time is it? There's no clock in here because who needs a clock with the constant companion everyone has nowadays? I manage to emerge from the bedroom and snake my way down the hallway. Finding my purse hanging on the coat rack, I rummage through the mess searching for my phone. It finally lights up and gives me some guidance in the dark. Pulling it out, I see its 1:07 a.m. and I have a ton of missed texts and calls. Five missed calls and 11 texts to be exact. All from Jeremy. Fuck. Well, this is quite the predicament, isn't it?

I shove the phone back in my purse and go into the office. I gather what's left of my clothes from the floor and slip back into them. Unfortunately, the corset is unwearable, and still on Cade's bedroom floor, so I'm left to just my panties, slacks, and jacket. No bra. Perfect.

Ok, ok. Think. I just need to take a deep breath. I can get through this. I blow out a huge burst of air as I try to gather myself and think through what I need to do. First things first, I need to get home. I can avoid Jeremy until our counseling session. Ugh, counseling. We really need to cancel those. They're a huge waste of time and money and... stay on track, Mil. I can worry about counseling later. I need to get home first.

I walk back to Cade's bedroom to let him know I'm going to go home. It's the last thing I want to do. What I really want is to jump back in that bed with him. Mold myself into his warm body, let his hands travel wherever they please, and have steamy, middle of the night sex. Scream his name to the ghosts who move around at this hour. I can't though. Not yet anyway.

Walking next to the bed, I see he's already fallen back asleep. Arms sprawled out to the sides, sheet barely covering what's below his waist, full lips slightly parted, letting his rhythmic breath in and out. He's so beautiful. So damn beautiful. Jesus, I should be slipping back into this bed with him. I silently curse the situation I've gotten myself into and decide against waking him up. I'll send him a quick text and let him know I snuck out. I don't have any clothes or toiletries here, so he'll understand. He just looks so peaceful. I can't wake him up.

I force myself away from the bed, and grabbing my purse before I leave, close the door so quietly it wouldn't even wake up someone sleeping right beside it. Tiptoeing down the front steps, I close my jacket tighter around myself. It's getting colder and without a bra or undershirt, the air is cutting right through to my nipples. I drop into the front seat and start the car. I turn on the heat full blast knowing it won't heat this car up any faster, but I don't care. I also need the noise. The noise to drown out my anxiety so I can think for a damn minute.

What the hell am I going to tell Jeremy this time? I haven't ever been out this late. I told him I was meeting with clients. He must have felt this sometimes, right? When he was telling me he was working late because his helpers called off or that he was going to events out of town. He had to have felt these crazy rushes of anxiety wondering what he was going to tell me if he ever slipped up. If I ever further questioned him. Which I didn't. I didn't because I was completely oblivious. So completely trusting of what he said he was doing. Why wouldn't I trust what my husband was telling me? My husband wouldn't lie to me about something like that. He certainly would never cheat. Yet here we are.

What would Jeremy have told me if he had come home this late? What would his excuse have been?

The kitchen was filthy after all the event prep we had to do.

I bought the guys a round of drinks as a thank you for all their help. I'm so sorry I got home so late last night.

Maybe I should start by looking at my phone. See what he knows.

The car finally starts to blow semi-warm air on my face as I scroll through my waiting texts.

Jeremy: I'm making steaks. Hopefully you'll be able to get away soon.

Jeremy: Steak was delicious. I hate that you had to miss it.

Jeremy: Steak is in the fridge with green beans and roasted potatoes.

Jeremy: Do you know when you'll be home yet?

Jeremy: I love you. AND miss you.

Jeremy: It's getting pretty late, Mil.

Jeremy: I'm telling myself not to worry but it's getting late, and I still haven't heard from you.

Jeremy: Mil... please answer me. I just want to know you're ok. That's all.

Jeremy: 11:30 and I still haven't heard from you. I know restaurants stay open late, but you should've at least called me by now.

Jeremy: If it gets to midnight, I'm calling Celeste.

Jeremy: Cel said you had a little too much to drink. I feel better that you're at least safe, I just wish she would've told me earlier. Anyway, I love you. Sleep it off and I'll see you in the morning.

Great. He called Celeste. Now I have two messes to clean up and more excuses to make. On the bright side, she covered for me. Although I don't know at what cost. She doesn't know how much I owe her for that. Before putting the car in drive, I scan the radio stations to see if there's anything worth listening to for my torturous ride home. I settle on "Supermassive Black Hole" by Muse and as I head toward my house, I think about the supermassive black hole I'm falling down faster and faster. In the back of my mind, I know I'll hit bottom eventually. All I can hope at this point is that I don't hit hard enough to kill me.

There are no lights on as I pull into our driveway and park my car. I feel about an ounce of relief knowing Jeremy is asleep and won't see me. I can figure out the rest of my lie before we're in the car together on our way to counseling. That word, counseling. Just thinking about it is giving me a headache I know will last most of the day. I just need to tell Jeremy we're not going anymore. I need to tell him it's not working. That I can't work on this anymore. That we're done.

I never should've agreed to work on this in the first place. That was stupid of me. To think I'd be able to get over what he'd done. What he'd done with Samantha. I'm not even sure why I chose to stay and try to let him make it up to me. Was I scared to be alone? Scared to start over? Ashamed? *Oh, look there's Mil. Didn't you hear? She's getting a divorce. Her husband cheated.* A chill runs over me as if I can feel the imaginary peoples stares and whispers. Maybe I was afraid to believe it was over. Everything is salvageable, right? Love conquers all. That's what the priest said anyway. Or was I afraid of the grief that would follow. As if I didn't experience grief anyway. It was almost worse having him in the house, in my face, next to me in counseling. The constant reminder that my husband was unfaithful to me.

Or, maybe, I was afraid to lose the future. The what could have been. Not celebrating my successful business venture with him. Him excited about the prospect of opening his own restaurant one day. Me surprising him with a positive pregnancy test and him lifting me into his arms, spinning us in circles with joy. Him looking down at me, sweaty and swearing, with tear-filled eyes as I pushed our child out into the world. Coming home with a newborn, watching her toddle around the house, growing up, and becoming whoever she was going to be. Watching the grey hair slowly make appearances on each other. The wrinkles that would make it obvious how old we were getting. Sending our daughter off into the world to do something great. Watching her fall in love and finding her own happily ever after.

I make my way onto the porch, close the front door behind me and let my body slide down it, landing on the floor. I bring my knees up to my chest and rest my forehead on them. None of those things can be though. Not now. Not after he decided to bring Samantha into the mix. Not after he decided Samantha was worth more than the future he and I could've had. God damn him! Why didn't he just talk to me? Why did he have to go somewhere else? Why did he feel like he couldn't come to me? Why did he have to make me miss out on our future together? Why am I the one that's left crying on the floor mourning all the things that could've been?

I wonder if I would've been over this by now if I hadn't agreed to stay. Did staying together just prolong all these *feelings*. Would I be at Cade's house right now, snuggled close to him, peacefully dreaming about the future that we might have? Maybe I wouldn't have even met Cade had I left Jeremy immediately. I guess I can look at that as the silver lining in all this. My tears start to fall faster as the reality of not meeting Cade sets in. Where Jeremy once was my world, Cade has taken his place. I don't want to think about my world without Cade in it. Now I need the courage to tell him that. I'm just not sure I could handle his rejection after Jeremy. After my own husband wanted someone else over me.

'Mil?'

My head jerks up at Jeremy's voice and I find him standing at the top of the stairs.

'Mil? What's wrong?' he asks, brows furrowed, as he starts to hurry down the steps.

'Nothing, nothing.' I start to get up, but Jeremy is there already, on his knees and taking me into his arms.

A sob chokes out of me as the certainty of what I need to do sets into my bones. Jeremy's arms wrap tighter around me as he tries to soothe my pain. A pain he created.

'It's fine. I'm fine.' I disentangle myself from his hold and get to my feet. I grab my purse and sit it on the sideboard and put my keys in the dish. Jeremy stands back, giving me the space he's promised from the beginning. I stare down at the floor so I can get my bearings before climbing the stairs to the spare bedroom. By myself. With my husband in the other room.

'Mil? Where's your shirt?' he asks as I turn toward him. I stop and lower my eyes down to my bare stomach peeking out from my open jacket. My very visible cleavage making it obvious that I not only do not have a shirt on, but I also do not have a bra on.

'Mil?' his voice breaks across my name.

'I... I stayed over at Celeste's... and I got too drunk,' I fumble to find the words I need, 'when I woke up on the couch, I couldn't find my shirt and bra. I... just grabbed what I could. I wanted to get home.' I start to step toward him, to reach for him. He takes a step back, running a hand down his face and all I want in that moment is for him to take me into his arms and say *it's fine. I get it. You got drunk.*

'I'm sorry Jeremy. I must have taken all my clothes off before I passed out on her couch.' I'm trying to salvage what I can. I don't want to end things this way.

'Right,' he slowly brings his eyes to look at me, and when they finally make landfall on mine, I see the tears forming.

'Right, well, we better get to bed. We've got an early counseling session.' He goes up the steps so fast I'm not even sure he touched any, leaving me with no confirmation on whether my lie was convincing enough or not.

I jump as the door to our bedroom door slams shut. I pull my jacket to cover my nakedness and let my abasement carry me up the stairs. Stopping in front of our door, I raise my hand to knock, but let my arm fall back to my side as I decide it might be best for my mouth to stay shut the rest of the night. Or morning rather. Its already after two in the morning and our appointment is at 9:00 am.

I strip my clothes off and leave them in a pile by the bed. Slipping under the covers, I want to transport myself back to Cade's. This bed is cold and uninviting. The tension is rolling in from the other room, making it even harder to find comfort in being home. I roll over and pull the covers over my head, leaving only my nose to stick out. My body shudders with unspent tears, and I bite down on the sheet to keep any sounds muted. Tonight, the tears will carry me to dreamland.

Chapter Nineteen

'Babe, wake up.'

I wake up to Jeremy shaking my shoulder. His tone a little too joyous for wondering where his wife's shirt was the night before. I roll over, peeling hair from my cheek and rubbing my eyes, not wanting it to be time to crawl out of bed yet. Once I've successfully dismantled the sleep from my eyes, Jeremy comes into view as I sit up.

He's ready to go. He looks… handsome. Really handsome. He's clearly taken some time to get himself ready this morning. I fight the instinct to hide under the covers knowing I probably look similar to something that crawled out of the woods. He waits patiently for me to get my bearings, holding a cup of coffee in a to go cup.

'Get up already,' he says, yanking the covers from the bed, 'I've got breakfast sandwiches ready to go downstairs. We have to leave in 10.'

'Where are we going?'

'Mil… counseling.' He almost hides his irritation, but I hear it in the clip of his voice.

'Right,' I say as I stand up and stretch my arms above my head, 'I'll be down in a minute.'

Jeremy's eyes scan my body and for the first time this morning, I realize I'm naked. I drop my arms down to my sides and scoot around him to our bedroom. Try as I might to disappear into the abyss of the closet, clothes are already sticking out the door, I have so many. I grab a sweater and some jeans and turn to throw them on the bed, Jeremy stands in the doorway staring at me. Taking me in.

'What?' I stop and hold my hands out to my sides. Of course, this gives him an even better view of my body and I notice the approving look in his eyes.

'Nothing. Just admiring.' He smirks. He rounds the bed and brings his arm around my waist, slamming my body into his. His hand gently pushes my hair behind my ear and skates along the bottom of my jaw, seemingly wanting to move further south. His eyes drop to my lips and back up again. And damn it if my heart doesn't start to race. He brushes the tip of his nose against mine and I feel the hint of his lips on mine.

'Hurry your sexy ass up,' he whispers too close to my lips. He slaps my ass before turning and walking out of the room.

What the hell? This is not the interaction I was expecting this morning, especially after he clearly caught me coming home from somewhere I wasn't supposed to be. And why is my pussy throbbing with want because of it. Damn this body and its stupid fucking indecisiveness. No, no. That's not fair. I mean, come on. Jeremy is a very attractive man. Hell, he's sexy. Any woman would die to have him railing them into oblivion. Like Samantha did.

Yeah, Samantha, remember. Thankfully the thought of Samantha has cured my wet pussy and I can move on with the morning. I throw on my clothes, pull my hair into a low bun, rinse my face, brush my teeth, and I'm ready to face the world. Sort of. I'm ready to go sit in counseling knowing I can't continue this charade. Knowing I'll never be able to move on. Knowing the man I'm really craving is lying in his bed about 35 minutes away.

I grab my phone off the nightstand and check to see if I missed anything in the last six hours. My heart flutters when I see Cade's name across the screen. And it immediately drops when I see I also have a message from Celeste. Shit.

Client – P. Alderidge: You left me.

Oh? Is this him missing me?

Me: I'm sorry. I had an early appointment.

Client – P. Alderidge: I know.

Client – P. Alderidge: As your Dom, I need to advise you to ask permission next time.

Oh. Damn. My excitement is quickly extinguished. He's referring to himself as my Dom. Well, I guess that puts this relationship into a little more perspective for me. I'm still a business client to him.

Me: Apologies, sir.

I fight back the tears as I press 'send'. Jesus, Mil, you idiot. Of course, he doesn't have feelings for you. You hired him to do a job and that's what he's doing. What did you expect? That you would just end things with your husband and run off into the sunset with Cade. Your Dom. The guy you hired to spank you. The guy you hired to take your mind off your husband. Which, he did. The only problem now is he's the only thing on my mind but I'm not having the same effect on him.

'Mil. We have to get moving,' Jeremy yells from the bottom of the stairs.

'Coming,' I choke out and make my way to meet my lovely

husband.

I've found a thread to pick at on this God forsaken couch. Now that my fingers have found it, they can't unfind it. My inability to focus on the sessions is becoming quite a problem. A problem that not only the doctor is picking up on but also Jeremy. He knows I'm not in the room. Why can't he be the one to give up? Why is it going to have to be me to end this?

'Jeremy, you've mentioned quite a few different ways you've tried to reignite the spark between you and Millicent. How are you feeling about that? Do you feel like progress is being made?' Dr. Johnson asks, tapping her pen on the top of her notebook.

Jeremy clears his throat and adjusts himself on the couch. I didn't realize the answer would require so much preparation. When he doesn't answer right away, I turn to look at him. Elbows rested on his thighs, he's rubbing his hands together, keeping his gaze down, seemingly not wanting to answer the question.

'I felt like we *were* making progress.'

He's using past tense.

'Were? What's changing?' Dr. Johnson reads my mind and her gaze flits to me as if this is my fault. As if the stalling of progress has everything to do with me not being accepting and nothing to do with the fact that he cheated on me.

'Well... I was feeling really positive for a while. It felt like we were dating again, getting to know one another again. Mil was even letting me in more. She broke down one night after remembering when I confessed about Samantha, and we talked through it. Just like you recommended...' he trails off, wringing his hands more and more, turning his head toward the window. No doubt trying to avoid my gaze.

'That's good. This is good.'

'We, uh, we ended up having sex and, uh, it was amazing. Really good actually.'

My face flushes with embarrassment and bring my hand over my eyes. Jesus Jeremy. Do we need to give her this much information. Are you going to tell her the position we were in next?

'There's nothing to be embarrassed about, Millicent. Really. This is great news and sounds like progress is being made.' My fingers part over my eyes and glare through the crack they create at her. I'm not paying for a sex therapist; I'm paying for you to fix us. Fix me. To make me want to stay with my husband. To make me not want Cade.

'Jeremy please, continue.'

'Since then, since we had sex...' God, why does he keep saying that? Stop telling her about our sex damn it.

'Things feel off. I don't know... maybe I'm... maybe it's just me. I almost feel like we're going backwards again. Like having sex was a mistake. Maybe it happened to soon.'

'Would you stop saying sex already?'

Jeremy's head snaps in my direction, fixing me under his scrutiny.

'What's wrong with it, Mil? We had sex. We're paying this woman to help us through this. And... and I feel like since we had sex, you've been pulling away from me again.'

'Jesus,' I mutter, turning my attention to the doctor, 'is this really necessary?'

The sharp sound of Jeremys breath leaving his mouth at my audacity makes my head jerk towards him.

'I think it is, actually,' Dr. Johnson interrupts. These two are going to give me whiplash this morning. It's too early for this. Entirely too early for this. The only thoughts that seem to be swimming in my head now is that I wouldn't be sitting here if I had just ended it. If I hadn't let him talk me into staying with him, I wouldn't be sitting here whipping my head back and forth at these two and their silly ass remarks.

I went to Celeste's house that night. After I left Jeremy, sobbing and yelling out for me after he had told me about Samantha. The second Celeste opened the door, she took one look at me, and wrapped her arms around me. The gates to the flood immediately opened. I cried into her shoulder, standing there in her doorway, until all that was left were the salty trails down my cheeks.

She led me into her house, sat me down on the couch, went to the kitchen for a bottle of wine, poured us both a glass, and we just sat. In silence. Until I was ready to tell her why I was there and what had me so torn up. I couldn't seem to get the words to come. They sat like mud on my tongue. Every time I thought I could let it pour out, the mud would get thicker, and I'd take another drink of wine. I was three glasses in before the buzz from the wine cleared the mud enough for me to utter the words.

'Jeremy cheated on me.'

There it was. Out in the open. The information hitting someone else's ears. Celeste wrapped me in another hug. The tears came again, my ducts pulling water from the wine. There we sat. Me encased in her arms and her letting me soak her shirt through once again.

One bottle turned into two and, not long after, three bottles. I couldn't talk about it. I couldn't talk about what it all meant just yet. And I am so thankful for Celeste knowing that. She knew the last thing I needed right then was to rehash what I just went through with Jeremy. No, what I needed was a good wine drunk and to forget about reality even if just for a night.

That night turned into three days. I wore Celeste's clothes and laid like a slug around her house, mourning the destruction of my life. Jeremy blew my phone up with messages and calls. Eventually Celeste gave him a bit of relief and called him to let him know I was alive. Her short tone on the phone concealing nothing and letting him know he had fucked up in the worst way. She walked out of the room away from earshot so I'm not sure what all she said to him, but it clearly led to him stopping by her house the following day.

The sound of the doorbell barely registered in my brain as I continued my staring contest with the wall.

I flinched when I heard his voice.

'Mil, baby, can we talk, please?'

I fixed my stare on Jeremy, already on his knees in front of me. His eyes begging me for anything I was willing to give at that point.

'I'll be in the kitchen if you need anything,' Celeste announced from the doorway.

'Thanks, Cel,' Jeremy responded.

'I was talking to Mil.' Jeremy's head turned to Celeste just in time to catch her back as she walked down the hallway.

'Mil, I can't even begin to tell you how sorry I am. I… I can't lose you. I would do anything to go back. I would. I swear.' His words curl around sobs as he tries to continue.

'Please, Mil. We can get through this. It was a mistake. She's completely out of my life. I don't know what I was thinking…. I can't lose you.' His hands wrap around mine and he lets his head fall into my lap.

I can't even react. I don't know how to react. How am I supposed to react to my husband pleading, begging, for me not to leave him after he stepped out on our marriage? They don't put this in the 'preparing for marriage' handbook. They leave that part out. The 'how to prepare for when your husband inevitably cheats'. I should've known, right? Every other relationship I had been in, every other man, cheated on me. All of them. The only difference being I was the one begging. I was the one begging them to stay when they decided to leave me for the other woman. I was so stupid. Begging these men to stay with me after they cheated on me. But now the tables have turned, and the man is begging for me for once.

Should that matter? It probably shouldn't but my heart pangs at the subtle difference. Those guys, the ones before Jeremy, weren't willing to try again. They didn't care enough too. Maybe he really is sorry. People make mistakes, right?

'Please baby, please. I will do anything to make this up to you. I will spend the rest of our lives together doing whatever it takes for you to trust me again,' he manages through gasping sobs. My hands are wet with his tears and his kisses.

I owe him this. I owe him to stay and work through this. 'For better or for worse', right? I can't just throw away us from one mistake. The future that still waits us. If he never does this again, and I don't stay to work on things, then I'll miss out on all the good he has left to offer me. The thought of starting over makes me sick to my stomach. The thought of him with Samantha makes me want to vomit all over Celeste's living room.

I should tell him to get the fuck out. I should tell him to go cry to Samantha. But then she wins. She shouldn't win. Why should she get my husband for the rest of her life? If he's promising not to do this ever again, shouldn't I benefit from that? Not her? God damn it! Why? Why did he have to cheat? Why did he have to do this? Why couldn't he have just maxed out our credit card or bought a car without discussing it with me? Why did it have to be him choosing to sleep with some slut?

'I've already called a counselor. We have an appointment in a couple days. I want to show you I want to fix this. That I want you and only you. I swear to you, Mil. I swear to you on everything I hold dear, that this will never... never happen again.' Jeremy leans up, gripping my face and wiping the tears I didn't know were even falling from my cheeks.

'Please just come home Mil. We can take this one step at a time. Let's just get home and we can start fresh. I can start fresh and show you just how much you mean to me.' His eyes peer intently into mine and I can tell he's holding his breath, waiting on my response.

My response is the slightest nod of my head and Jeremy immediately plunges his head back into my lap. He wraps his arms around my waist, pulling himself as close as possible to me. My hands fall onto his back and in his hair and my eyes cloud with tears again as my heart starts to break all over again.

I can do this. We can do this. It was a mistake. It won't happen again. I can trust him again. Everything will be back to normal in no time, and we'll be all the stronger for making it through to the other side. I hope.

'Can you give me some specific examples since, since you've had sex, that are making you feel like the two of you are moving backwards?' I wipe the tears from my cheeks as Dr. Johnson directs her question to Jeremy, hoping no one takes notice.

'Just, the nights, the nights are getting later that she's working. I try to get her excited to come home to me as fast as she can but there's always something. I know she's busy but it's starting to feel like she's coming up with things to stay away longer.' Jeremy continues to stare at the floor, elbows perched on his knees.

'Millicent?'

'I can't help I have a business to run.'

'Can you understand where Jeremy might be coming from?'

'I don't know, maybe.' Of course, I can. I'm gone all the time. I'm with Cade all the time.

'I guess I wouldn't feel this way if it at least felt like you wanted to be home. Like you were excited to be coming home to me. Even when I offer to have dinner ready, I'm met with 'I don't know when I'll be home. Don't bother. Don't wait up.'

'My texts go unanswered. I don't even get a 'be home soon' or 'wish I was home instead of this showing'...'

'I'm busy when I'm working Jeremy, I can't help that.'

'Even on nights when you don't have an open house, you're meeting with Celeste, or in the office, you're not at home.'

'I just have a lot going on.'

'What about today then? After counseling? You don't have anything going on. Let's get away for the night. We can go wherever you want. Please. I just want to be with you, Mil.' Jeremy's eyes plead with me from the opposite end of the couch. They want me to jump up, hold out my hand for his, and for us to run off to wherever together. Happily together and with no plan. But we're tainted. He's tainted us.

'I can't... I have to go into the office...'

'Since when?' he cuts me off.

'Since I have a job and I need to get ready for an open house tomorrow.'

'This is what I'm talking about Mil. This. Right here. I didn't even know you had to go into the office today or that you had an open house tomorrow. You didn't tell me! You don't tell me anything. Hell! You asked for a raincheck for some time this weekend for the dinner I wanted to take you to last night. That's obviously not going to happen either!'

Jeremy can no longer disguise the hurt on his face and my chest strains against the guilt as he stands up and moves toward the door.

'Where are you going?' I demand.

'I'm done for today. I'll be in the car whenever you're finished.' The slam of the door makes me jump. A coldness gathers under my skin as I stare at the door he just escaped through.

Dr. Johnson clears her throat and I remember she's still here. That I'm still here. Sitting in her office.

'I'm sorry, he… I…'

'It's ok, Millicent. These things are hard. The road will not be without its rocks. You'll get through it,' she says cutting me off from my stuttering. She stands and places her hand on my shoulder. The weight of it feels so foreign. She's never touched me before and it covers my body with a weird uneasiness.

'Let's continue next week, ok?' She smiles at me, and I nod in agreement. She walks ahead of me and opens the door, holding it for me, and waits for me to move through it so she can get onto someone else's shit life.

I drag my cement legs through the door, and it shuts behind me. I grab my jacket from the coat rack and begin the walk of humiliation to the car. The car where my husband waits for me. Hopefully. The last thing I want to endure right now is a long walk home.

Chapter Twenty

Jeremy is waiting on me in the car when I come out of the counselor's office. Which is great since I don't want to walk but also sucks since the last thing I want is to ride home in a silent car.

And silent it is. Jeremy weaves in and out of traffic, never taking his eyes off the road. I keep my stare out the passenger window and think about what it would be like to be in anyone else's car besides this one. The couple glances I steal, Jeremy's hand is white knuckling around the steering wheel while his left hand holds up his head against the window. If this were in any other stage of our relationship, I'd ask him what was wrong. I'd drag it out of him. I would not let him just sit in the car not speaking to me, clearly upset. Now, I find myself counting down the minutes until I'm free from this speeding cage.

That just leaves being at home. My moving entrapment traded for an immobile one. My home used to be a sanctuary, but it hasn't felt that way for the past few months. Now, I'm a feral beast pacing back and forth, looking for any hole I can escape through. Today my escape is going to be to the office. Even if it's only for a little bit, I need to be able to breath. To think about my next move.

Jeremy pulls up to the house and puts the car in park. Neither of us make for our doors. We both just sit there, staring forward at our home. The silence floods my ears, and the air thickens. The urge to run begins flowing through my bloodstream and makes its way throughout my body. Getting me ready to bolt. Taking a deep breath, I reach up for the door handle.

'Mil...' Jeremy utters finally, just as I've gained the confidence to remove myself from this car.

'Mil please,' he says, adjusting himself to face me. My head drops slightly as I decide whether it's worth listening or not.

'Jeremy,' I reply turning my body toward his, planting my back against the door.

He brings his body almost across the center console and reaches to take my hands in his. I look down at our hands together. My hands are sweaty in his and it takes everything not to pull them away. I realize then that he's trembling. His hands are shaking so hard they vibrate into my own.

'Mil, I...' he barely manages and clears his throat, 'listen, Mil, I know, I know this has been so damn hard. I know I asked the impossible when I asked you to stay with me, to work through this together.'

He's pausing now. I can see him trying to keep it together. Trying to harness all of his emotions so he can get whatever he needs out. I give him the room to do this. Feeling his hands earthquaking in mine is enough for me to know he's also hurting. This might be just as hard on him as it has been me.

'I know I've made promises and broke them and then made more promises. And I've asked you to find it in yourself to trust me again. I know you're trying; I do. And I see how much this is tearing you apart. How much I've torn you, us, apart. But I'm begging you, I'm begging you as your husband, as the man you fell in love with, as the man who broke your heart into irreparable pieces and wants so badly to glue it back together, as a man who cannot fathom the thought of losing you, please, please do not give up on us. Please. Help me help you come back to me. All of you. All the broken pieces. Help me put them back together so I can put us back together.'

I search his bloodshot eyes for any hint of malice as I listen to the blood pound in my ears and around my body. My cheeks mirror his, made wet from the tears he's created on his face and mine. How can I feel anything for this man? This man that wrecked me so completely and yet I want to hold him and tell him it'll all be ok. Is this what true regret looks like? Is this the face of a man who knows he's about to lose everything and will do literally anything to keep it from happening? I want to punch him in his throat then wipe away his tears. Hold his head in my chest. Stroke his hair, his back. I want him to take me inside, make love to me, show me what I'll be missing if I choose to walk the other way. I want to string him up by his ankles and beat him for putting me here. For putting us here. I want him to suffer and end his suffering at the same time.

My only response to his pleas is the faint nod of my head. And that's all it takes for him to barrel across the center console and pull me into his chest. He holds me tightly and I let my arms wrap around his back as I listen to his heart slow from the hyper-speed it was beating.

He pulls away from me and leaps out of the car so quickly you'd think we were on fire. I can't even wrap my head around exactly what's happening before he's on my side, opening the door, pulling me out, picking me up and cradling me to his chest, and striding toward the house. Somehow, he manages to unlock the door, open, and shut it all while holding me tight against him. He must have grabbed my purse as he took me from the car because he drops it on the floor before hauling us up the stairs.

Jeremy walks us into our bedroom and sits me gracefully down on the bed. He stands in front of me and grabs each ankle to slip my shoes off before stepping out of his own. He steps up to the bed, forcing my legs to part so he can stand between them. He leans forward, placing his hands on either side of my thighs and pecks my lips lightly. The kisses so swift and light he seems to be learning my lips all over again.

My heart races as I kiss him back. Quick, teasing kisses, with promises of more to come later. He parts his lips on mine and his tongue traces along its outline, encouraging my mouth to let him in.

He starts to put his weight in to the kiss and I let him push me back onto the bed. The second my back makes contact with the plush covers; our kisses turn hungrier than ever, and we devour each other. His arm wraps behind my back as he pulls me further up the bed effortlessly, and my head lands softly on a pillow. My pillow. In the bed we used to share.

His hand finds my face and his thumb pulls and grips on my cheek. His other hand starts to trail up my sweater igniting a line of fire up my stomach. His lips leave mine as they trace down my jaw and to my neck as a slight moan breaks the silence of the room. His cock starts to harden between my legs as his hips begin to rock into me. My back arches off the bed as his hand finally reaches beneath my bra. His knowing fingers reach my hardened nipple. He starts to roll it between thumb and forefinger, sending a wave of pleasure straight to my pussy that in no way should be throbbing.

He comes back from my neck and our mouths clash again, breathing moans into each other's mouths as we both start rocking to a silent rhythm only our bodies can hear. Reaching my hands down to unbutton his jeans, I find the zipper, the teeth absurdly loud as they unhook from each other. I push his jeans down his hips and free his cock. Gripping it in my hand, the veins pulse against my warm palm as I start to move my hand up and down, leaving him groaning into my mouth.

'I want you so bad, Mil,' he confesses as his tongue dips in and out of my mouth.

'Then take me.'

He wastes no time pushing up to his knees to pull off his shirt and finish removing his jeans. I stare down at him. This body that lingers above me, all mine, muscles, hard cock, and all. My teeth bite savagely into my bottom lip as I watch his cock twitch in anticipation.

He pulls me into a sitting position and removes my sweater over my head, then unclasps my bra and tosses it aside. He bends to kiss me again, all tongue and lips, and I let him push me back against the bed once more. His tongue continues to slide against mine as he unbuttons and starts to remove my jeans. Sitting back again, he pulls my legs straight up in front of him and strips the jeans the rest of the way off. My legs fall back to the bed, straddling him, and I'm completely open to him, wet pussy bared for him.

His hungry eyes find mine as he crawls forward, arms on either side of my head, hands in my hair, and cock pushing against my pussy, soaking up the feel. The weight of his body sinks me further into the bed and I'm lost in him as his mouth meets mine. Fingers gripping my hair, he tips my head back, giving him even more access to my mouth and I hear his name slip through the opening of my lips.

'Jeremy, oh my God, I'm so wet.'

'Just how I want you,' he says, his voice like gravel, 'soaking for me.'

He reaches a hand down and slips his cock effortlessly into my waiting pussy. My pussy clamps around each inch of him as he slides in. His name slipping from my mouth once again as the pleasure builds beneath the surface like a volcanic eruption. Our tongues and teeth clash together as we rock against each other, eliciting carnal sounds from the depths of our bodies.

Everything seems to hit all at once and I can't hide the sob that bursts from me. Jeremy pulls his face from mine for just a moment and then starts to kiss where the tears are staining my cheeks. Something in my chest seems to split and break apart as his smooth lips clean up the sadness. My arms wrap under his and run my hands along his muscles as they contract on his back as he fucks me slowly. Drawing out the pleasure for both of us.

His eyes find mine and we watch each other move closer and closer to coming unglued with each other. For each other. My core starts to ache for the orgasm to roll over me as he slips in and out of me torturously.

'I love you, Mil,' he breathes.

'I love you, Jeremy,' I manage. His mouth smashes into mine again and drives into me until my pussy tightens around his cock. I scream into his mouth as he drags the orgasm out of me. And that's all he needs before he's spilling his cum into me.

He continues pulling out and pushing back into me in languid motions, our lips kissing and tongues playing as we come down from the sex induced high. Jeremy rolls onto his side, taking me with him and land in a tangled mess of legs and arms. I smell the pine and citrus scent emanating from his gleaning skin as his fingers twirl the ends of my hair. He kisses into my hair, and I let myself sink a little bit deeper into his warmth.

I wake up in a knotted, sweaty Jeremy mess. I forgot what it was like to sleep with him. It's been months since we've been in the same bed, and he is a hot box. I didn't really mind before. The heat that radiated off his body was a reminder of his love. The love I let blanket me every night. It's hot tentacles wrapping around every inch of me and lulling me into a blissful sleep. Now, all I want is to shower.

I slip out of the roaster that is our bed and make my way to the bathroom. I turn the knob all the way to scalding and turn to face the mirror while I wait for the water to heat up. I pull the hair from my neck that got stuck there during the hottest nap of my life and suck in a lung full of air.

What the fuck is wrong with you, Mil? My other half asks as she stares coldly into my eyes.

She doesn't need to say anything further. I already know what she's thinking. I'm running around with another man while my husband pours his soul into us. I let him make love to me and tell me he loves me. I even say it back. It's not a lie though. I can say that much. I do still love Jeremy. He'll always hold a place in my heart whether we're together or not.

Someone else is holding a place in my heart now. Taking up even more space. The biggest problem is I can't shake the feeling that I owe this to Jeremy. I owe it to him to stay and see this through since he's trying so hard after he fucked up so royally. Where does that leave me though? Feeling forever inadequate in my marriage regardless of the goddess treatment from my husband. The daily thoughts of Cade swimming in and out of my brain. The chill that travels from my spine to my fingertips and back when I think about the things we've done together. How my heart swells from just seeing his name on my phone screen.

I stare at myself with circling thoughts until the steam clouds the mirror. I wipe the fog away to give myself one last glance, before getting in the shower. I let the water sting my skin and roll down my body. For once, my mind clears and it's just me and the stream of water. I almost feel at peace.

The shower door sliding open breaks through my quiet mind, and Jeremy's arms snake around my stomach, his chest pressing against my back.

'You should've woken me up. You know I love showering with you.'

'I didn't want to wake you.'

'You can wake me anytime, you know that.'

Jeremy's hands roam around my middle, skirting just below my tits and just above my pussy. His cock stiffens against my ass as I try to drown myself in the water. The fact that my nipples and pussy are reacting to his touch is becoming an annoyance. His teeth graze up the side of my neck and my mouth betrays me when a moan slips between my lips.

Its ok, Mil. I remind myself. *You are allowed to be turned on by your husband.*

Wet fingers grip my jaw, pulling my face to look over my shoulder. His tongue invades my mouth in a rough but sensual kiss. A kiss of assurance. Of love. Of apology.

His assault on my mouth continues as his free hand slides between my legs, fingers slipping around my clit and playing at my swollen entrance. His teeth sink into my bottom lip, tugging slightly, before releasing me. His darkened eyes burn into mine and my eyelids slowly flit open. My body starts to quiver as his palm increases pressure against my clit. His fingers slide in and out of me with ease as he starts to pick up the pace.

'That feel good, Mil?' he asks as his tongue glides along the shell of my ear. His iron grip tightens around my throat like a vice as the orgasm swells beneath my surface, threatening to explode out of me.

'So tight and wet.'

I gasp for breath as the water continues to pour over my body and the electricity that Jeremy has created starts to shoot out from all directions. I transform into a boneless heap as the orgasm wrecks me from within.

'Oh, Mil, come all over my hand.'

Jeremy continues to pull the orgasm out of me as I slump against him from the combination of the burning hot water and the pure ecstasy washing over me like waves. Just when I think he's done with me, his hold loosens on my neck, and I find my face and chest pressed against the wall. Grabbing my hip with his hand I soaked, he pulls my ass back to meet his cock.

Releasing his grip on my hip, he circles the tip of his cock around my pussy, testing my readiness before sinking balls deep into me. I start to push away from the wall, but I'm put right back in place as his hand settles between my shoulder blades. My face slides against the shower wall and my hands fumble around for something to hold onto as he pumps in and out of me, decimating me from the inside.

He's taking everything from me making me his. The water splatters off our bodies as his hips slap against my ass while our names echo around the steaming abyss. I writhe against him as he jerks inside of me, both of us spilling onto each other. Sliding out of me, he lets me stand a little straighter but keeps me pressed against the tile. His soft mouth kisses along my shoulder as remnants of my orgasm shutter through my body. Shivers travel along my spine with every touch of his lips as the water starts turning lukewarm.

He turns the water off before stepping back. My legs weaken further as I push myself off the wall.

'Good girl,' he snickers as his hand stings across my ass.

I spin around, his comment catching me off guard. He's never said that before. He steps out of the shower, grabs a towel, and hands it to me with a wink before walking out of the bathroom.

My head spins as I towel myself off. The air once thick with lust, grows thicker with guilt. The thought that Jeremy is somehow onto me ravages my brain, but I quickly stuff it into a dark, untouched corner to deal with later. I just need some fresh air.

'What would my love like for dinner?' Jeremy asks as I walk into the bedroom, towel wrapped firmly around my body.

'Oh, I don't know. I'm not really hungry.'

My stomach lets out a grumble that could shake the neighborhood and we both stand there, just staring at each other. A smile slowly starts to pull at Jeremys lips as my face flushes with embarrassment.

'Right,' he says matter of fact, pulling a sweatshirt down over his head.

'I need to run and get some work done first. I'm gonna head to the office for a bit.'

I need to get out of this house. I need to think. I need to get Jeremy's eyes off me. The longer I stand here in front of him, the deeper he can see into my mind, and I can't let him see what I'm hiding underneath.

'Oh, yeah, I forgot.' He gets visibly smaller right in front of my eyes. The confidence of having made love to me and then fucking me against the shower wall waning as I shoot him down for dinner.

'I shouldn't be long.' I add to try and placate him a little. I'm finding myself trying to restore some of the high we were both feeling just moments ago. I hate that I'm the reason the light just left his eyes.

'Ok, well, I'll see you in a bit then,' he buries the unmistakable hurt on his face and crosses the room.

'Don't be too late,' he whispers before pulling my head into his kiss. His lips resting on my forehead, not wanting to let me go again. Almost as if he already knows this is all going to come to an end sooner or later.

Chapter Twenty-One

I shouldn't care but I hated leaving Jeremy after the day we had. Something about him making himself be ok with me being busy and seemingly not making time for him is starting to wear away at the edges of my broken heart. The desperation he tries to hide. The complacency he oozes when I walk out the door to do something I'm not supposed to. The lies I know he accepts. He just can't put his finger on what the lie is. He thinks I'm needing space, time to think, time to digest what's happening in our relationship. And he gives it hoping it'll make things better but also desperate for me to include him on working through this.

The house is cold as hell as I walk in the front door.

'65?!' I squeak, checking the thermostat before making my way up the stairs to my office, and instantly cranking it up to 74. Even if I planned to do any work, my fingers will never cooperate at this temperature.

I listen for the heat to kick on and hope the heater isn't going out. That's not something that needs to be added to my plate right now. I kick off my shoes as I round the doorway and drop my purse onto the velvet couch. I cross the room to my mini fridge and pull out a small bottle of pinot grigio. I don't care what anyone says, wine is always the answer.

I pull the chair out and fall into it, propping my feet up on the desk. I twist the lid loose and flick it the rest of the way off, sending it flying across the room. It clacks against the wall, falls to floor, and I watch as it rolls over to the couch, disappearing underneath. The cold wine washes over my tongue as I swallow a gulp. I let my eyes close and rest my head on against the chair.

There should be a book on how to handle life. Out of all the books out there, no one has thought to write one describing scenarios with ideas on how to deal with them. I suppose there probably is something in existence on *how to face a failing marriage after a husband has cheated*. I wonder if it would recommend finding a Dom to take your mind off things. To relinquish your control so someone else can take the wheel for a while. Even if someone out there suggests it, I highly doubt they would further suggest finding the Dom while you're still married. I also suspect they wouldn't suggest falling for him.

I wish someone would tell me what to do. If I could get even a hint of what my life will look like if I stay with Jeremy. If I leave him. If I choose Cade. If I stay alone. Knowing deep down, I wouldn't stay alone, though. If I leave Jeremy, there is no doubt I will run straight into Cade's arms. The part I'm not sure about is if Cade's arms would be waiting openly. Part of me believes he wouldn't hesitate to pull me in but there are still those shreds of doubt telling me I'm no more than a business deal among other business deals.

I try to not let the latter get to me knowing it would completely destroy me. I bring the bottle back to my lips, letting the wine invade my mouth and wash away the hurt of Cade not choosing me before its even happened. I let the image of leaving Jeremy into my mind. What emotions come up? Of course, I feel some hurt. It does make me sad thinking about leaving Jeremy. He's the love of my life... or was. I'm not sure anymore. The contrition takes over when it becomes obvious that the level of sadness I feel about being separated from Jeremy pales in comparison to the utter fracturing of my soul when I picture my life without Cade.

I finish off the bottle before wiping the tears from my cheeks. I need to come to terms with the fact that my tears are for Cade and the idea that he may not choose me. The tears that come for Jeremy are the ones I should've cried a long time ago. The tears of grief from what we should've had. What we could've been. What he ruined. What we won't ever have.

'Need another one?' I open my eyes to Celeste walking across the room to my mini fridge. Damn her and her silent steps.

'Uh, yeah, actually.'

Grabbing two bottles and turning, she steps toward me to make my wine delivery. I take the bottle and open it before she has a chance to make it to the couch. Her eyes drill into my own as she sits, opening her own bottle and taking a drink. This whole exchange is made so much worse since I already know she's mad... and why. Not only am I betraying my husband, but I'm betraying her friendship knowing damn well how she feels about cheaters. I can only hope she'll simply be upset I didn't come to her for advice and that she'll settle for being disappointed in me for what's going on with Cade.

'You got my message.' It's not a question. She knows I got it.

'Yeah, sorry. We had counseling this morning and then, we were busy, and yeah. Now I'm here.'

'How is that going? The counseling?'

Sweat starts to gather around my hairline as she drags this out and I find myself wishing she would just rip off the band aid and get to the point. I'm overwhelmed already with relationship drama and can sense I'm not far from being buried alive. *Here lies Millicent – buried by her inability to make a decision.*

'It's going.'

She takes another drink before leaning forward. Her eyes

bore into me more viciously than I thought possible, lacerating my soul. I never realized how intimidating Celeste could be. Her normally cool, friendly demeanor is gone, and I won't lie, it's a little unnerving. This is a side she must save for special occasions. Boy, am I glad I was invited.

'It's going? Mil,' her pause excruciating, 'how long have we been friends?'

'Um, I don't know, like six years probably.'

'Eight, actually. Eight years we've been friends, Mil.' I see the hurt flit across her face at me not remembering the exact timeline as my face scrunches a little with shame.

'Do you think after knowing you for eight years I don't know when there's more? That I wouldn't know when you're leaving something out?'

'I, uh, no I guess not. I'm sorry, Celeste. Just with everything going on... Jeremy and... the apartments...'

'Stop. Stop right there,' she interrupts, and I immediately seal my lips, 'I don't want to hear about these damn apartments. There is no extra work you could possibly be doing that I couldn't be helping with. And if there really is, then you're just being a bad business partner. But we both know the apartments are a cop out.

'The real shit that's going on involves Jeremy. And, from the call I got from Jeremy in the middle of the night last night, there's a hell of a lot more shit going down than you're leading on to.'

My throat constricts as I swallow hard and stay quiet as Celeste calls me out on my bullshit. My shirt starts to stick to my back as the sweat begins to seep from every pore around my body. I tighten my fingers around my wine bottle, fearing it might slip from my grasp, as my temperature rises. The arm of the chair feels clammy under my slickening palm.

'Yeah,' my voice cracks, 'I suppose you're right.' I adjust myself in my seat so I can give my best attempt of facing her like an adult even though I'm desperate to slink underneath this desk where I can only hope she'll leave.

'So, what the fuck is going on? Because I lied to your husband last night, Mil. I lied and told him you got drunk after the client meeting. I told him I didn't want you driving home, and you were sleeping it off in my spare bedroom. I told him I was sorry for not letting him know earlier because I was also buzzed, ya know, from the client meeting...' Her voice continues to rise as she recounts the lies she fed Jeremy while I was cuddled up, nice and warm and blissfully unaware, in Cade's bed.

'Do you know what I did last night? I certainly didn't go to a client meeting, get drunk with you, and give you a place to crash after. I sat at home, by myself, drinking wine and binging true crime shows. Something I *used* to do with my best friend,' she adds almost as an afterthought, 'until I got a phone call from Jeremy, freaking out about the whereabouts of his wife. His wife who wasn't answering the phone and hadn't heard from in hours.'

Her rage seems to vibrate around the room, and I know I'm not meant to interrupt. Not that I would be able to anyway. She has hardly let herself breathe as I watch her resentment for me grow with every word she speaks at me. Her anger, carrying sentence after sentence out of her, has given me no time to respond even if I wanted to. It starts to become all too clear that she's not going to take what I've been doing lightly. This very well could be the beginning of the end for Celeste and me.

'Please tell me, Mil. How was the client meeting last night? Did I have fun? Did we nail down a sale?'

'Cel, I...'

'Don't!' Her wrath forces my mouth shut. 'You'd better think real hard before you feed me some bullshit lie like you did Jeremy. The thing is, Mil, I'm most upset I had to hear I was tangled up in your lie from Jeremy. You didn't even have the courtesy to tell me ahead of time. So I could prepare. Damn! Do you not trust me? Is that it? I thought I was your person. I thought I was the person you would come to about this. You did in the beginning anyway. You know my door is always open. If you're needing to get away from Jeremy, my house is a safe place. It always has been. You don't need to be hanging out here and at the damn bar.'

I watch as the tears cascade down my best friend's face. The hurt she's feeling because I wasn't letting her in. The hurt she's feeling because I wasn't running to her for help or, at least, letting her know I needed help working through this. The hurt I caused with her thinking I've been alone in all this when, in reality, I've been letting another man comfort my broken soul.

'I wasn't here… or at the bar…'

'Where were you then?' Her brows pinch together as confusion rolls over her. It's now or never.

'I was with someone… a man.'

'I don't understand. What man?'

'I've been seeing another man.' My words are barely above a whisper as I utter them out loud for the first time. As I tell someone else about Cade for the first time.

'You've been seeing another man? Someone other than Jeremy?'

'Yeah.' My cheeks sheathe in guilt as they grow even more red with my confession.

Celeste stares at me trying to work out what I'm telling her. A myriad of emotions swim across her face as she considers what her response will be. Her eyes fall to the floor, and I can only watch as her head starts to shake slowly from side to side. Finally, as her head lifts, she averts her gaze from mine, focusing on the windows to the side of the room, eyes brimming with unshed tears.

'So, let me get this straight… you've been seeing another man, while you're married to your husband, who cheated on you, but you've agreed to work on things?'

'Yeah, that about sums it up.'

Celeste's eyes flick to mine and the glare carries a fire that could burn straight through me *and* whatever else is behind me.

'How long?'

'A few months.'

'A few months?' she scoffs.

'Yeah.'

'Are you fucking serious right now?' her voice raises octaves as mine lowers.

'I'm sorry?'

'You are fucking another man, while your husband, who I understand cheated on you, sits at home wondering where you are?! I get it, Mil. I do! You're hurting. Hurting so bad. Probably more than I'll ever be able to truly understand. But your solution to it, to mending your heart, is to fuck another man. All the while your husband is doing everything in his power to make you realize he fucked up. To try and win you back. To mend everything he screwed up. To treat you like the goddess you are so he can show you how important you are to him?'

'Well, when you put it like that.'

'You're just as bad as he is, Mil. Do you not see that?' she implores.

'I, I know, its… it's probably not the best way to handle things but…'

'Not the best way to handle things?! Are you fucking kidding me?'

'Cel, I just, I didn't know what else to do…'

'You go to fucking therapy, Mil. You eat a pint of fucking ice cream. You spend days at your friend's house crying and drinking wine. You scream at your husband and beat your fists on his chest until he grabs you, pulls you in, and holds you while you unleash your sorrow. That's what you do, Mil! That's what you do. What you don't do, is go fuck some other dude. What you don't do is tell your husband you're willing to work on things. You don't make him think you're all in when you're just out there letting some dude be all up in you.'

I watch as Celeste's chest heaves from the verbal berating she's giving me. I knew she'd be pissed but a part of me was still holding out that she would understand. Even if it was only a little bit. I was hoping she would still be a shoulder for me. An ear to let me vent. Someone to offer me advice in an impossible situation. I didn't account for her to hate me. Right now, I'd give anything for her to slap some sense into me and then take me in her arms. I can tell now though, that that would be the best case scenario and currently, I'm staring into the eye of the worst case.

'Hello? Mil, you up there?' Jeremy's voice echoes gently up the stairs and into my office. What the hell is he doing here?

I don't have time to respond before he strolls into my office, stopping as soon as he sees the scene in front of him.

'I brought you some dinner,' he says, holding up a bag, concern etching his face. His eyes flick back and forth between Celeste and me.

'Cel, everything ok?'

'Yeah, sorry, just having a moment, ya know,' she keeps her eyes on mine as she answers Jeremy. His look of confusion shifts to me, urging me to provide further explanation.

'I'm sorry to interrupt,' he stalls, 'there's plenty here... if you're hungry.'

'No. No thanks,' she says abruptly and stands, gathering her coat, 'I'm just heading out.'

She walks toward the door but stops short and places her hand on Jeremy's shoulder. Jeremy's confusion multiplies as he looks from the hand on his shoulder to her face as she gives it a comforting squeeze.

'Uh, see ya later, Cel,' he sputters as she walks from the room, not sparing me another glance.

'Ok, that was weird,' he states, turning his attention back to me, 'what's going on with her? I've never seen her that upset. That sad. Or mad. I'm not even sure what she was.'

He's in front of me, placing the bag of food on top of my desk before I can fully wrap my head around what just happened.

'Mil?' he asks when I don't immediately respond, my eyes still glued to the doorway Celeste just vanished through.

'Sorry, yeah, she's just... under a lot of stress. With the, uh, the apartment deal. That's all.'

The lie thickens and sours in my mouth as realization smacks me in the face. I've just destroyed my best friendship.

'You'll get through it. You've been friends too long to let a business deal come between you two.'

'Yeah, you're probably right.' I whisper around the boulders in my throat.

'You guys have been friends for like eight years, haven't you? You'll be good, promise babe.'

My eyes finally slide to his. Jesus. Even he knows how long I've been friends with Celeste, and he wasn't even in the picture when we met. I really am a shit friend. Fuck me.

Chapter Twenty-Two

It's a Sunday like any other Sunday except I have the whole day to myself. For once. Jeremy left early this morning for a wedding and has a couple corporate events out of town. So, technically, I have until Tuesday to myself. The silence of the house wraps around me as I saunter down the hall into the kitchen. Bacon demands my attention as its smell wafts into my nose from the island.

I reach the island and grab the note sitting next to the plate of pancakes and bacon. Warmth emanates from the plate so he must not have left as early as I thought. He was down here making sure I woke up to breakfast. Damn him and his benevolence. Groaning, I unfold the paper.

Mil,

I hate that I'm leaving you for two days but hopefully this breakfast will keep you warm for at least a little while. I also threw together a lasagna. It's in the fridge and just needs to be baked at 350 for 55 minutes. That should keep you full until Tuesday.

I miss you already and I love you even more.

-Your loving husband who is over the moon for his Mil,

Jeremy

I can't help the eye roll as I refold the note. Why does he have to be so nice? Why does he have to be trying so hard? If he weren't, I could've already walked away. I could already be on my way to seeing what sort of future I might have with Cade. But no. He's over here pouring his all into this. Into us. And here I am being an ungrateful bitch about it. I suppose I'm mad because I'll be the one that ends things eventually. Won't I? Won't I have to end this?

I grudgingly grab the plate from the counter and slide the silverware drawer open in search of a fork. I force myself into the nook seat and stare down at my breakfast. Of course, it looks delicious and smells even better. Fucking Jeremy.

My mind roils as I mull over the inevitability of the situation. The thought of being completely done with Jeremy is making me sick. The decision might be easier if I knew exactly where Cade stood with us. He may not even consider an *us*. Is that what's really happening here? Am I worried about being alone? Am I worried about settling for Jeremy? Or am I ultimately worried about being rejected by Cade?

The question now becomes what I'm supposed to do if I end up alone? Start to rebuild, I guess. I undoubtedly can't stay with Jeremy. He's done something I'm never going to get past. And the fact that Cade is even in the equation shows that my heart isn't in it with Jeremy anymore. I wish I could move on with him, wish that therapy was working, wish he had never stepped out, but the reality is, it happened and now we have to deal with it. I can't keep this charade up any longer. For both Jeremy and my mental health.

I finish my breakfast, clean off the plate and stow it away in the dishwasher, and decide it's never too early for mimosas. I grab a glass from the bar car and set out for the champagne and orange juice waiting for me inside the fridge. The cork explodes from the mouth of the champagne bottle and sails through the kitchen. I'm instantaneously transported back in time to our first night in this house. Such a happy time. We didn't even bother with glasses, just passed the bottle back and forth to each other. They were packed up anyway and who has time to go digging when you've got celebrating to do. We certainly didn't.

One bottle turned into two as we gazed around at our amazing new house, talking about all the memories we'd make here together. Two bottles turned into three and Jeremy's face buried between my legs as I sat on the edge of the island. The tricks his tongue pulled off that night were unmatched. The first of many orgasms that would echo through the house, sinking into the woodwork, laying claim to what was now ours.

I'm sure a lot of couples celebrate events with sex eventually but there was something that stood out that night. Jeremy climbing up my body after making my thighs quake around his head, the wild look in his eyes as he licked his lips, completely satisfied with his work. The anticipation that quickly built up again from simply watching his body move over mine in the most primal way, knowing he couldn't wait to have his cock buried inside of me. The way his hips aligned perfectly with mine, his cock teasing my entrance before sinking into the warm abyss. His hands gliding up my arms, forcing them above my head. The way he gripped my hands while he slowly fucked me into oblivion. Whispering into my ear, reminding me of how much my pussy turned him on, how he couldn't wait to do this every night, that we might even do it in this very spot.

I remember how my body arched off the granite, almost fighting what he was doing to me. My finger mindlessly grazes along my bottom lip as the phantom of his bite lingers. Wanting to make sure the entire house knew exactly how fucking good he was making me feel, I whimpered his name out to the ceiling with every passing stroke. Our bodies sticky from sweat once we were both satisfied, not wanting to even move, but to just keep laying there on the counter together forever.

The whole episode plays out in front of me as if I were the director as I stand at the island sipping my mimosa. I watch as Jeremy finally comes to terms with the fact that we can't sleep on the island. He gets up slowly, not wanting to leave me, and digs out a kitchen towel to clean me up. He reaches for my hand to help me up, but before my feet can hit the ground, he throws me over his shoulder, grabs another bottle from the fridge and move swiftly upstairs to ravage me again in our new bed, in our new room, in our new house.

I finish my drink and pour another. I walk grudgingly up the stairs, my legs moving like they're encased in cement, and try to decide if it will truly be relaxing to be home by myself. If I'm only going to be reliving all the amazing sex Jeremy and I had while simultaneously wishing I could be in Cade's bed, I might be better off finding something to do. Standing in front of my closet, I decide on some jeans and a Rolling Stones t-shirt. I gather my hair and tie it into a messy bun, swipe on a little mascara, and decide that whether I go out or stay home, this is enough.

I'm met with a flashback of Jeremy and I on the stairs after we could barely make it through the door as I make my way back to the first floor. We had just got home from celebrating our third anniversary and he couldn't keep his hands off me the entire drive home. He started undressing me as soon as we hit the porch, fumbling with keys to get the door unlocked, between frantic kisses. Once he finally got the door open, we burst through like a couple of teenagers getting ready to fuck for the first time. I hit the first step and he was on me like a predator taking down his prey. Pulling my pants down right there, unzipping and freeing his throbbing cock from his pants, wasting no time and driving into me at full force. He had never done anything like that before and my pussy reacted in the best way possible. It was some of the hottest sex we had ever had. The fact that he couldn't wait coupled with the forced nature of it right there on the stairs.

My pussy start to throb at the memory when I remember we had been celebrating in the bar where Samantha was working. And the whole night he was distant. I could barely keep his attention. But then took something out on me when we got home. I was so thankful for the change that I couldn't see what was happening at the time. I reaped the benefits that night but only because he was dealing with some kind of feelings about her. Did he even really want me that night? Or was he taking his frustration out on me that he didn't get to fuck her that night? Was he picturing her writhing underneath him on the stairs while he plunged in and out of me? Motherfucker. So much for the good memories. Even more evidence that everything is tainted by that whore.

I find myself at a bar in a somewhat seedy area, cocktail in hand, and well on my way to pushing reality farther out of my mind and into orbit. It's just busy enough in here that the noise drowns out my racing thoughts but not too busy that the bartender hasn't been able to keep my glass full. The last thing I probably need today is bourbon, especially after the three mimosas I had a little while ago but no one's here to stop me. I tell the trendy hipster behind the bar to keep the old fashions coming and he doesn't question me.

I scroll a bit on my phone, but everything seems so stupid when I think about what's going on in my own life. I'd like to call Celeste and tell her to meet me so we can get drunk together, but I know she hates me. I could call Cade to see what that hot piece of ass is doing but I have just enough of a buzz that there's a high possibility of me confessing my love for him, and my shaky mental state wouldn't be able to handle a dismissal right now. Drinking alone it is. Well, I'm not alone per se, Jake, my new bartender friend, is here to keep me company. Although, him calling me bro is starting to give me a headache.

This bar seems to be at odds with itself. The outside looks fresh and modern while the inside resembles a hole in the wall bar where the locals hang daily, turning their heads simultaneously to stare down newcomers as they enter. By the looks of Jake, I'd say this is a popular college hangout but I'm here far too early to see that crowd. Most likely, any college student is still in bed attempting to recover from all the shots of liquor to the face and poor decisions made on a Saturday night. Or they're making that wonderful walk of shame back home in last night's underwear belching up PBR and regret.

The music selection doesn't match the vibe in this place either. When I walked in, the speakers were floating a Rolling Stones tune around the bar. Since then, I've heard songs from Maroon 5, Muse, Morgan Wallen, Hozier, and an even more random throwback to Britney Spears. I'm thrown for an even larger loop when "Closer" by Nine Inch Nails queues up.

Jake places my third, heavy handed old-fashioned in front of me without a word before turning to greet a newcomer at the other end of the bar. I watch as he grabs a bar napkin and drops it onto the counter in front of her. In front of Samantha. Fucking bitch. My blood is instantly set to boil as I take in her unnaturally colored hair. Somewhere between fire red and burnt orange, she's attempted a beach wave but ended up channeling Mufasa instead. The flicked on splattering of freckles across her nose and cheeks partnered with the overdrawn beauty mark above her lip, she's looking as artificial as imitation crab. Her slightly wider set eyes are beetle like and, not surprisingly, the exact color of shit after you've binge drank and ate taco bell to quell your hangover.

This is Samantha. This is the woman that my husband cheated on me with. The woman he deemed worthy enough of losing his wife and everything that comes along with a marriage. I'm not vain enough to consider myself a knockout but surely, I'm more desirable than the slight framed female across from me who decided on a boob job so big she has to resort to relieving the enormous sacks on the bar top to counter their weight. Why wouldn't I find the one bar she comes into? This is probably where she picks up all her married men so she can keep her business of homewrecking going. I wonder what marriage she's currently ruining. Maybe she's switching gears and going for the young ones so she can ruin them early.

It's crazy to me, in the beginning, I felt sorry for her. I thought

Jeremy had pulled the wool over both our eyes but no, she knew. She knew the whole time that he was married. She was a snake in the grass waiting for me to get busy with life and for my husband to become desperate for attention. Now, she's just as bad as him, if not worse. I've heard through the grapevine that she has a habit of bagging the married ones and walking away unscathed when the wife finds out. Leaving the husband to fend for himself and take all the blame. So much for clearing my head.

I avoid her gaze like the plague, not wanting to draw attention to myself.

'Whose got you simpin' bro?' Jake asks in his chill, *I'm so cool*, voice.

'Sorry?'

'Who are you thinking about so hard?'

'Uh, what... no... no one. Uh, can you just cash me out?' I need to get out of here.

'Sure thing bro,' he replies smoothly through his toothy smile as he pushes off the bar and heads to the register.

I slip off my stool and head to the back so I can use the bathroom. There's no way my *three old-fashioned* bladder will make it home. I find the least dirty stall and go about my business. Taylor Swifts voice grows loud for a moment as the door opens then closes, muting the sounds outside the bathroom once again. The music in this place is almost as ADHD as me. Finishing up and making my way to the sink, I wash my hands and swipe a couple flakes of mascara from my cheeks. The stall behind me opens revealing the devil herself. I focus all my attention on my reflection in the mirror and then to my overly rinsed hands as Samantha makes her way to the sink next to mine. After barely washing her hands, she pulls lipstick out of her clutch and starts to reapply the horrid plum color painstakingly slow to her collagen filled lips as I continue to pretend she doesn't exist.

'I thought that might be you. How's Jeremy?' she asks, rolling and smacking her lips dramatically to ensure full coverage of the ugliest color I have ever seen in a lipstick.

'Excuse me?'

'How's Jeremy? You know, your husband? Or is he not your

husband anymore?' she snides.

'That's really none of your business,' I retort, turning my body toward her while gripping the sink and placing a hand on my hip to steady myself. Anything not to swing on this woman.

'Oh, Millicent,' she pouts, 'the only person you should be mad at is yourself for not being able to please him. I'll take a thank you for taking care of what you couldn't.'

I'm left speechless and stare bewildered at her as she recaps the lipstick and tosses it back into her clutch before turning for the door. A monster burns with fury from within and wrestles with the little girl I've buried deep inside who cowers at the first sign of confrontation. My body moves on autopilot and before I know it, I'm behind her as she reaches for the door.

'Here, let me get that for you,' I grit as I let the monster takeover. I seize the back of her head by fake hair and slam her little slut face into the bathroom door. Not once, not twice, but three times I drill her plastic ridden face into the steel blockade as a sliver of retribution sweeps over me. Her scream pierces the stale vomit air, and her hands fly up to the door to brace herself from any more hits. Releasing her, her hands instinctively cover her nose as she falls back against the wall. I watch as the blood starts to trail from beneath her hands, flirting with her chin to eventually get to her neck. A purple hue has already started to peek out around her fingertips that are pressed to the corners of her eyes showing the first hint of a broken nose.

'You fucking bitch!' she grumbles stuffily through the pain and the blood.

'Just my way of saying thank you,' I say with a saccharine smile before leaving her alone in the rancid bathroom to lick her wounds.

Taylor Swift is still polluting the bar with "Look What You Made Me Do" and I can't help but to roll my shoulders back with confidence and crack my neck with satisfaction to what just may be my new theme song as I return to the bar. I gather my debit card and purse before walking out the door, feeling a sense of justice served as the sun pelts my face.

I should probably continue this little party at home.

Chapter Twenty-Three

I spin around in my desk chair until I'm sure I'm going to projectile vomit. Coming to a stop, I rest my heels on the edge of the desk and find my trusty spider that hangs out in the ceiling corner for my staring pleasure. The last couple days have been relaxing without anyone breathing down my neck so why don't I feel any better? Probably because I know I still have big decision to make. I was just able to push them off for a little bit.

My phone dings and I grab it off the desk. My heart immediately filling with joy when I see his name on my screen.

Client – P. Alderidge: I'd like to see you earlier tonight.

Cade is requesting not demanding. This is a strange change-up. I'm still not sure when Jeremy will be home since he didn't know when he'd be done but I'm positive I can swing meeting him earlier than normal. Besides, after not seeing him, I could go over now and never leave. I could turn into his bedroom troll, never to see the light of day again, and die a happy woman.

> *Me: I should be able to do that, sir.*
> *What time did you have in mind?*

I check on my spider again while I wait for his response. I hear the door open downstairs and assume it's Celeste coming in, dread sinking into my bones. I haven't spoken to her since Saturday night, and I have absolutely no idea where we stand. I just hope she can find it in her heart to forgive me eventually.

> *Client – P. Alderidge: My mind was thinking about*
> *an early dinner and then back to my place. 4:30?*

Dinner? We've never been out to dinner before. Shit! Is he asking me out on a date? If this is a date that certainly means I'm more than a business deal, right? A date is wanting to get closer to someone. A date is showing the person you like a good time and wanting to treat them. But business partners also have dinner all the time. I hate this. Every time my hopes soar, I effectively tear them back down. That's it. I'm going to lay it all out there tonight. It has to be tonight. Then, when I see Jeremy, I'll break the news to him. We can't continue this way. *I* can't continue this way.

> *Me: Sounds great, sir.*

> *Me: Should I meet you somewhere or at your place?*

'Hey.'

I look up to see Celeste, leaning on my doorframe and wringing her hands.

'Hi,' I reply hesitantly, placing my phone face down on the desk. I'm having a hard time reading her and start to brace for the worst.

'I got a call from another investor on my way over here. They want to see the apartments tonight. Also, Dominus wants to see it again as well.'

'Tonight? Uh...'

'Is that a problem?' she interrupts. I'm taken aback by the brashness in her tone. The lack of anything left for me is evident.

'No, no. of course not. What time do we need to be there?'

'You'll need to be there by 5:30 p.m. They should be there at 6:00 p.m.'

'Are you not going?'

'No. You're on your own tonight. I've got another commitment.'

'Cel, I...' I start and her hand immediately comes up warning me that I had better not move from behind my desk.

'Don't, Mil.'

I stand, gripping my desk, trying like hell to keep myself from falling over. Is she leaving me? I mean, is she quitting me?

'I need some time. I'm going away for a couple days.'

'Ok.'

'Once the investors see the apartments tonight, I'd give everyone until Friday to make their offers and you can go from there. Looking at the offers we already have, Dominus, LLC will get the building by a landslide.'

'Stop talking like it's only going to be me.'

Her eyes drill into mine inducing a shot of acid to my core. It is just me. She's not going to be here and doesn't know if she's coming back.

'You're not coming back, are you?'

'I don't know Mil... I don't know.' I watch as the tears gather at her eyelids. When the weight of them becomes too much, single tears slide from each eye, moving down her cheeks to dangle from her chin, just waiting to meet their dry fate on her jacket. With that, she turns and leaves.

My head starts to pound from the blood rushing inside my skull. My own tears silently spilling down my face. I just lost my business partner. My best friend. My only friend. Our history flushed down the toilet because I couldn't even be honest with her. Or adult enough to make a fucking decision. I already know she won't be back in this office. Even if she's saying she doesn't know. I know her mind is made up. She just needs to give herself a couple days to let her decision soak in. What the hell am I going to do now? Hire someone? How am I supposed to find someone I trust like Celeste to be in business with? My heart thunders against my chest as my vision blurs and I sit back in my chair before I pass out.

Shit. Shit. Shit. I wipe sweaty palms across my cheeks to clear away the tears. Get it together. We can figure this out. You can figure this out. My last grasp at finding some motivation falls short as I remember I'm supposed to meet Cade tonight. Can this day get any worse?

Client – P. Alderidge: Lets meet at my place. I'll wait in my car though. Since I know if you come in, we'll never make it back out. ;)

The streams from my eyes fall again. I sniffle and wipe my nose with the backside of my hand and down my wrist. How attractive, Mil. I don't care at this point though. I just want to be in Cade's embrace as he tells me I'll figure this out.

Me: I just got some bad news. Another investor wants to see the apartment building tonight. I'll have to raincheck.

Client – P. Alderidge: Can we just meet for dinner then? We can meet back up at my place after you meet with the investors.

Me: I have to be there at 5:30. With it already being 1, I have to get a bunch of things ready. Can we meet tomorrow?

Client – P. Alderidge: I really need to see you tonight.

Why the urgency? Any other time, I'd receive a punishment for pushing appointments and we'd move on. But this isn't a regular appointment. He asked me to meet early. And for dinner no less.

> *Me: I'm beyond bummed this came up, but I have to get this investor in before the offer deadline. Can I call you when I'm done, if it's not too late?*

I watch the dots across the screen, Cade taking too long to respond. I feel like I'm upsetting him but I'm not sure why. I can always go over after. If Jeremy isn't home that is. I can definitely make sure I see him tomorrow evening, if not tonight.

> *Client – P. Alderidge: Yeah, sure. Apologies.*

Oh, fuck. He *is* upset. Why though? Why is he upset? Can't dinner wait? He's waited this long to ask me to dinner, what's another night?

> *Me: I'm sorry. I'll get ahold of you later.*

I wait for a few minutes before realizing he isn't going to respond. Unfortunately, I don't have the luxury of waiting. I need to get a list together for tonight. I need to get to the apartments before 5:30 p.m. if I'm going to make sure they're ready for a showing. Since its just one investor, and Dominus, LLC wanting to see it again, I should be able to shove everyone out fairly early. Hopefully. Fingers crossed.

I grab my phone and send a quick message to Jeremy to head him off before he blows my phone up when he finally gets home.

> *Me: Cel just dropped a last-minute investor visit on me for the apartment building tonight. I'm hoping it doesn't take all night. I'll see you when I get home.*

> *Me: Safe travels*

Safe travels? Who am I? I want him safe but when the hell have I ever said anything remotely like *safe travels* to him?

There. That's better. Now, let's sell this damn building. I adjust my invisible crown and get moving.

I glance down at my watch, trying not to make it obvious I want to get the fuck out of here. My wrist taunts me with the time of 8:15 p.m. Clearly, I am not getting out of here early. The investor that requested to see the building has taken phone call after phone call while I tried to take him around the building and talk to him about it. We'd start to make some headway and he'd inevitably hold up his finger, signaling the need to take the call, put the phone to his ear, use his business voice to say 'Maxwell' into the receiver, then walk away from me down the hall. Fuck Maxwell and his popularity.

Meanwhile, the chick with Dominus, LLC has been measuring rooms and halls and running her fingers along the walls. I have no idea what information she needs exactly. According to Celeste, the offer they already gave us pretty much assures the building to them. Last minute checks, I guess. Whatever it is, it's really impinging on my night with Cade.

'I think that's all I need for tonight. You've received our offer already, correct?'

I spin around from the window of the first floor apartment I was daydreaming out of and face the woman from Dominus.

'Yes, yes, we have it. Are you sure there isn't anything else you need from me? We'll... I'll be taking a look at the offers over the next couple days.' The quick pinch and release of her brows shows she noticed my correction but doesn't address it.

'No. I believe I have everything I need.'

'Perfect. I look forward to doing business with you.' We walk towards each other, and I wipe my hands on my slacks before shaking her hand. My hands seem to be perpetually sweaty nowadays and

I surely don't want her taking that back to her business partners.

She flashes a pearly white smile framed in red lipstick, turns on her heel, and disappears as fast as she appeared. Why couldn't she have been this fast doing all her measuring and calculating? I sneak another peak at my watch and walk into the main hallway. Jesus. 8:30. I have no idea where Maxwell ventured off too but he's no doubt on the phone doing other business or gossiping. I have no idea at this point. What I do know is that I am putting a last viewing date on any future buildings like this. And it will be firm. If you don't make it before then, so be it.

'Millicent.' The sultry voice snakes into my ear making my hands fall to my sides and my eyes spring upward, no longer concerned with the time.

Cade stands in front of me in leather loafers, grey slacks, black belt, white button up, with the top couple of buttons undone, hands held behind his back. His facial hair casting the perfect shadow on his jaw line. His mouth hitched up slightly on one side. His piercing green eyes looking at me as those he's seeing me for the first time.

'Cade… what are you doing here?' I fumble around my words.

'I'm happy to see you too, Mil,' he smirks.

'I'm sorry, I just didn't, I didn't expect you to show up here.'

'I told you, I wanted to see you.'

'Right, yeah,' his face seems to falter a little as though he realizes he made a mistake. 'I just still have an investor here. Somewhere anyway. He keeps getting phone calls and… anyway.'

'Just tell him I'm another investor when he comes back. Maybe that will up the ante.' He steps towards me, holding out his hand, and I instinctively take a step back.

'Cade, I can't. You have to go. This building has been exhausting enough already.'

'Hey, I'm sorry, Mil,' he says holding his hands up. 'I just needed to see you. It couldn't wait.'

'Well, it has too. Please, just go before he sees you and thinks my boyfriend has shown up here unannounced.'

'I'm your boyfriend now?' I don't miss the twinkle in his eye as he asks the question.

'Cade, please, can we have this conversation later?'

'Just tell him I'm an investor. You wouldn't be lying.' He takes another step closer and this time, I stay put.

'What are you talking about?'

'Dominus, LLC? Mil, I own it.'

I stare at him speechless. He *owns* Dominus, LLC? Like, it's his company?

'I'm surprised you didn't put it together sooner.'

'You own Dominus, LLC? Why wouldn't you tell me that?' I feel anger rising to the surface. Why didn't he tell me this? Why was he keeping this in the dark? Not that we've been super forthcoming with each other but still. He knew I owned the company that was showing this building. He came here and fucked me three floors up. No wonder he knew I was here. No wonder no alarm bells went off when a man in a suit walked in to look around. The stupid woman that was here earlier works for him.

'I had some stuff to work out before I told you I was buying your building.'

'You had some stuff to work out? What kind of stuff might that be?'

'The kind of stuff that involves feelings. Mil, I...'

'I need some air.' I break away from Cade before he can finish his sentence and storm out the front door. I stomp down the couple steps and find myself on the sidewalk.

'Mil, I'm sorry.' Cade calls desperately from behind me. I spin around and he's on me so quick I barely have time to react. His hands are on my shoulders and his lips are on mine, taking me right there in front of the building.

'Mil, I love you.' He claims, leaving me speechless after that kiss.

'Cade...'

'Stop. I love you, Mil. I know I should've told you sooner. I should've also told you I own the company that's buying this building. I've been beating myself up for weeks over this. I'm leaving for Italy tomorrow to meet my brother. That's why this couldn't wait. I'll be gone for a few weeks, and I couldn't go without telling you how I feel.'

'What about the diner? What about your other clients?' I step back trying to catch my breath and let my brain catch up. All this new information is making my head spin out of control.

'Victoria's? Mil, I own it.'

'You own it?' I scoff in disbelief.

'I do...,' he snickers, 'actually, I was simply filling in when you started coming. I've been fighting you for a while. And, while I was seeing other clients when you first started, I haven't seen them for months. I stopped the second I knew you were more than just a client to me.'

My eyes brim with tears at Cade's words. He loves me? He hasn't been seeing other clients? He owns the diner? Have I been walking around with my eyes closed for the past six months? I've been dying to hear all of this from him and he's finally laying himself bare.

'Mil, look at me.' His hands are on my shoulders once again. I bring my eyes to his and his feelings for me seem to pour out and into my soul.

'I fucking love you. I fucking love you so much.' A sob wracks my body as his words puncture my body. His love, forming thread, starts to stitch together the open wounds I've been carrying on my heart.

'Mil?' We both jerk our heads to the right and the strings that were just sewing my heart together, immediately unravel.

'Who are *you?*' Cade demands from the man standing mere feet away from us. A bouquet of flowers hanging down in one hand.

'I could ask you the same thing. Who are you and why are you telling my wife you love her?'

'Your wife?!' Cade's hands immediately drop from my shoulders as he takes a step back. The loss of his palms settled on me fills me with an emptiness I've yet to endure in my lifetime.

'What the fuck is he talking about Mil?' Cade's eyes drill into me while his hand points to Jeremy.

'Cade, I...'

'I'm her husband, Cade. Or didn't she tell you?'

I let my head hang as tears collapse the barrier of my eyelids. I want to puke. I want to run away. Being buried alive would be better than this. I feel completely out of my body as if I'm watching a movie, starring Mil, the cheater, who broke not only her husband's heart but her Dom's. And her best friends.

'You know, I didn't want to believe Celeste when I ran into her on Sunday. I really didn't. I told myself Mil would never cheat on me. I know I fucked up when I was with Samantha, but Mil has forgiven me and she's in this. She's in this, she's told me that. She would never do this. But Celeste asked me about the sex we've been trying out. And I was shocked, considering we haven't been having sex. Aside from lately and that wasn't anything crazy. She mentioned this building and you leaving with handcuffs. The same day you came home *sick*. My confusion was clear.

'Then I remembered how upset she was last Saturday. I asked her why she was so upset. She didn't tell me. Your friend isn't like that. But that's all I needed. That's all I needed for it to all come crashing together. She told me you slept in her spare bedroom, and she gave you pajamas when I couldn't find you last Friday. But when you came home, you didn't have your shirt. And you said you passed out on her couch and must have taken your clothes off. That you were grabbing in the dark for them so you could get home. I asked her about that. I watched a tear roll down her face as she said, 'I'm sorry, Jeremy,' and then walked away.'

'You were with me last Friday. You were with me last Friday while your husband was at home waiting on you? You've been married this whole fucking time? God damn it! I'm so fucking stupid.' I can feel the rage burning inside of Cade.

'I can explain!' I plead as he starts to walk away. I reach out for his arm, but he tugs it away.

'Do not touch me, Millicent.' My full name on his lips hits me like a Mack truck.

'Cade please!' I scream at his back hoping with everything he'll turn around and let me explain this mess.

'Don't! Don't you dare call me that. That names reserved for people I care about,' he barks. The wrath in his tear stained eyes and words freeze me to the spot I'm in. My heart, in two halves at this point, bangs around in my chest demanding to be released. I clench my fists and feel my nails bite into my skin. I try to make something hurt more than my heart does right now but I'm pretty sure even death wouldn't make this feel any better. I watch as

Cade, what could've been my future, walks down the street and disappears into the dark.

I don't try to hide my choking sobs even though there would be no controlling them at this point. I turn slowly back to where Jeremy stands. I find his gaze and it sends a jolt through my body. His eyes are void of emotion. They're tired. Just tired.

'I got these for you,' he says roughly, handing the flowers out to me. I don't know what else to do at this point, so I reach up and take them from him.

'I want a divorce,' he continues matter of fact. Taking one last look at me, he turns to walk off into the darkness, just like Cade. The two pieces of my heart being drug off in opposite directions with them.

I stare after him. I can't do anything else. My body won't let me. My body is finally making me sit in my feelings. In all of my feelings. And now, instead of grieving my marriage, I get to grieve my friendship, and my new relationship all at the same time. Aloneness consumes my soul as a scream barrels from my throat. I scream so loud that someone is bound to call the police, but I don't give a fuck. I unleash my scream into the night sky with blinding outrage.

The scream finally subsides, and I stand panting in front of the building. I try to slow my breathing but I'm sure I'm on the verge of a full on panic attack if I'm not in the middle of it already.

'So, I'm gonna go....' I turn slowly to find Maxwell standing at the door of the apartments. 'Thanks for letting me see it at the last minute. I don't think I'm interested though.'

'Pleasures. All. Mine,' I grit out. I convince myself I can burn holes into his face if I stare hard enough and I think he convinces himself of the same thing because he completely skips the steps and speed walks to his Toyota Corolla. A Toyota Corolla? Are you shitting me? He wasn't even going to buy this building! He was probably talking to his mother on the phone the whole time. Maxwell is the reason my whole night went to shit?! The car fires and he almost burns the tires completely off trying to escape from the horrid scene that is my life.

I walk back into the building, slamming the door behind me,

and drop to the floor. Tears, spit, and heaving breaths threaten to destroy my body as I crumble in the empty apartment building. Completely alone.

Chapter Twenty-Four

Somehow, I've managed to make it to Friday. I haven't heard from anyone. Anyone being Jeremy, Celeste, or Cade. Cade. Just his name makes my chest constrict with an agony so unbearable I have to find anything else to think about. I've been staying at the office since Tuesday night but need to face the music. Obviously, Jeremy and I are over. So, I need to at least clean that mess up and figure out what the hell I'm going to do next. Being single is clearly in my future. I can deal with that after Jeremy and I hash out whatever we need to.

Over the past three days, I cleaned the entire office space. And by cleaned, I mean I was on my hands and knees cleaning floors, scraping gunk from corners with a toothbrush, washing couch cushion covers, making sure the screens on the faucets were free of debris. When I was done with all that, I started over again. Anything to keep myself from spiraling further out of control.

Wednesday morning was the worst by far. I don't know how I made it back to the office Tuesday night but when I woke up in the morning, my floor was littered with empty wine bottles. I even found a wine bottle in my pocket. Maybe I was saving it for later or didn't want to misplace it. Who fucking knows. The most intriguing thing about waking up at my office, was the fact that I was face down on my desk. The drool making my face half stick to the surface, hair sopping and smashed to my face and neck. I got drunk, I guess. Obliterated.

The only productive thing I've managed this week was getting the information out to Dominus, LLC for accepting their offer. My heart needed Cade to be the one I would speak with when I called but, sadly, I dealt with the woman. It isn't surprising anyway. He's in Italy. With his brother. Probably talking about the bitch in America that fucked him over. Broke his heart. Now, I'll only deal with the woman and her with me. Since Celeste is doubtfully returning. Out of any of them, I might have the most luck in winning her back. But I already know things will never be the same even if she does forgive me. It hurts thinking about her meeting the man of her dreams, getting married, buying a home together, having kids and knowing I won't be there to celebrate by her side. I hate that I'm going to miss out on all the amazing experiences with her. Even the sad ones. I'd even take holding her hand and letting her sob on my shoulder when her mom finally passes at this point. I know that's selfish of me, but I can't stand the thought of not holding her through her grief.

I should've come to her as soon as I was thinking of seeing another man. Or at least, came to her when things started progressing with Cade. She would've been upset but she would've been able to help me. If I had went to her, maybe I wouldn't be without Jeremy and Cade right now. She could've talked some sense into me, and I would've stayed with Jeremy. Or she would've encouraged me to leave Jeremy since I was already thinking about someone else, and I could've seen where things went with Cade. I could be with him right now. But that's all gone now. Now, I have to figure out how to put the pieces back together by myself.

Even though I knew things with Jeremy were over, I'm still sad. I didn't want everything coming to a head the way they did. I wanted to sit down with him and break it to him in my own way. Not him showing up in the middle of the other man professing his love to me. He shouldn't have found out that way. I should've been more up front. I had plenty of chances at home or even in counseling to say what I was feeling. Instead, I led him on. Letting him think we were going to be ok while I was choking on Cade's cock. I know Jeremy will be ok. That's who he is. He's probably fine now. He's probably just waiting on me to come home so he can kick me out. as he should. It's what I deserve.

Its why I just pulled up to our house. I have to face this. I let myself have some time, but I need to get this over with. Not only do I need to set myself free, but I need to set Jeremy free. He needs to be able to start healing and I can't waste anymore of his time. My hands are shaking so bad I can't believe I was even able to keep the car on the road. And the sweating. The damn sweating that has become a steady, unwelcome friend over the past few months. My palms should be studied for how much water has come out of them.

Is this what Jeremy felt like before he told me about Samantha? Was he this nervous? Was he dreading that I would tell him to get out as soon as the secret left his lips? Did he know he deserved it? If he felt anything like I'm feeling right now, I commend him for coming out and telling me. I really do. I am not half the person he is if this is even a fraction of what he felt before spewing the words *I had an affair.*

I decide to leave my purse and keys in the car. I doubt I'll be here long. While I do love this house, I also don't think I could stay in it without Jeremy. Or, after Jeremy rather. If I have to start over, I need to really start over. I may not even be able to stay in this town after everything that's gone down. The last thing I want is to run into Celeste, seeing her laughing with a new friend over food at a restaurant, or see Jeremy and his new girlfriend, hand in hand, happy as ever, him completely engulfed by her. And Cade. There's no way I could stomach seeing him with another woman. Would it be another client turned girlfriend? Would she like him throwing her across his lap, loving the feel of his palm slam against her ass? Would he make her smother his face with her pussy and lick her until she was writhing against his mouth? I shake the thought from my mind as I stand on our porch. Not quite ready to turn the knob.

The only thing worse than seeing Cade with his new woman would be to see him alone. Knowing I was the reason he couldn't give himself to anyone. I would be the reason he couldn't trust another female because I was married the entire time we were fucking. I never let on to that. My only defense being that I didn't expect our relationship to bloom into anything beyond business. But I had many opportunities to tell him after I started having feelings for him. This really is all my fault.

I realize the door is opening but my hand isn't turning the knob. I let my arm drop to my side and take in Jeremy's appearance. His red rimmed eyes, the beard that hasn't been shaved in several weeks, his shirt and sweats I'm guessing he has been in since at least yesterday. I did this. He looks like this because of me. He looks worse than when he came to bring me home from Celeste's after I left following his confession. This is not what I wanted. Not at all.

'Mil, what are you doing?'

'How did you know I was here?'

'I heard you pull up a while ago. Were you going to come in or just stand out here like a weirdo?' his voice is strained, and I think he was trying to make a joke but neither of us smile.

'Right. I'm sorry to bother you. I figured we should talk at some point.'

'You're not bothering me. This is still your house too you know,' he says as he moves out of the way and ushers me inside.

'I know, I just… I didn't… I'm sorry.' I can't latch onto anything. I've failed him in a huge way, and I know no matter what I say, the words will come out wrong.

'Yeah, me too,' he says bitterly as he passes me in the hall and stalks toward the kitchen. A wave of sorrow and regret wash over me as I follow him.

I stay in the doorway as he crosses to the bar cart grabbing a couple glasses and a bottle of wine.

'Wine?' he asks, turning toward the nook table. My gaze follows him and that's when I see it. The huge manilla folder sitting on top of the table. The manilla folder that no doubt holds white papers filled to the brim with black ink waiting to scream *'you're getting divorced, you idiot'.*

He sits at the table, opens the wine, and pours two glasses. The wine comes all the way to the brim, threatening to spill over any second. The same way the contents of my stomach are getting ready to spill.

'Mil, sit.' He looks at me, still standing in the doorway.

My cement filled legs carry me reluctantly to the table. I sit down across from him and hate that a part of me thinks he's handsome right now. If it weren't for the evidence of him hurting, the beard looks amazing on him. His shaggy hair gives him that youthful look. I find myself wishing he had taken on this look before our relationship crumbled. I would've liked to enjoy him looking so good. God. What the fuck is wrong with me? My soon to be ex-husband has been crying for days, from the pain I've induced, and all I can think about is how sexy he looks. I am at the bottom of the barrel.

Wanting to silence my inner whore monologue, I grab the glass of wine and drink half of it down immediately. Maybe this will shield the blow. I watch as Jeremy spins his glass slowly in his fingertips, watching the wine slosh around.

'Is that what I think it is?'

'Divorce papers? Yeah.' His eyes cut to mine. I can see the remorse in the depths of his brown pools. He doesn't want this. Which is why he begged me to stay in the beginning. He didn't want it then and he doesn't want it now.

'Right.'

The silence ensues again as the word *divorce* hangs in the air above us. I finish off my glass of wine and pour another. This is brutal. Us not talking, addressing the elephant in the room, is worse than if he would just scream at me and tell me to get the fuck out. He could've just sent me these in the mail. I'm sure he knew where I was even though he didn't bother to text me or call me.

After Tuesday, he knew I wouldn't be holed with Cade somewhere. And he surely knows I wouldn't have been welcomed at Celeste's.

'Jeremy, I...'

'Please don't Mil,' he interrupts me, instantly silencing me, 'I've tried for three days to not be mad at you. To make excuses for you. I fucked up first. I had an affair and asked you, begged you, to take me back and forgive me.'

Even though he's stopped talking, I don't say anything. I know he's gathering everything he's thought about over the past couple days. The past few months. And I let him have his moment. He deserves it.

'Every time I think I make sense of what you did, every time I think I can forgive you and maybe we can continue to move forward, I get stuck on the fact that you were lying to me the entire time. And I get it, Mil. I do. I lied to you. I lied to you about the nights I wasn't coming home, about the events I needed to work, about the phone calls I needed to take. I get it. But, when I asked you to stay and work through this, and you agreed, I had made a promise to myself, a promise to you, that never again, while I am breathing, would I be the cause of your tears ever again. Unless they were happy tears that is,' he snickers with a shake of his head.

'But you,' his eyes like lasers, 'you told me, more than once, you were in this. That you wanted to work through this and see it through to the other side. You let me think you were just hurting, and it would take time to fix everything. You let me think I just needed to give you space in the beginning and then later, you let me think if I just worked a little bit harder, I'd be successful. That you would forgive me, and all would be fine. That we would be able to love each other as if nothing had happened if I just gave you more. I made love to you, Mil. I made love to you more intensely than I ever have just last week. I thought we had some sort of break through! Did it even mean anything to you? I poured my heart out to you. I tried to be understanding. I tried to show you, not just tell you, how fucking sorry I was and how something even slightly related to an affair would never fucking happen again!' his voice breaks over a sob. I can see the hatred rising in his eyes. I'm worse than he ever was.

'All the while I was trying harder, giving you more and more, trying to love you harder than I ever had, trying to make you see I had made a huge mistake and I couldn't live without you; you were just out with him. Weren't you?'

I nod my head yes because there's no use in lying at this point. The huge ass cat is out of the bag. The only thing I can do now is make sure the lies end here. This is how I start moving forward. He harrumphs and drinks his wine down to the bottom of the glass and pours another. There's nothing like getting drunk with your husband while you talk about each other's affairs over divorce papers. Someone should write a book about this.

'How long have you been seeing him?'

'For a few months.'

'Jesus, Mil. We've been trying to fix us for a few months. Were you ever trying with me? Was there ever even a chance I was going to be able to fix this?'

'I don't know.' And I don't. I met Cade so early on and I was so desperate for someone else to take control and wipe away my grief that I have no idea if Jeremy ever stood a chance.

'The worst part about all of this is that I still love you. I still fucking love you.' Jeremy rubs his hand down his face and looks out the window as he stifles a sob.

'I know it probably doesn't mean much at this point, but I do still love you, Jeremy. I really do. I can't explain exactly why I did what I did. All I know is that I was hurting so badly I didn't care what fixed it. I just needed it fixed. I certainly didn't plan for this. This was not some ploy to make you feel what I felt when you told me about Samantha. Please don't think that. I didn't want this.'

'Do you love him?' he asks as he turns his head to face me again.

'Jeremy...'

'Just answer the question, Mil. Believe me, it can't hurt any worse than seeing you with him the other night.'

'I do,' I whisper, 'but that doesn't matter anymore anyway.'

'Yeah, that's what I figured. I could tell you wanted to say it back to him. I knew as soon as I saw you two standing together, before I could hear anything he was saying, I had lost you. Lost you for good.'

A tear falling down my cheek is my only response. I hate that I'm the one that hurt him. Even though I do love Cade, I hate that this will never be fixed. That this really is the end. There is no fixing Jeremy and I. The future we could've had is no more and anything we shared is in the history books only to be remembered. The good memories forever tainted with the moment he confessed about Samantha and the moment he realized I did the same thing. The moment that all was lost. I'm hit with the realization that, right now, sitting across the table from Jeremy, watching as our relationship finishes crumbling in front of our eyes, that I am just like the men that hurt me before Jeremy came along.

'Happy anniversary by the way.' Jeremy holds up his glass as the realization sweeps over me. It's our 4th anniversary.

'Cheers,' he says, clinking his glass to mine.

'Cheers,' I choke out and take a sip to smother the cries.

Chapter Twenty-Five

'That's no problem at all. Ok… uh huh… sure, absolutely. Ok, yes, you as well. Have a wonderful day.' I press end on my phone and let my mask drop. That was a ridiculously long phone call for absolutely no reason. I really need to hire a secretary or something. Someone that can field these calls and I can give them the information to pass on so I don't get stuck talking to all these clients. I guess I shouldn't complain, business is booming. And since that's the only thing that has been good in my life lately, I should be happy to answer and sit on the phone for hours at a time.

Jeremy and I's divorce has been finalized for about three

months now. We both agreed we had hurt each other enough so it was amicable. The cars were already in our own names. The only thing to decide on was the house. We decided to sell it and split the money and pay for the divorce from the profit. Neither of us wanted to stay in the house and be constantly haunted by memories of the other. We certainly couldn't see ourselves with a future partner there either and we didn't want to curse any future potential relationships.

We still talk every once in a while. I guess when you've been through something like that, it's possible to still care for the other person and want the best for them. I do want the best for Jeremy. He screwed up but he certainly didn't deserve what I put him through at the end. I know he would never let what happened with him and Samantha happen again either. He was regretful enough with me that he wouldn't make someone else endure that kind of crippling hurt.

He told me last he's started seeing someone. They've been on a couple dates and things seem like they could progress but he's taking it slow. He doesn't want to scare her off just coming off a divorce. A divorce where both parties cheated on the other. Not a great ice breaker I suppose. Even if it doesn't work out for him with this one, I know he'll find the woman of his dreams. Someone who wouldn't imagine putting him through the same thing I did.

I'm coming to terms with the fact that I'm not the worst person in the world. I made a mistake, just like Jeremy did, and people make mistakes. Some are just bigger than others and require slightly more clean up. I just wish there hadn't been so many casualties with mine. I found a new therapist and I couldn't be happier with her. I didn't think it was appropriate to continue with Dr. Johnson and besides, I hated her. Loathed her, really. I can't say I'm completely healed or happy, but I do know I'm getting there. And I feel better every day. I'm busy enough not to dwell on everything that happened but not too busy that I can't sit with my emotions and deal with them as they come. And do they come.

Celeste finally broke the news to me she was moving on the week after Jeremy caught me with Cade. I knew it was coming but it didn't make it any easier to hear. She took a position with another realty company and is super successful. Although she hasn't forgiven me, maybe never will, she is still my friend. I'm not sure if we'll ever be the Mil and Cel we were a year ago, or even before Jeremy's affair, but we're trying. Eventually I think she'll be able to let me completely in, but she surely won't ever forget. I've made it my mission to make her understand how much I love her and value her friendship in my life even if she's only giving me a small percentage of herself. I was right about everything. She was more upset that I wasn't honest with her, and I pulled her into my web without her knowing. She hates that I was cheating on Jeremy, especially after he was giving me double his all, but she's understanding in the sense that I was drowning and didn't know what to do so I grabbed the nearest float I could find.

A float that blew up in front of my eyes six months ago. I know Cade left for Italy the day after he spilled his feelings onto the sidewalk in front of the apartment building and Jeremy, my husband, and I didn't expect to hear from him while he was away, but I'd be lying if a little part of me didn't hold on to the hope that he might reach out when he got back. Ok, a huge part held on to that hope. A huge part is still holding on. I know it's not healthy to dwell on something that's over and that will never be, but I do still love him. I think I always will. He saved me from the deep waters of grief, whether he knows it or not, and I will always be thankful for that. He also showed me some things I never knew about myself. Like the fact that I love being spanked and I miss it every. Fucking. Day.

Not a day goes by that I don't dream of Cade showing up to my office and demanding I lift my skirt and lean over the desk. I listen to his belt slide from the loops of his pants and my pulse quickens as he steps nearer to me. The anticipation of the first lick of the belt crashing onto my ass. He'd give me the worst punishment I've ever had, and I'd take it willingly everyday if it meant he'd forgive me. I shouldn't be getting turned on right now but who wouldn't be thinking about Cade. He's probably got some amazing woman that bends to his every command and is giving her every orgasm, she's ever wanted. And love. He's probably loving her as well. She's soaking up the love I could've had. And I hate that.

If I could go back, I'd do so many things differently. I don't know that I would've left Jeremy immediately following the affair because I do think that event had something to do with me meeting Cade, but I do know I wouldn't have continued to string him along. And I would've told Celeste everything so I wouldn't have been so alone. I think that's ultimately what led to my demise. My brain couldn't function with all the grief swimming around and I wasn't thinking clearly. Now, I would've told Jeremy we were through the same night that Cade left me alone, naked on his desk. That was the night I knew. The night I knew I loved Cade. I'd do anything to even feel that level of pain again. To feel him pull away from me, tell me he'd see me on Tuesday for our appointment, and walk out of the room leaving me to stand against the cold desk just having been ravaged by him. I should've gone home that night and told Jeremy I couldn't do it anymore. But I didn't. And now, there's nothing I can do about it. Other than make sure if I do meet someone, I can be whole for them and be completely honest.

I close my laptop and gather my bag to head home. I bought a townhouse a few blocks from the office, so I don't even need to drive anymore. It's kind of nice. I've lost a few pounds from my new way of commuting and have been working out regularly. I haven't been drinking either. Not that I was ever a drunk but there toward the end with Jeremy, I was definitely on the verge of a problem. So, instead of hitting the bar on the way home, I stop into this new little coffee shop. It's just the pick me up I need to get me through my walk home and through my workout.

All this is different from my lifestyle before but its good. I think I'll keep it around for a while. It's certainly helped get me through the hardest parts of rebuilding my life the past six months.

The sun feels good on my face as I lock the door to the office. It was a long winter and its time I start soaking up some more vitamin D. I start down the sidewalk in the direction of home. I pop my headphones in, turning on my go to playlist, and let Vessel carry me to the coffee shop. A few steps into my walk and my headphones announce an incoming call.

Celeste.

I pause the music a little too anxiously and answer her call.

'Hello?'

'Hey girl. How was work?'

'Oh, you know, not the same without you, but I got through it.' I smile and offer a laugh. I don't try to make her feel bad for leaving. I think it helps me even more being able to joke about it.

'I knew you would.'

'So, what's going on?'

'Not much, just leaving a showing. I thought maybe we could grab dinner later. Unless you already have plans?'

'Well, you know I'm usually so busy on Friday nights... of course, I can have dinner. You know I don't have anything going on.'

'Stop it,' she giggles, 'you're going to have to start dating sooner or later you know.'

'Uh no. I think I can hold out for a little while longer. Besides, I'm busy and haven't even had to the time to think about it.'

'Ugh, fine. Anyway, you know the new restaurant over on Hanover Street everyone's been raving about? Foods great and wine is even better, I guess. Wanna try it out?'

'I'll be there. I'm just leaving the office now. I'm going to grab a coffee but could head out in a couple hours. What time were you thinking?'

'I can call and get us a table for 7:30 p.m. or 8 p.m. Does that give you enough time?'

'Plenty. I won't even have an excuse to miss my workout.'

'Perfect. I'll see you in a few hours.'

'Sounds good.'

Ending the call, Vessel's voice sneaks its way back into my ear canals. I stuff my phone back in my bag just as I come up to the coffee shop. I could skip it but if I'm going to dinner tonight too, I should probably take advantage of the extra caffeine.

The door chimes over the music as I walk in, and the smell of coffee brewing soothes my mind. There's only one person in line since its Friday and most people are working off pure adrenaline from it being the weekend not needing the extra shot of espresso. I order my coffee once the woman in front of me is finished up and start to plan my work out for when I get home. I should really go for a run. I haven't went running in a couple months because I like to run outside but the weathers been shit. Its only in the 50s today but the sun is shining, and the bitter cold is starting to melt away. I check the weather on my phone to make sure there's no chance of rain. If it's all sun, I'm running. "The Love You Want" by Sleep Token launches and there's nothing I can do as a small shiver of sadness overtakes me. Not really the mood I'm looking for, but I've vowed to deal with the feelings as they come. Its somber and slow and intense, dredging up emotions from my depths every time it plays.

'For Millicent? A vanilla chai latte?'

'Millicent?'

'Oh! that's me,' I startle and grab my coffee.

I turn and try to shove my phone back in my bag and not drop my coffee all over the floor. I've endured enough embarrassment lately; I don't need to add that to the list. I manage to shove it in a front pocket of my coat instead and when I lift my head, my eyes catch on him sitting at the corner table in the window.

Green eyes pierce through me as our gazes meet and I'm stopped in my tracks. A guy walks through the door and is forced to walk around a couple tables since I'm frozen in the middle of the aisle leading to the counter. At least I didn't drop my coffee.

I can't tear my eyes from his and everything I've worked so hard to push out of my brain over the past few months comes hurdling back in, this song not making it any easier. I reach up and pause my headphone as my heart fills instantly and breaks all over again knowing what happened. Seeing him sitting there. Remembering his full lips against mine. The taste of bourbon on his tongue as it played along in my mouth. The perfect way his cock filled my pussy. The feel of his rough palms skating all over my body. Touching every inch of skin I have. The heat from his body radiating through mine. The weight of him comforting me. His entire existence consuming me.

I take a deep breath and decide I just need to smile and be on my way. It's a fluke we are at the same coffee shop right now. I come here almost every day and he does live and work in Chicago. It's not completely crazy that we ran into each other. I hate that I wasn't more prepared for this moment that was bound to happen.

And that it still hurts so badly to see him sitting there, eyes on me, knowing he's not mine anymore.

I will my legs to start moving me toward the door, but no amount of brain power will carry me out of here.

A slight smile starts to form on Cade's lips, and he nods his head toward the empty seat motioning for me to take it. My legs wouldn't move a second ago, but I basically break into a sprint to sit in the chair at his table wanting to take up residence across from him before he rescinds the invitation. I slide into the chair and he's even more beautiful than I remember. His eyes seem greener somehow. The sun hits his face just right, shadows contouring his face in all the right places. His minty cedar scent inhabits my nose and I'm taken back to the last time I was face to face with him. He looks so fucking good.

'Hello, Mil,' he rasps. His smile growing.

'Hello, Cade.'

Acknowledgements

Whether they know it or not, this book was a group effort, and it wouldn't have made it this far without these people:

To Nicole, the inspiration for this book's dedication, I'm thankful Krista's bitch ass convinced me to go to that haunted prison with you. Between sending musical bangers back and forth and seeing our favorite band together, I love what our friendship has become. I still wonder if the owner of the wrong email I sent the draft to ever read it....

To LeAndra, it was love at first fart. You've been my ride or die since 7th grade. You are the friend that, even when life gets in the way, I know is still there rooting for me. Along with Nicole, y'all provided the motivation I desperately needed and the feedback to get me through to the end of this book.

To Shelby, my drunken Nashville bestie turned person for life, thank you for listening to me talk through scenes to make sure the words were just perfect. Being neighbors would still be too far away from you for me.

To my book club, which is made up of the coolest bitches you'll meet (don't let that go to y'all's heads), thank you for constantly asking 'when can I read it?!' and dealing with my scatterbrained nonsense. You all were the people that read the rough draft of my first chapter and let me know I should keep going. I love each and every one of you. Except Jessica.

To Sleep Token, listening to your music has allowed me access to an untapped creative space that's been buried in the depths of my brain (and, not to mention, a mask kink).

To Sam Fistere, beta reader extraordinaire, I so much appreciate the constructive feedback you offered. I hope you know you made this book that much better.

To Amanda Bryk, fellow published author, and friend, thank you for guiding me through this process, offering support, and for being my first friend in the author world.

And finally, to my husband, for making sure certain scenes would, in fact, work. And, of course, for loving me.

ABOUT THE AUTHOR

Between having her nose buried in a book, her two children and husband keeping her on her toes and keeping track of the rabid squirrels running loose in her brain, sightings of M.A. Carter out in the wild are rare. Besides spending time on her small homestead and giving Captain Planet a run for his money, she enjoys hassling her book club, forest bathing, and a good rabbit hole.

Follow M.A. Carter:
Instagram @macarterwriter
Facebook MA Carter